CHASING
AIR

CHASING AIR

A Novel

CAROLINE PRINCE

DEWPOINT
CREATIVE
VENTURES

Published by Dewpoint Creative Ventures, Carmel-by-the-Sea, CA
www.authorcarolineprince.com

Edited and designed by Girl Friday Productions
www.girlfridayproductions.com

Cover design: Kathleen Lynch
Project management: Abi Pollokoff
Editorial production: Katherine Richards
Image credits: Cover, Morgan_studio/iStock (background), Arand/iStock (car), tapui/iStock (airplane); chapter open illustration, Joanna Price

ISBN (paperback): 979-8-9925026-0-2
ISBN (ebook): 979-8-9925026-1-9

Library of Congress Control Number: 2025909997

First edition

To a time when life was simpler—kind of.

*To my husband—your unwavering support, love,
and patience made this journey possible.*

*To those who pick up this book—thank you
for giving my words a chance.*

*May these pages bring a smile, a spark,
or simply a moment to breathe the air.*

PART ONE

CHAPTER ONE

The rain came down in sheets along the Gualala coast. It was late in the season for such storms, but given California's desperate need for water, Allison welcomed the sight of it streaming down the windows, dripping off the Chinese pistache in the side yard and cascading off the patio toward the ocean below.

Her body ached—a dull, persistent reminder of the years of physical strain she'd endured. Every joint, every muscle, protested in unison, staging a rebellion against any hint of movement. Rainy days like this, though soothing to the soul, did little to ease her discomfort, and they dissuaded her from her daily hike. After years of pushing her body to the limits, hiking was one of Allison's last bastions of deep physical exertion. But today, the trekking poles would remain untouched in the corner of the garage, the kinesiology tape for her hips and glutes unused, the knee brace snug in its drawer beside the bed.

Allison sighed, sinking into the rhythm of the downpour. Stretching exercises crossed her mind, but the invitation to rest felt far more tempting. Wrapped in the afghan her mother had crocheted—a comforting blend of forest green and earth brown—she gave in to the stillness, allowing herself to simply lie down.

From her bedroom window, she watched the rain-soaked Japanese magnolia tree in the yard. It looked bedraggled now, its pink blossoms beaten down by the storm, but it still held a special place in her heart. Nineteen years ago, when she'd first moved into this house with Tom, the tree had greeted her like an old friend. Though Tom had built the house long before their paths crossed, it always felt like he'd constructed it with her in mind.

Tom had left early that morning, slipping out before she'd awakened. These days, she worried about him constantly. The risks he and other doctors had started taking since February, out there among the infected, left her with gnawing concern over what once was a routine workday. And she couldn't rely on swimming, golfing, and biking—the activities that used to occupy her days—as a distraction. The pandemic had shifted everything.

As Allison mulled over her thoughts, her gaze wandered out to the cliffs beyond the patio. Through the sheets of rain, she caught sight of a dark figure standing near the edge of the bluff. He stood still, a solitary silhouette against the churning ocean below. Though she couldn't make out his face, she knew who it was. She turned away.

On the bedside table, a small transparent pillar caught her eye. Nestled at the top, encased in Lucite, was a globe slightly smaller than a golf ball. She picked it up, turning it over in her hands. Its smooth exterior gave way to a mesmerizing interior—variegated shades of blue flecked with brown and white. It was an alternate world, a tiny universe she'd always loved getting lost in.

Returning the globe to its stand, she lay back down, closing her eyes. The afghan's weight was reassuring, anchoring her against the swirl of thoughts in her mind. Her memory drifted back to another magnolia tree on another overcast day. It was a tree from her childhood, one she used to climb during hot Georgia summers. Beneath its sprawling branches, she'd inhale the lemony scent of its blooms. Sometimes, she'd sit at her second-story bedroom window, watching its leaves quiver in the breeze. Those were safer days, simpler days, at least for some.

Allison's memories wandered through their vault . . .

In her mind, Allison was three again. Kneeling on an upholstered wing chair near the window of her childhood home, she watched the last few petals of the magnolia tree drift away on a November wind. The tree shuddered, as if reluctant to surrender to the approaching winter. She loved this room, especially on days like this, when she could gaze down at the world outside.

Her neighborhood in Sunflower, Georgia, wasn't particularly lively. On warm days, neighbors lingered on lawns or porches, gossiping about minor scandals involving other people's children or spouses. On colder days, once she'd wrapped herself in the green-and-brown afghan—the same one now draped across her—she'd watch as they retreated inside, their presence marked only by the occasional flicker of a curtain.

As a child, Allison would often watch the street below, imagining the lives of passersby. She especially loved the rituals before bedtime. After her bath, one of her parents would draw the shades and close the curtains. Dressed in homemade pajamas, she'd settle into the wing chair for a story before being tucked into bed.

One gloomy afternoon, the muffled hum of her mother's vacuum cleaner blended with the faint rhythm of distant drums. Curious, Allison wandered down two flights of stairs to the recreation room in the basement. There, her mother stood motionless before the new color television, tears streaming down her face.

"Why are you crying, Mother?" Allison asked, her small voice breaking the silence.

Startled, her mother wiped her eyes and turned. "Oh, Allison. It's the president's funeral. They're taking him to the cemetery."

Allison's eyes widened. "They killed him, didn't they?"

Her mother nodded, her lips pressing into a thin line as if trying to keep herself composed. It was the first time Allison understood the weight of loss, even if only through the emotions of the adults around her. That dark day became her earliest memory—a world shifted by tragedy, a loss too vast for her young mind to fully comprehend.

An unforgettable voice entered Allison's mind next.

"Come in, dear," Mrs. Maye said.

Everyone on Huguenot Street thought that Mrs. Maye was odd. She would wander the neighborhood in her nightgown and bathrobe and greet everyone she'd see. But she meant no harm. After all, she hadn't always been odd. She'd only taken to her pajamaed strolls after Mr. Maye died, a few years before Allison was born. Until then, she'd been a normal third-grade teacher at Bedford Forest Elementary. And her barely dressed treks besides, she never left the house without washing her short, wavy white hair until it shone and applying her favorite lipstick, Certainly Red, as well as a little eyeliner and eyebrow pencil, as if she were going to school to teach her thirty students math, reading, social studies, and art.

Mrs. Maye once asked Allison's mother, Emma, if she might invite her five-year-old daughter over once a week or so in the afternoons. Mrs. Maye's grandchildren lived in Jacksonville and didn't visit often. Later, once she was older, Allison figured her mom must have thought Mrs. Maye was starved for the companionship of children, which is why she agreed. After accompanying Allison to the house a few times, where Mrs. Maye would serve her milk and graham crackers, her mother said that it was fine if she went on her own.

Sometimes, Mrs. Maye would read poetry aloud; sometimes she asked Allison to read. Her favorite poet was Mary Oliver, and often, they read from a collection of her work called *No Voyage and Other Poems*. Allison liked this well enough, even if she didn't always understand the poems, which at least weren't very long.

"That's all right, dear," Mrs. Maye would say after gently quizzing her on what she thought a poem might mean. "Just enjoy the sound and rhythm of the words. Sometimes that can be quite enough."

She also encouraged Allison to write her own poems, and Allison did.

What Allison really loved, however, was the *World Book Encyclopedia* in the little study off the dining room. Bound in forest green and ivory, with a mottled texture that felt good under her hands, she loved the shiny pages, as much for the aroma that rose off them as the pictures and sentences that she was just beginning to understand. When she asked Mrs. Maye about that smell, Mrs. Maye said, "That is the bouquet of a good book."

Allison would pick a volume at random and look through it, always feeling a thrill of gratification when she came across the colored transparencies that illustrated complex systems like the human body or geological formations.

"What are we looking at today, Miss Blanchet?" Mrs. Maye would ask, setting a glass of milk and a plate of graham crackers on the coffee table.

"This."

Mrs. Maye, who was no more than five feet two and at most weighed 105 pounds, looked over Allison's shoulder.

"Japan. Try reading me a paragraph."

Allison read the first paragraph, about Japan's geographical location.

"Very good, especially for someone who's five. I don't know anyone else your age who can read as well as you."

"Thank you."

"You're welcome."

Allison's attention was soon drawn to the photos of women in traditional Japanese dress.

"What's this one?" she asked.

"Well, what does it say in the caption?"

Allison read it carefully. "A Japanese bride wears an *uchikake*." She pronounced it "OO-chee-cake."

"And then what does it say?"

"A formal wedding gown." She studied the dress. Its shape reminded her of a picture of the Liberty Bell that her mother had shown her. It was black with sinuous silver stems flowing around it, and silver-and-gold flowers. The hem was bright red. "I want one!" she said.

"My dear, you'd have to marry a samurai. Have a graham cracker instead."

Late one afternoon, as the shadows of the magnolias and black gum trees lengthened, Mrs. Maye brought Allison down a hall into a bedroom, the door to which had always been closed. When they entered, she was confronted by a room full of dolls. They sat on the bookshelves, the bureau, the rocking chair, and the armchair; they were propped up on the pillows against the headboard of the bed. They colonized every flat surface. Only the windowsills were empty, because they weren't wide enough.

Allison stared. The dolls—all of them girls—stared back.

"Here are my other children!" Mrs. Maye laughed. "They want to meet you!"

But Allison did not want to meet them. She was unnerved by the sight.

She grimaced and ran from the room, out of Mrs. Maye's house, and across the street to her own room, where she shut the door and grasped herself tightly in the safety of the upholstered wing chair. She determined never to go back to Mrs. Maye's, even if it meant forgoing the *World Book* forever.

Try as she might, Allison's mother could never convince her to visit with Mrs. Maye after that. Allison had made up her mind never to see all those doll eyes again, nor even return the old teacher's hellos on the street. Eventually, after one too many friendly greetings went unanswered, Mrs. Maye ceased acknowledging the little girl who lived across the street.

And on and on the memories came, filtering through Allison's mind like a movie as she lay safe and sound, wrapped in her afghan, imagining her own life just as she'd imagined the lives of strangers so long ago.

CHAPTER TWO

Allison liked the company of older people, perhaps because her parents were older. She had two twin sisters, Susan and Sarah, and two brothers, Jerry and Will—all much older and gone from the house by time she attended school (she came to refer to them in shorthand as the Old Ones). Emma and Doug, Allison's father, were in their forties then. Emma would tell her later, "After raising your brothers and sisters, I was tired by the time you came along," which accounted for the way in which Allison often came and went on her own, doing pretty much whatever she pleased.

When she was eight, as if someone had pulled a switch or pressed a lever, Allison began riding her bicycle like a demon. She'd begun bicycling a year earlier, just to go somewhere nearby, or to play with the Whitmore sisters. Now she began riding fast, and on her own.

Emma countered by constructing a steel-reinforced enclosure of activities meant to keep Allison out of trouble and designed to be as difficult to escape as one of Houdini's trunks. Of course Houdini got out, and so did Allison.

Over the years, this edifice housed piano lessons with Mr.

Priest, the nice young man who lived with his mother, and in case the piano lessons didn't take—which they didn't—there was another nice young man who came to the house to teach Allison the guitar, which did, at least for a few years. There was ballet, which was a good outlet for all of Allison's physical energy, but two years into Allison's instruction, the school closed when the teacher was injured in a car crash. Dance was replaced with English riding lessons. The church choir met on Wednesday afternoons. For a time, she attended the Maude Cullen Butler School, where she learned poise and ballroom dancing. She took golf lessons at the country club, although it would be many years before she learned to appreciate its contemplative pace.

Despite all of Emma's attempts to contain Allison's attention and energy within these constructive, creative, and safe activities, Allison slipped through the tracks of time on her English racer. The first few times Emma saw her tear down the driveway hell-bent for wherever, she called her back.

"Where are you going so fast, Allison? I don't want to spend my afternoon scraping you off the pavement. Ride that bicycle like a lady."

Allison, who had no such intention, learned to ride slowly to the corner of Eleventh Street, where the school bus turned. Once the watchful Emma was satisfied that she wasn't going to plow into Mrs. Maye or a random pedestrian or be flattened by a teenager taking the corner like a demon in his pickup—that is, as soon as Allison was out of sight—she would take off like a rocket. Soon, she stopped riding with the Whitmore sisters and the other neighborhood girls, who were too slow and easily distracted.

Instead, she started riding with the boys. They didn't ride on the sidewalk like the girls did. They rode in the street, with as little care for their personal safety as their older brothers who had just learned to drive. They rode on dirt tracks, steering with one hand, holding a can of RC Cola in the other. They did wheelies and taught Allison how to do them too.

Allison didn't know why she suddenly wanted to go so fast, or why she cared more about the ride itself than where she was going. It was an urge. Once, flying over the roads in Montgomery Park—a few blocks down the hill from Huguenot Street—under the laurel oaks, red maples, and loblolly pines, she felt a freedom that she knew she needed, even if she didn't know what that meant. Getting to wherever she ended up was never as exhilarating as the journey there; often, she had no destination. Sometimes she would pedal as fast as she could go—which was easy on the park's flat roads, riskier on the dirt paths—and then coast, with the wind blowing her auburn hair behind her, enveloped by the silence that thrilled her, that called for more speed.

"Allison!" Emma stood on the front doorstep. "Dinner! Allison!"

No answer.

"Allison! Dinner!"

Still no answer.

"I swear. That child."

It was the evening ritual, finding Allison for dinner. Emma could see Angel, one of the Whitmore sisters, playing jacks in the Whitmore driveway a few houses down.

"Angel, have you seen Allison?"

"She went off with Bobby Sewell, Mrs. Blanchet."

"Did she say where to?"

"No, Mrs. Blanchet."

"Thank you, Angel." Emma went inside. "Oh, Lord preserve us," she said to herself.

She walked into the kitchen, where Doug was sitting on a low stool near the refrigerator. It's where he always sat, his long legs splayed out, when it was just him and Emma in the kitchen.

"Any sign of her?" He had just loosened his tie and was in the process of untying his shoes.

"Angel said she went off with Bobby Sewell. She *knows* not to do that before dinner."

"What else is new? He's an okay kid. Even if he does have the habit of climbing every tree he sees."

"And inviting Allison to climb up with him."

"Well, it could be worse. They could be teenagers, getting up to all kinds of things in those trees."

"I'm not worried about her being up *in* those trees, even though I've told her a hundred times not to go around climbing them. It's falling *out* of them that I worry about."

"Well, she doesn't do that too often, does she? And don't you always put her back together?"

"How often is too often, Doug? You're not around when I have to wash the blood off and put on the Bactine and the Band-Aid. It's not the way a twelve-year-old girl should be behaving."

"Let's arrange for her to fall out of a tree on a weekend, then. If I'm not playing golf, I'll clean her up." He had a thought. "Or maybe I'll take her to the club with me and she can climb a tree there. Then I'll be on the spot to apply the disinfectant and the bandage." Emma ignored the suggestion.

"All I have to do is walk into Singleton Pharmacy and they say, 'How many boxes and bottles, Mrs. Blanchet?' And then I have to repair the overalls or the blue jeans. Or the dress."

"So, we're doing our bit for the local economy. And it occurs to me that it would do me some good if you didn't mend every pair of blue jeans or overalls." Doug was vice president of sales for the Britmar Textile Company, which manufactured mostly denim.

The back door slammed.

"I'm home!" shouted Allison, running up the short flight of steps leading to the kitchen. "What's for dinner?"

"Let me look at you," Emma said as Allison flung herself into the kitchen. "Were you climbing trees with Bobby Sewell?"

"We only climbed one." Emma turned her around, looking for damage. "And I didn't fall out."

"Praise the Lord for that."

"See?" said Doug, standing up. "Miracles happen in our time. Since you're dirt-, blood-, and bruise-free, Radish, give me a hug." Radish was his personal name for her. When she was born, Doug looked at her and said, "Why, she's as red as a radish." Then her hair turned out to be red, and that just confirmed it. For him, she would always be Radish.

She happily complied. "Can I come to work with you next week? You promised I could come."

"Are you traveling next week?" Emma poured him a glass of bourbon and added a little water.

"Nope. Next week I'm going nowhere. So I guess you can come one day."

Bourbon in hand, he walked through the dining room, where he picked up the newspaper from the dining room table, and proceeded to the living room, where he sat in an armchair, putting his feet up on the footstool. Allison followed, taking a seat, as ladylike as she could, on the sofa.

She watched him light a cigarette, look at the front page of the *Sunflower Enquirer*, and sip his drink. She loved everything about him: his tall, lanky frame; the face that everyone said resembled Jimmy Stewart; and what she considered to be his sophistication, apparent by the way he sipped his drink, pulled on his cigarette, and read the paper, all with the air of a man who didn't have a worry in the world. He traveled often for work, gone for two or three days at a time, and he flew on airplanes—something Allison longed to do. And she loved the fact that he rarely got angry, and when he did, the anger dissipated almost as soon as it appeared. Emma, on the other hand, whom Allison loved the way many daughters love their mothers—with less fairness and more scrutiny—could be volatile. Perhaps she had been looking forward to a little peace and quiet once the last of the first four children left the house, and was surprised, at the age of forty-three, to be pregnant again. She was not always as happy as Doug was to see Allison, regardless of the circumstance, but as far as Allison could tell, she seemed unhappy when she *couldn't* see, or couldn't find, her fifth child. In those early years, before she had devised the rigid cage of activities meant not only to keep Allison from falling out of trees but also to groom her for the future, Emma's temper would flare as she searched for her wayward young child on the street, on the playground, in the park, after school, and on the weekends. There were only so many bandages she could apply, only so much Bactine and Desitin she could rub on a wound before she felt as if the wound were her own, open and stinging. Once or twice she'd even resorted to taking a switch to Allison if the dinner was going to be late again because she was out searching the neighborhood.

Emma, however, was neither monster nor authoritarian—she was just, as she said, tired. She was also devout and, on Sundays, attended St. George's Episcopal Church. Once upon a time she would make quite the entrance shepherding her brood of four children and, if she could convince him, Doug, who preferred to commune with his maker on the eighteen holes of the country club. These days, it was usually just her and Allison. She remained a minor celebrity in her fifties, still bringing a child with her to services, just as she'd been doing for a quarter century.

She was devout enough to be troubled on those rare occasions when she punished Allison physically, even though she knew it was a parent's duty to discipline her children. She certainly didn't believe in the fire and brimstone that some of her neighbors did. Nor did she swallow doctrine whole. "The

Bible is not a cookbook," she instructed her children. "You have to think it through for yourself. God gave you a brain, so use it."

She was relieved when she discovered that Allison actually enjoyed church. She had a good voice and, when she was old enough, joined the choir. She loved all the hymns, but her favorite was "Lord of the Dance."

Allison eagerly sang in the choir. She was also drawn by the ritual, austere though it was compared to the Catholic church she'd once attended with Angel Whitmore. Years later, after she'd left the church, she could still recite the service by heart (impressed upon her not only by the music but courtesy of the baritone voice of Reverend Hewett, whose rich, cadenced sound, combined with his good looks and commanding presence, kept fragments of his sermons ringing in her inner ear long into adulthood).

After church, as Emma was preparing lunch, Doug, if he wasn't on the golf course, would launch into his own ritual.

"How was church?"

"It was fine. Allison sang beautifully."

"How could you tell?" Allison would ask on the weeks when she didn't have a solo.

"Well, you didn't stick out."

"I love church," Doug would say, patting Emma on the rear. "Great place to meet girls." Emma would blush. That was exactly how they'd met, and that was exactly why Doug had come the day he had, sitting in a rear pew.

"Why don't you come more, then?" Allison would ask.

"Because I don't need to meet any more girls."

A few nights later, the phone rang. Doug picked up in the kitchen. He listened more than he spoke.

"All right," he finally said. "Please keep us informed." He hung up, swallowed hard. "Emma!" The tone of his voice brought her up quickly from the rec room.

His face was ashen. "It's Will."

"Where is he? Is he all right?"

"That was the Coast Guard. They say he's somewhere north of San Juan, but they've lost contact with him. Big storm."

Emma sank into a kitchen chair. She thought of her youngest son, lost at sea. Doug sat next to her at the table.

Thanks to his independence and travels, Will was already something of a legendary figure in the neighborhood, much talked about, seldom seen. His visits to Sunflower were rare and highly anticipated, and also a source of anxiety, as Emma and Doug nervously awaited his arrival as he sailed alone from Caracas or Saint John in the Virgin Islands.

She said nothing. She looked down at her hands.

"All we can do is wait," he said.

After a moment, she said, "We have to do something." She stood again.

"They said to wait," Doug said again as she left the kitchen. "What can we do?"

She went down to the rec room, where Allison was watching television. She took her by the hand. "Come with me" was all she said, and Allison followed.

"Doug!" she called when she reached the living room. He came in from the kitchen. "We're going to pray."

While they waited for news from the Coast Guard, the Blanchets could think of little else. Over the next several days, Emma notified the two older sisters, Susan and Sarah, living in Atlanta, to stand by, as well as Jerry, who now lived in Richmond. Doug sat in his office at Britmar, shuffling papers and staring out the window. Emma skipped the bowling league and lunch at the country club to stay by the phone. Allison, too, hung around the house, not riding her bicycle, not playing with the Whitmore girls or climbing trees with Bobby Sewell. She spent her time staring at books and the television but after a few minutes realized that she couldn't remember what she'd read or seen. When Emma and Doug came upstairs at night, they would find her on the floor, asleep next to her bed, having drifted off in the middle of the long extra prayers she had added for Will's safe return.

A week later, Emma, Doug, and Allison sat in the rec room with Will, who had arrived home, tired but otherwise all right, the night before. He was tall like his father, lean, and with a face tanned and already weathered by his solitary trips down to the Caribbean in a wooden boat he'd built himself called *Perseus*. Allison sat next to him on the brown leather love seat. He was twelve years older, the youngest of the Old Ones, and, as a wanderer, the sibling she identified with the most and saw the least.

He shrugged off this latest incident, saying little more than that he'd had to secure himself in his hammock as the boat tossed and flipped and righted itself for two days and nights. He made jokes about it on phone calls with his fellow Old Ones. He was not one to regale family or neighbors with stories of adventures in exotic places; a part of him remained locked away somewhere else.

Emma and Doug resisted the temptation to hover. For one thing, they knew it got under Will's skin and would only lead to his departing again sooner rather than later. In any case, being demonstrative wasn't their way.

Allison, however, rarely hesitated to express herself. During long walks with Will in Montgomery Park, she begged him to stay. She regaled him with all the attractions that Sunflower had to offer.

"You could get a bike and we'd take rides. We could take guitar lessons together, or go horseback riding. You could join the choir at church."

"That's your thing, not mine. Besides, I can't sing as well as you."

"But why do you have to go sailing around the world all the time?"

"Because . . ." He thought a moment, since he couldn't remember being asked that question before. "Because I have to. I have to find out how far I can go."

"But if you go around the world far enough, you'll only wind up back here anyway."

"Well," he said, taking her hand as they walked past the teeter-totters toward the high school, "that's a good point."

What he *would* talk about was his growing interest in Buddhism. This was slightly shocking to the good Christians of Huguenot Street. Allison was curious, though, until Will told her that desiring objects led to suffering. "I know that," she'd say, "but the suffering goes away once I get what I want." She wasn't about to give up her bicycle, for example, and she still loved to look through the *World Book Encyclopedia*, even if she now had to do it at the library. (Mrs. Maye died when Allison was ten. She'd harbored vague hopes of acquiring the set then, but Emma had discouraged her from asking the relatives who'd come to take away the late widow's possessions.)

"You have a lot more than we ever did," Will said to her.

"Mother says that's because there were so many of you at once and Daddy was just starting out. It's not my fault I came at a better time. And besides, I don't have *everything* I want."

"What don't you have?"

"I don't have the new James Taylor album. And I don't even have *Sweet Baby James*."

"You had it; you told me you did. What happened to it?"

"Bobby Sewell ruined it with his pocketknife."

"Why'd he do that?"

"We were trying to put more lines in it so we could add more songs."

He looked at her.

"Because it didn't have enough songs already?"

"That's right."

"Like I said—you have too much stuff."

"You have a yacht! A hundred-foot yacht!"

"It's not a yacht and it's not one hundred feet. It's thirty-two feet."

"It's a big boat. *I* don't have a big boat."

"You're spoiled." Since he didn't say it angrily—in fact, he always said it with a smile—she didn't hold it against him or take the criticism very seriously.

One Sunday at lunch after church, the family did the ritual.

"How was church?"

"It was fine. Allison sang beautifully."

"What did you sing?" Will asked.

"'Lord of the Dance,'" Allison said. "My favorite song."

"That's your favorite song?" Will asked. "Why do you love *that* song?"

"Don't you?"

"No."

"Why not?"

"It's creepy."

"It's not creepy!"

"It's not?" Will sang:

> *I danced on the Sabbath*
> *And I cured the lame;*
> *The holy people*
> *Said it was a shame.*
> *They whipped and they stripped*
> *And they hung me on high,*
> *And they left me there*
> *On a cross to die.*

His voice was as good as Allison's.

"It's gruesome."

"It's about dancing. I don't pay attention to those other parts." She stood up from the table and sang:

> *Dance, then, wherever you may be,*
> *I am the Lord of the Dance, said he*
> *And I'll lead you all, wherever you may be,*
> *And I'll lead you all in the dance, said he.*

"That's all that it's about."

She started dancing there in the kitchen. She began deliberately, singing as she danced, emphatically pounding out the beat:

> *Dance, then, wherever you may be,*
> *I am the Lord of the Dance said he . . .*

She danced faster, whirling around the kitchen, singing breathlessly:

> *And I'll lead you all, wherever you may be,*
> *And I'll lead you all in the dance, said he.*

As she spun, her left hand knocked a vase of tulips off the kitchen counter. It landed on the floor, sending spurts of water and shards of pottery flying.

"That's enough!" said Emma, throwing her napkin down. She was intending to shake some sense into Allison, but Will got to his sister first, and, placing firm hands on her shoulders, he knelt and sang, softly, to the same tune:

> *'Tis the gift to be simple, 'tis the gift to be free,*
> *'Tis the gift to come down where we ought to be,*
> *And when we find ourselves in the place just right,*
> *'Twill be in the valley of love and delight.*

Allison began to calm down, and Will continued:

> *When true simplicity is gained,*
> *To bow and to bend we shan't be ashamed,*
> *To turn, turn, will be our delight,*
> *Till by turning, turning, we come 'round right.*

"That's what you should sing," Will said.

"Well," Doug said, wanting to bring the meal to an end, "I like *that* version, Will. But I think Radish can sing whatever song she wants to."

CHAPTER THREE

The following week, Allison accompanied Doug to his office at Britmar. The company was housed in two century-old two-story redbrick buildings in the old industrial part of town. One building held the offices of the textile firm, the other was the mill. A covered walkway connected them at the top floor; the shabby gray bridge sagged about a third of the way out from the office building, rose as it approached the center, and sagged again as it reached the mill, a minor carnival ride that had early ambitions but then gave up.

"Welcome to the brain trust," Doug said, as he often did when he brought business associates, as they climbed the worn wooden steps to the second floor of offices.

"Good morning, Mr. Blanchet," said a young woman seated at a desk near the entrance to the large open room as Doug, followed by Allison, entered through the swinging doors with frosted windows.

"Good morning, Mary," Doug half sang.

A few desks away from the door, a short, stout man with thinning brown hair waved a sheath of tables and graphs in Doug's direction.

"Who's the little lady?"

"This young woman is Allison, my daughter. You remember her, Oscar."

"Do I?" Oscar looked her over. "When was the last time you graced us with your presence, young lady?"

"A long time ago," Allison said, feeling immediately at home. "Years!"

"Really?"

"I've been busy."

"Wish I could say the same for your father."

Doug laughed and lit a cigarette. Oscar handed him the report.

"Good news?"

"Not necessarily." Lines suddenly appeared on Oscar's brow (already glistening with perspiration). "The problem with being popular with the hippies is that they have no money in their pockets, even if we made the pockets. Meeting with the big guy in fifteen minutes."

"Ah. Okay. Come on, Allison. Let's get you settled in the office, where you can make the big decisions. We'll inspect the mill later."

They walked toward Doug's office at the far end of the room. Several workers waved.

"Morning, Charles," he said, as he poured himself a cup of coffee at a small station.

"Morning, Doug."

"Lovely day, Sarah, Betty." Stirring his coffee, he tossed a well-received, genial smile at all the women working away behind their desks. There was something almost regal about him, Allison thought. And while he was tall at home, striding across the wooden floor he seemed even taller here.

"Janice," he said to a young woman at a desk near his door, "you remember Allison."

"Of course I do." Janice, who was in her twenties, came out

from behind her desk and shook Allison's hand. "Isn't that a pretty pinafore."

"My mom made it."

"And Allison's learning," Doug said. "She's in a sewing class."

"This is my third summer."

"My. You'll have to teach me."

"Any messages, Janice?"

She handed him a few slips of paper.

"And Mr. Swift wants to meet all the VPs in his office at nine thirty."

"Right. Thanks."

They walked into his corner office. While he stood by his desk, looking through the messages, Allison sat in the comfortable leather rolling chair behind it.

"Are there lots of VPs?" she asked.

"Some would say too many."

"But that doesn't include you."

"Oh, no. I'm the most important one."

"I thought so." From his desk she picked up a small Lucite ball, smaller than a golf ball. It looked like a globe, but it didn't resemble the ones in school or the earth as shown in the *World Book*. In place of polar ice caps were dark-blue patches, darker than the surrounding blue. They resembled oceans broken up here and there by browns, blacks, and whites that might have been continents, islands, and other geographical formations. White spots could have been snowcapped mountains like the Himalayas. An alternate world. When she put it back on its small transparent pillar, it seemed to float in midair. "I want to be a salesman. Not someone who works in a department store," she went on. "I mean like you."

Still standing, Doug was looking through the report that Oscar had handed him. His brow now wrinkled too.

"Why is that, Radish?"

"You get to travel. You fly somewhere, and someone else pays for it."

"That's funny. I always think that I pay for it in the end."

"And you get to eat out a lot."

"That's true. But I like coming home to your mother's cooking. And your mother."

"And," Allison added, "everyone likes you."

"They put up a good front." He perched on the window ledge. "Okay. Do you want to know the secret to selling, since you're going to be a salesman—a saleswoman?"

"Tell me."

"You don't try to sell anyone anything."

"You don't?"

"The surest way to blow a sale is to try to sell someone something."

"Then what do you do?"

"You listen. Hard. You try to connect with them, learn what their problem is and then work with them to find a way to solve it. Sure, you want them to buy what you're selling, but they never will if you don't understand their problem. You have to buy their story before they'll buy your product. That's the truth."

"You have to buy their story before they'll buy your product," she repeated.

"You're a natural-born salesman. I've got to go to a meeting, see the big guy. Half an hour, maybe. After that, we'll go over to the mill."

"Okay, Daddy."

He handed her that morning's *Sunflower Enquirer*.

"Here's the paper. See what's going on in the world, and don't cause any trouble."

"In the world?"

"Start in the office here." He gave her a wink. Walking across the office floor, he waved at a couple of secretaries before disappearing into a big office catty-corner from his.

She read the horoscope and a few comics, but soon lost interest. The comics were for kids. She looked through the front section: articles about the upcoming 1972 election, in which eighteen-year-olds who were being sent to Vietnam would be eligible to vote for the first time. Battles on the border between Pakistan and India. Of more interest was the imminent opening of Disney World in Orlando.

She looked at the ads for turtleneck pullovers, shift and granny dresses, and, of course, jeans, which were more compelling to her than the dresses. There was also a short article about the invention of something called a microprocessor by a company in California named Intel. The article said it was the size of a fingernail and slimmer than a human hair and contained twenty-three hundred transistors and would be used in new computerized adding machines.

Allison put the paper down and wandered into the main office. As she walked around the periphery, she didn't see women in any of the offices like Doug's. They were all at desks in the center of the big room and, like Janice, worked for the men. She walked up to the desk of one who had waved at him a few minutes earlier.

"Excuse me," said Allison.

"Yes, dear?" The woman, whose name, according to the silver nameplate on her desk, was Miss Gandy, looked up from her typewriter. Unlike Janice, this woman had a hard, middle-aged face that said, *Don't bother me when I'm working.*

"I'm Mr. Blanchet's daughter."

"I know. Can I help you with something? I'm a little busy right now."

"Did you always want to be a secretary?"

Miss Gandy stiffened.

"That's a personal question. I'm not sure it's any business of yours."

Ignoring Doug's advice about listening, Allison pressed on.

"I don't want to be a secretary. I want to be a salesman, like my father."

The secretary looked at her, her mouth pursing into a line.

"Good luck to you," she said, and returned to her typing.

Allison stood across the desk for a moment, wondering whether she should say anything or consider the conversation closed. Miss Gandy was taking no notice of her, so she turned her back and walked away. She was halted by the woman's voice.

"Don't expect anyone to give you anything, Miss Blanchet." She paused, as if she'd said enough, but something changed her mind. "No one's going to give you a job that belongs to a man."

Allison turned, watched as Miss Gandy pulled a sheet of paper out of the typewriter, and saw her hand trembling. The secretary ignored her as she put another sheet behind the platen, jabbed a button, and waited for it to roll through.

Allison walked back to Doug's office. This was why she liked men more than women. She was going to be like her father.

A few weeks after Allison visited the offices of Britmar Textiles, Doug arrived home from work as usual. Watching through the kitchen window as he walked from the garage to the back door, Emma thought he looked tired. He didn't have the usual kick in his step saying the day was behind him and he was looking forward to her company, his cigarette, and his bourbon.

Allison, as usual, was out. With the end of summer, her web of activities had at last dissolved, which meant that she was probably tearing around with Bobby Sewell after rehearsal at the State Theater. Emma had enrolled Allison in the young persons' theater program there a year earlier when she turned eleven, and because it gave her the opportunity to sing, Allison didn't object. She'd already played Marta von Trapp in *The*

Sound of Music, and after that, she was, unhappily, relegated to a member of the Indian chorus in *Peter Pan*. Now, what seemed like a further demotion—working backstage shifting scenery for *Jesus Christ Superstar*—didn't bother Allison at all. She wouldn't have a chance to sing, but it meant that she could hang out with the other stagehands, most of whom were boys.

After an early rehearsal, she met Emma at the beauty parlor for a ride home. "He's a hunk!" she cried out as she entered. The ladies in the chairs looked up. Emma, who was paying at the counter, closed her eyes.

"Who is, dear?"

"Jesus!"

"Oh, for goodness' sake!" said Evelyn, who owned the beauty parlor and who regularly attended the Methodist Church of the Redeemer.

"He's a hunk! He's got the bluest eyes you've ever seen!"

"Emma," said Evelyn, more in anger than in sorrow, "would you please take that young woman elsewhere?"

"Let's go home, Allison." Emma tried to take her hand.

"I love Jesus!"

"That's enough." Emma hustled her out the door.

Allison turned to give the hard-staring, frowning ladies a last bit of good news.

"I'm going to marry Jesus!"

"I hope you'll be very happy," said Emma as they got into the car.

On this day after rehearsal, however, the news was not so good, and the atmosphere when Allison leaped up the stairs from the back door wasn't very happy.

Doug was sitting on the kitchen stool. "Hi, Radish," he said. The usual lilt in his voice was absent as he swirled the glass of bourbon in his hand.

"You better sit down," Emma said, sounding concerned.

Allison sat at the kitchen table. There was silence as

she looked from Doug to Emma and back to Doug. "What's wrong?"

"I lost my job, kiddo."

Allison sat, uncomprehending.

"What happened?"

"Well, kiddo, we used to be a big fish. But we've gotten smaller." He sipped his bourbon. "And we just got swallowed up by a bigger fish." He paused and looked at the glass in his hands. "That happens in business sometimes."

"Is it going to be all right?"

"Everything will be all right."

"That's almost the name of a song in the show." Ordinarily, she would have launched into it, but it felt wrong. She didn't need the look she got from Emma to keep it quiet.

"I'm still going to go to school, aren't I?"

"Of course you are," Doug said.

"And can I keep working on *Jesus Christ Superstar*?"

"Absolutely," said Emma. "That won't change."

Other things changed. Doug and Emma resigned their country-club membership. Doug started playing on the public course, but only once or twice a month. They no longer attended the club's monthly Mr. & Mrs. Dance event, where they were routinely the best dancers on the floor. Emma stayed in the bowling league but no longer joined the other ladies for lunch afterward.

Before her marriage, Emma had taught elementary school. Now she enrolled in some classes and became a teacher's aide in the special education classes at Bedford Forest Elementary.

Subtly, she cut down on the meat at dinners and introduced more vegetables. She'd always been a good cook, but now, inspired by the limitations of a restrictive budget, she found ways to combine the fresh fish and shrimp that came up from the Alabama shore with mustard greens and butter beans, or sweet potatoes and collard greens. She discovered that she could recall the recipes of her childhood. Her father had been a mill worker and the family had grown up on the wrong side of the Sunflower and Chattahoochee tracks, and her own mother had always been vigilant when it came to spending. Emma had learned some culinary skills and tricks in the ensuing years, and so she combined what she remembered from those years of perennially tightened belts with her newer knowledge, and neither Doug nor Allison, nor anyone who came to dinner for the next several years, left her table unsatisfied.

For years, Emma had made many of her children's clothes. Now she began making Allison's jeans. Allison was not pleased.

"I don't like them," she said as she tried on the first pair, although they were expertly made.

Emma looked at her as she frowned at the mirror. "What's wrong with them?"

Allison showed her. "They don't flare enough at the bottom. And the waist isn't high enough."

"It's high enough for you. But I'll flare the legs out a little more."

Doug struggled to find a new job. That he'd been a top salesman, and then, as a vice president, the supervisor of top salesmen, at the now former Britmar Textile Company, that he had a shelf of awards from a once grateful manufacturer, didn't matter. He was over fifty; that's what mattered.

Finally, the job he got was one he gave himself. He and a friend from the country club, who had retired early (and was looking for a way to amuse himself and make some extra money), started a business selling hydroponics equipment designed to grow tomatoes and other plants in water. When Doug made a big sale to some young folks a few miles outside of town—clad in jeans and denim jumpsuits—he wasn't too surprised when they politely declined the complimentary packets of tomato seeds. Nor did he raise an eyebrow when they paid him in cash. Doug had never judged people on whatever they did with their denim fabric rolls when he sold them; he wasn't about to start now.

The market for hydroponics didn't grow in a big way, despite Doug's sales and marketing skills. So the family stayed on a budget. As far as Allison could tell, neither he nor Emma minded very much, not nearly as much as she did when her allowance was cut (though only slightly) and it took her a few more weeks than it once had to afford the new albums by Carole King and Billy Joel.

"It never felt so good not having to wear a tie every day," Doug told her not long after he was let go. "And I'll never have to buy another as long as I live." But when she overheard him ask Emma how she could have maxed out the credit card at Casual Corner, she knew she didn't want to live like this the rest of her life—no matter what Will, who in any case had gone off again to the Virgin Islands, said.

PART

TWO

CHAPTER FOUR

he mood was tense in September 1975, and not just in Sunflower. In Boston there were riots over school busing, and President Ford criticized the federal judge who had ordered it. Closer to home, in Washington, North Carolina, a female inmate in the Beaufort County Jail killed a prison guard who had attempted to rape her, then she escaped. In August, the woman, known as Joan Little, was acquitted.

That fall, busing came to Sunflower. Ordinarily, Allison would have gone to Sunflower High in Montgomery Park, less than a mile away, but the students who lived on Huguenot Street were ordered to go across town to Braxton Bragg, an all-Black school near downtown. Emma and Doug didn't object to desegregation; they told Allison that it was a necessary step toward building a better society. However, because they didn't know any of the families of the other children who would be on the bus, they, along with the Whitmores and other families on the street, decided it would be preferable to drive their children to school themselves.

Had it been up to her, Allison would have chosen the bus. She didn't exactly enjoy it when Doug pulled up to Braxton

Bragg and discharged her, the Whitmore girls, and Bobby Sewell from his Cadillac DeVille backfiring smoke.

"Yo, Lovey!"

It was Lillian. Her family had moved into a small house at the end of Huguenot Street when Allison was in the fourth grade. Allison's attempts to befriend her at school weren't rebuffed; they played politely at recess. Lillian came over to the house once for milk and cookies after school and, in a quiet voice, returned the invitation. Lillian's mother was polite when the girls arrived, but Allison felt a coldness she hadn't recognized on more familiar ground. Suddenly, there was little to talk about, and she was glad to go home when five o'clock came.

When Emma asked if she'd had a good time, she said only, "It was okay."

When it was clear that she had no more to say, Emma said, "Don't expect it to be like going over to the Whitmores'. Lillian's family has probably led a very different life."

"How different?"

"We'll talk about it later."

Allison and Lillian didn't play much after that. It was as if each had performed an unspoken duty and then moved on.

A couple of years later, Allison saw Lillian in Montgomery Park carrying a tennis racket. Tennis was another of the activities with which Emma was trying to corral Allison's energy, and, tired of always beating Angel Whitmore and of Bobby Sewell's always hitting the ball out of bounds, she asked Lillian if she'd play.

Lillian sized her up as if she'd never seen Allison before.

"Sure," she said. "I'll play you."

She had a forehand and a serve too powerful for Allison to return, and it was Allison's turn to be easily beaten. Lillian, however, was not a gracious winner; she rarely acknowledged Allison's congratulations or her offers to go for a Coke afterward. Lillian began calling her Lovey, since she'd often take games without Allison scoring a single point. She'd say, "*That* was easy, Lovey," and walk off the court. Under other circumstances, Allison would have had it out or refused to play with her anymore. But playing with a Black girl seemed somehow the right thing to do these days. Weren't they still fighting for their civil rights? It mattered, Doug had said, that Atlanta had recently had its first Black mayor, and that Barbara Jordan and Andrew Young were the first African Americans from the South to be elected to Congress in the twentieth century. So, she bit her lip. It ceased to matter after a month, when Lillian and her family disappeared from the street.

"I said, 'Yo, Lovey!'"

Allison grimaced. She hadn't seen Lillian after her family had left Huguenot Street, but since her first day at Braxton Bragg, Lillian hadn't missed an opportunity to torment her.

"Daddy's drivin' you to school again? Lucky you. You don't have to ride the bus with the white trash."

Allison didn't understand why Lillian seemed bent on making her life difficult at school. She would purposefully bang into her in the hall; a few times she shoved her hard against the lockers, followed by a cheerful "Sorry, Lovey!"

Allison fumed, but what was she going to do? She wasn't about to be put down by anybody, particularly when she hadn't done anything to deserve it, but she knew that if she took Lillian on, she'd be pounded into dust. It's not as if she could rely on the Whitmore girls in a fight; they clung to each other in fear as they skittered through the halls between classes. She hadn't been at Braxton Bragg long enough to make friends, and she wasn't entirely sure that she could. Most of the students were different from the ones she'd known before. From what she could tell, most didn't have the things she did, beginning with the up-to-date (if mostly handmade) clothes. For lunch they brought sandwiches made with baloney, not with baked chicken or a roast beef left over from a Sunday dinner made by Emma. Their music wasn't hers either: She didn't hear anyone singing Billy Joel, Carole King, Joni Mitchell, or even Queen. She heard the Pointer Sisters, Wild Cherry, Chaka Khan.

Of course, there were other white students. Bobby Sewell was one, but Allison didn't know what was up with him. She never saw him between the time they piled out of the car in the morning until they were picked up again in the afternoon, and sometimes not even then. She never saw him at lunch. He rarely talked about his day or who he hung out with, or if he was hanging out with anyone.

However, a week after arriving at Bragg, she discovered a group of white students smoking under an apple tree in an oak grove next to the school. She'd taken seriously the warnings Doug had given her about the health risks that cigarettes posed, but as far as she could see, her need for friends at Braxton Bragg was far more immediate than the risk of getting cancer. In any case, Doug's warnings were undercut by the fact that he and Emma both smoked a pack a day. So, leaving aside the long-term concern for her health, she took up smoking and hanging out with the kids at what they called the smoking tree.

The girls there were cliquish and off-putting; they held no fascination for Allison. The boys were more approachable, and at fifteen, Allison discovered that she was willing to be approached.

One was particularly interested in approaching her. She'd known Buddy at the State Theater, where he was a lighting assistant, but as he was seventeen then and she was twelve, they were merely passing acquaintances. She hadn't seen him since then; her membership in the theater ended at her thirteenth birthday, a casualty of the Blanchets' financial retrenchment and Allison's waning interest in putting on elaborate costumes and makeup only to sing in the chorus.

"What are you doing here? Haven't you already finished high school?" she asked him. "Or didn't you graduate?"

"Senior year!" He took in her skeptical gaze.

His body had filled out since the last time Allison had seen him at the theater. She was tall for her age, but he was taller, and broader at the shoulders than she remembered (had he been working out?). Some people's eyes are hard and push observers away, others' are soft and invite a watcher in. Buddy's large green eyes, behind the thick honey-brown hair he was constantly pushing away from his face, welcomed Allison in. Neither his lips, which he was in the habit of pursing, nor his eyebrows, which lifted on their own accord whenever he would speak, contradicted the invitation. Allison was fascinated.

"Aren't you a little old to be hanging around here?"

"Compared to who?"

"Me."

"Aren't you too young to smoke?"

"I'm not too young to have a job, so I'm not too young to smoke."

"You have a job?"

"I work Saturdays at Wendy's, handing out balloons to kids."

"That's an important job."

She couldn't tell whether he was joking or not.

"And you? Are you still hanging lights at the children's theater? Is that a job for a grown-up?" She only meant to ask what he was up to, but the question came out like a challenge.

"The one I have now is. They made me technical director last year."

Okay, she was impressed. But she wasn't about to let on.

"Why don't you take a ride with me in my Corvette and we'll talk it over."

"You have a Corvette?"

"Yep. A 1965 Sting Ray."

She'd never been in a Corvette. In fact, like most people in Sunflower, she'd never seen one in person. The offer was tempting.

She calculated the plusses and minuses. The plusses: At fifteen, the speed of her bicycle was less satisfying than it once was, and she was still a year away from getting her driver's license. She imagined taking on the hills and straightaways around Sunflower with Buddy at the wheel, her hair streaming out behind her—wait, did he have a convertible?

Another plus: the chance of discovering whether being with a boy was at all like the fantasies she'd been having for the last few years. Between the lack of any sex education in Sunflower schools and Emma remaining silent on the subject, she didn't know a lot. She didn't even know that Corvette Sting Rays had no back seat in which to get an education.

The minuses: Would she get a bad name for herself by riding in a fast car with a boy five years older than her? She'd never thought about her reputation before, and the opinions of the neighbors on Huguenot Street had never held any terrors for her. What would Emma and Doug think? Would they ground her?

She was hard pressed to come up with other minuses.

"No, thanks." The answer had come out before she'd finished thinking it through. "Some other time, maybe." No sense closing the door completely.

"Maybe." He pursed his lips. "Sure."

On Saturdays, after she'd handed out balloons at Wendy's and been bathed in the balm of french fries, Allison would stop by the lunch counter at Singleton Pharmacy. It was presided over by a legendary local figure known as the Captain. No one knew his real name; when asked, he would say, "My real name is the Captain." Everyone called him Cap. He was a Black man in his sixties or seventies, but his specific age was another mystery.

He claimed he'd grown up in Arkansas and done a stint in the navy, but no one knew for sure. They only knew that he showed up at the pharmacy one day not long after World War II and got a job in the kitchen. At some point—again, no one could quite remember when—he was running the lunch counter.

The most popular items on the menu were all his inventions. The bestseller was the Singleton Scramble, which had nothing to do with eggs. A pair of grilled hot dogs were nestled in buns and then smothered beneath a mound of chili, which was topped with crumbled saltines, and the *real kicker*? Sliced garlicky dill pickles. You could substitute onions and corn chips for the saltines, or just have the chili on its own.

Every morning, Cap whipped up the chili, a secret recipe of his own devising, in large vats. No one was allowed into the kitchen while the magic was working.

Whether on hot dogs, onions, or corn chips, Cap's chili was known for its lethal effect on the digestive system, and once that became abundantly clear, the pharmacy's owner installed a small display box at the end of the counter filled with rolls of antacids. Marvin Marx had put it there, he joked with friends, so that he wouldn't get sued. At first, Cap took this prophylactic measure as an affront to his culinary skill, but in a short time arrived at a more philosophical, not to say retail, view. "Mr. Marx knows everybody's gonna eat my Singleton Scramble and some of 'em won't have the necessary strength to deal with it. Sellin' those little pills might just give those folks the ability to eat more."

Late on a Saturday afternoon, Allison came in and took a seat at the linoleum counter.

"Hey, Cap!"

"Hey, Miss Blanchet. Somethin' to fire up that appetite before that good dinner I know Mrs. Blanchet's gonna make?"

"Just a small bowl of chili, please."

"That's all? You're not eatin' that stuff they call meat at that fast-food place you work at, are you? I wouldn't give that mess to a dog."

"I don't want to spoil my appetite."

"My chili never spoiled nothin', you know that." He smiled at her. "Comin' right up."

Instead of eating it, Allison would have loved to have rubbed the chili all over her arms to get rid of the french fry smell. On her way out, she bumped into Buddy in the parking lot. They had seen each other several times at the smoking tree since that first day, but he'd not asked her again if she wanted to take a ride with him.

"Fancy meeting you here," he said.

"I'm here at least once a week. Nothing fancy about meeting me here."

"I stand corrected."

"What's going on at the theater?"

"*You're a Good Man, Charlie Brown*. It's a fun show. You should see it."

"I'm too old for that."

"You would have made a great Lucy."

"You think so?"

"Sure. Where you off to?"

"Just home."

"Want to go for a ride?"

Would she have to make another decision on that now?

"In your Vette?"

"No, that's at home. In that." He pointed to a highboy red Ford pickup.

A Corvette *and* a pickup. Allison ran the calculus: Was it better, or at least less bad, to be seen with a twenty-year-old boy in his pickup than in his Corvette? And since the truck couldn't go as fast or take the turns as tightly as the Vette, would it be as much fun?

She looked at Buddy, taking in that tall frame, the green

eyes, and the sun-bleached blond hair on his arms that showed below the rolled-up sleeves of his plaid shirt. Where was he thinking of taking her? Perhaps someplace private?

"Sure," she said. "Where to?"

"Warriner's."

She relaxed. And was disappointed.

"The garden place?"

"Yep. I need a bag of mulch."

"Oh yeah. Sexy."

Buddy smiled at her. She looked at her hands. Modesty usually came hard for her; now it came unbidden. She fought against it and looked back. *I could like him,* she thought.

On the short ride to the garden center, Allison suddenly found herself feeling self-conscious.

"Sorry about the french fry smell," she said.

"French fry is one of my favorite smells."

She offered a wrist.

"In that case, wanna lick?"

Buddy took his eyes off the road for a moment and looked at her.

"Hmm." He paused. "Not while I'm driving."

Buddy bought a bag of mulch at the garden center. There was something about the salesman he was talking to that made her shudder, so Allison wandered the grounds. It was still fall; there were some flats of succulents and perennials left. But it wouldn't be long before the Christmas trees arrived. She wondered if Doug shouldn't work out a deal with the owners and get some of his hydroponic gear in here. She made a mental note to bring it up when she got home.

"There's something about that guy," she said once they were in the truck.

"Yuri? He's harmless."

"You think? He gives me the creeps."

"Is this because he's Russian?"

She scoffed. "No, of course not," she said, but secretly pondered for a moment the anti-Soviet messages that had been pushed on her as long as she could remember. Yet, no, it wasn't that, she convinced herself. He just felt off, in the same way Mrs. Maye's room full of dolls felt off years ago.

Buddy dropped her off at home.

"Don't want you to be late for dinner," he said, bringing the Ford to a stop in the driveway. "See you again?"

"Why not?" She acted noncommittal. She waited to see if something else might happen. He smiled; the eyebrows went up. That was all. She got out of the truck and watched him pull away.

"Hey, Dad," she said when she found Doug watching golf on television.

"What's up, Radish? How was work?"

"You know. Balloons, kids with greasy hands. Hey, have you thought about branching out a little?"

"What did you have in mind?"

"I was just at Warriner's with Buddy."

"Buddy from the theater?"

A pause.

"I stop by the theater now and then to say hi to people, and I've seen him a few times."

Doug looked at her. She held his gaze.

"Evidently, he's said hi back."

"Yeah, we're friends."

"And what were you doing at Warriner's with your buddy Buddy?"

"Nothing. He was buying mulch."

Another pause.

"And then he brought me right back." Two out of three statements were true. That wasn't bad, she thought.

CHAPTER FIVE

History was one of Allison's favorite subjects. In the fall, it was American history; on this day, the teacher, Mr. Bickerstaff, was discussing the Declaration of Independence.

"What did you learn from your reading?" he asked the tenth-grade class.

"Not much," Lillian muttered. A few students around her tittered. Mr. Bickerstaff, who might not have heard, pressed on in the otherwise silent room.

"Who had the primary responsibility for writing the Declaration?"

Silence. Then Lillian piped up.

"Some white dude."

"Whose name was?"

"Mr. I Own Slaves."

Mr. Bickerstaff tried to make room for Lillian's point of view. After all, although she was far from the most deferential student to ever sit in his classroom, it was clear to him that she could think.

"I appreciate the fact that you've done the reading, and yes, he did. But we're talking now about the Declaration of

Independence. Anyone else? Who had the primary responsibility for writing the Declaration?"

"Mr. Who Gives a Shit."

Now there was laughter. It annoyed Allison. She liked this class and Mr. Bickerstaff, even though he had less than half the charisma of Reverend Hewett and could not always control the room. She was sitting with the small band of white students in the back of the room, a few rows behind Lillian and the other Black pupils.

Without looking at her and without meaning to be heard, Allison said, "Why don't you just admit you don't know the damn answer?"

A tense silence. Allison knew very well who had written most of the Declaration of Independence but, in these circumstances, didn't want to be identified as the White Girl Who Knew the Answers. In her annoyance, she had spoken louder than she had intended. Now she was the White Girl Who Had Challenged a Black Girl on the Black Girl's Turf.

"Oh, yeah!" came a female voice from among the Black students.

"Watch out, girl!"

"What a motherfucker!"

"That's enough!" Mr. Bickerstaff tried to exert some control.

Lillian stood. "I'm gonna see you outside, Lovey." She pointed toward the door. Low laughter rippled around the room.

"Whoa!" said a voice from behind Lillian.

Allison said nothing. Suddenly, she had to consider how she'd get through the day without a broken nose or limb, and it was only eleven o'clock.

When the class ended, Allison looked straight ahead and tried to appear as if she weren't hurrying to the door. A knot of students in front of her blocked her path. She sensed Lillian, who had pushed three students aside, behind her just before she felt the shove below her shoulder blades.

"Let's go, Lovey," Lillian said, and shoved her again, pushing her into two students in front of her. From the corner of her eye, Allison saw Mr. Bickerstaff busying himself with a stack of papers, determined not to look in her direction.

Now they were in the hallway. Some students scattered, not wanting to be involved; others gathered around. Students coming from other classes, sensing that something was about to happen, joined the growing scrum. Allison retreated a few steps to give herself some space, and tried to think. There was no way she was going to back down. But she didn't relish the thought of getting her face bloodied or possibly losing some teeth.

As if on cue, the gathering crowd also stepped back, clearing a space, a little arena, for the match about to take place.

Lillian stepped into the middle of the impromptu ring. "Okay, Lovey. You and me. Been waiting for this."

Allison stayed back.

"What's with you, Lillian? All we ever did was play tennis."

"And I beat your ass."

"Yeah, so what's your problem now?" Her mind was racing, trying to find a way out of this.

"Quit stallin'!" a voice behind her shouted.

"Get it on!"

"Okay, bring whatever you got," Allison said, not knowing why she said it.

"Right on!" Lillian suddenly rushed Allison. The crowd whooped and pushed in for a better look at the impending bloodshed.

From out of nowhere, a large figure stepped in Lillian's way.

"Don't do this, Lillian."

She looked up at the tall, wide figure whose head loomed above hers.

"Out of my way, Wendell."

The young man she'd called Wendell put his big hands on Lillian's shoulders.

"Lillian," he said calmly, "you know you don't want to do this."

"Hell I do."

"No, you don't. You really don't."

Lillian looked at him hard for a moment, seeming to forget about Allison, who was still standing a few feet away, wondering who this boy was who was saving her life.

"Lillian," he said again. "Listen to me. It ain't worth it. You know what I mean."

Lillian pulled away. She was not mollified. She stared at Allison, the short path between them clear.

"This ain't over." She turned and walked away.

Allison took a few steps toward Wendell, unsure of what to say.

"Thanks . . . Wendell?" She said his name as if she wasn't certain she'd heard it right. She wasn't sure she'd seen him before.

He shrugged.

"I'm Allison," she said in the awkward silence.

"Okay then."

"I appreciate what you just did."

"If you value your skin, don't get up in her face."

"I won't. Don't worry."

"Okay then."

"But what if she gets up in mine?"

"Don't let it happen."

He walked past her and, joining the last group of Black students still hanging around, strolled off.

For a moment, she felt defenseless. Then, alone in the suddenly deserted hallway, she squared her shoulders and left the building. The hell with the rest of the day. She'd call Buddy. They'd go for a ride.

She was sullen for the first few miles as Buddy drove around town in the Corvette. She didn't want to talk about her humiliation. Finally, as they were leaving Sunflower to ride through the hills south of town, she told him. She hadn't mentioned Lillian before, so she started at the beginning.

"I never should have invited her over for milk and cookies," she said with some bitterness toward her ancient generosity after she described the events of the morning.

"Girl, you've got to stay away from that one."

"What I don't get is that from the beginning, she seemed out to get me. I mean, it didn't seem like it was enough just to beat me at tennis, she had to pound me into the ground."

"She probably has a lot to be angry at. Maybe you were the only one she could punish."

"Maybe then. But what about now? She couldn't find anyone else since then to punish for whatever she thought I did?"

At first Buddy didn't answer. Then he said, "It's ugly out there for a lot of people. The sixties are over, the backlash has set in. It's all about the silent majority now. They don't like it that Black folks are getting their rights. And Black folks don't much like us either."

"What's this 'us'? I'm not 'us,' I'm me. I didn't like getting beaten to dirt by Lillian in tennis and seeing her enjoy it, but I didn't hold it against her. Not for long, anyway. She's still carrying it around like it means something."

"I guess it still does. You'd be better off just staying out of her way."

"What am I supposed to do, hide for the next three years?"

They had reached the hills. Autumn was just settling in; the leaves on the beeches and oaks were still green. Buddy picked up speed along the winding road, and the sun sent streaks of light through the trees as they sped by. Allison let out a sigh. Her anger dissolved in the changing light, and she felt it being replaced by the thrill of speed, the sound and feel of the gears shifting smoothly from third to fourth. She felt the Corvette grip the road as Buddy took the curves. It all gave Allison that feeling of flying. She wanted more of it.

"Hey—can I drive?" She had to shout to be heard.

"What?"

"Can I drive?"

Buddy laughed. "No! Not till you get your license. And maybe not even then!"

"Why not?"

"This car'd throw you like a bucking bronco."

"That's what you think!"

"License first. Then we'll see."

She was still fifteen. She wouldn't get her license for almost another year. How could she survive the wait to go that fast, under her own control?

At lunchtime on a Friday afternoon in early October, Allison pulled on her denim jacket (made by Emma, although she didn't tell anyone this), put on an Atlanta Braves ball cap and, as had become her habit, went out to the smoking tree. Three other girls were there, part of the usual senior clique. When they saw Allison coming, they huddled up and ignored her.

Lighting up, she assessed her situation at Braxton Bragg. She had gotten into the girls' chorus and made a few friends there, where the barriers between classes weren't as impermeable as they were in the cafeteria, assemblies, or hallways. She was doing well in the subjects she liked (history, geometry, and biology), less well in the ones she didn't care much about. If she stayed out of Lillian's way, she'd be fine, although the thought of having to keep a lookout for the next three years, due to some nameless crime she didn't commit, didn't sit well.

As she stubbed out the cigarette, she saw Wendell, the young man who had intervened between her and Lillian, coming in her direction. Since that day in September, she'd say hello whenever she'd pass him in the hall or see him in the cafeteria. He would acknowledge her and walk on—not rudely but, like the other seniors, with an understanding that he lived in a different world.

"Wendell!" No harm in trying again.

"Yeah, hey," he said, not slowing his pace.

"Wendell!"

He raised a hand in what might have either been a wan *hello* or a brush-off.

"Wendell, hey, come on!" Allison hustled toward him.

"Yeah?" he sighed.

"Just wanted to say hi. Why don't you come over and have a smoke?"

He looked at her, slightly bewildered, as if to say, *Are you kidding me?*

"What? Come and have a smoke with me."

Wendell sighed again. "How long have you been here?"

"At school? Six weeks, maybe? Why?"

"Don't you know that that's the *white* smoking tree?"

Allison's face froze. She didn't know that. She'd been at Braxton Bragg for six weeks. She'd seen, but hadn't *seen*, that all the smokers at the smoking tree were white.

"I didn't. I guess I'm pretty stupid. I'm sorry."

"Not your fault. It's how it is."

"I know you smoke. Where do you go? Is there a Black smoking tree?"

"Back there." He pointed to a spot beyond the smoking tree.

"In the woods?"

"That's right."

"Well—could I come and smoke with you?"

Wendell sighed a third time. "What's your name again?"

"Allison."

"Allison. You know how it goes around here."

"Do I? I don't think I do. Are there rules for a smoking tree?"

"There are rules for everything," he said, "if you're Black."

"Well, I'm white. And I don't like rules any more than I think you do."

"How do you know what I think about rules?"

"Invite me to come with you to your smoking tree."

He said nothing for a moment as they came close to the woods. "No rules against you walking next to me."

It wasn't much of a woods, more a patchy clump of sweet gum trees, but their red leaves glowed in the mellow autumn light.

"Nice place for a smoking tree," Allison said. "Better than the white one."

"It's okay."

They approached a tree that stood out from the others by the wide circle of dirt covered with butts surrounding it. A small group of Black students who had been smoking and laughing stopped and looked at Allison and Wendell.

"Just a visitor," Wendell said. Like the white students, the Black students ignored them.

"Happy now?"

"Oh, damn, Wendell, I just want to be friends."

"It's hard here."

"If it's hard here, how's it going to be any better out there?" She gestured past the woods.

"Is this for you? You need to have a Black friend?"

"No, but . . ."

"Don't you know you're living in Sunflower?"

"Yeah, but it's 1976."

"Doesn't matter what year it is. It's still Sunflower."

"I don't care."

"If this is about you almost getting pounded by Lillian, I didn't do that for *you*."

"But you still did it."

"Lillian has a history. Sometimes she loses control. If she'd gotten her hands on you, they'd have kicked her out of school. And it wouldn't have mattered whose ass she kicked."

"Well, still. Thanks. I think."

"I'm just saying, if this has to do with that, well, that didn't have anything to do with you."

Allison felt defeated.

"I just wanted to be friends."

"Better leave it where it is."

She reached for a cigarette, feeling at a loss of what else to do, and discovered that she'd smoked her last one.

"Can I at least bum a cigarette?"

Wendell reached into his pocket, withdrew his pack of Newports, and let her take one.

"Thanks." She lit up. She looked at Wendell, who said nothing. "Well."

A few boys who were smoking and talking in low voices turned and looked at them.

"Thanks," she said again.

She walked toward what she now knew was the white smoking tree. Before she reached it, she ground the cigarette into the grass. She had no use for menthols. Then she walked back to her locker.

The next day, flyers appeared on bulletin boards around the school:

> Independent Powderpuff Football Team!
> Stick It to the System! Sign Up Today!

Allison read one posted in the cafeteria. *Stick it to the system,* she thought. *Sounds good to me.*

Tryouts were the next day on the football field. She showed up in sweats, determined to be quarterback or nothing. Will had taught her how to throw and catch a football, and although (because no one else would play with her) she hadn't handled one in a while, she felt completely confident in her abilities. Besides, falling out of a lot of trees had meant that her face had met the earth in a hurry plenty of times, so the thought of big girls coming after her as she attempted to pass or run didn't frighten her. Anyway, what would they do besides try to pull a flag out of her belt?

Coming onto the field, she saw about twenty other girls there for the tryouts. Three of them were white; they stood apart from the others, talking among themselves. Allison wondered where she should go, but before she could make up her mind, she saw Lillian. She didn't seem so formidable kneeling alone, tying a shoe. Still, Allison gave her a decent berth and walked toward the Black girls.

"Hey," she said.

One, another freshman named Tasha, whom Allison recognized from geometry, turned.

"Hey," she said.

The girls on the field were freshmen and juniors. The seniors had organized themselves into Braxton Bragg's first powderpuff team. There wasn't enough interest among the juniors to field a team, however, and the freshmen were too busy getting their scholastic and social bearings to start one, so a few doughty girls had stepped forward to create a team from anyone who wanted to try out. Allison liked their spirit of self-reliance. She thought of the Miss Gandys of the world, bitterly sitting behind their typewriters, waiting for the permission that would never be bestowed to become someone else.

Someone blew a whistle. Allison saw a Black gym teacher, Miss Ivey, walking toward midfield.

"Line up at the fifty-yard line," she announced.

The girls, most of whom appeared to be in no hurry, started for where Miss Ivey stood.

"I said, 'Line up at the fifty-yard line'! Now!" Miss Ivey blew her whistle again. The girls hustled over. Tasha moved with her friends past Allison, and Allison found herself at the end of the line. She braced herself as she saw Lillian walking toward her and then standing next to her.

"Coming out for the team?"

Lillian looked the other way. "Yep."

"If we're going to be on the same team, we might as well get along."

"No one said you're going to be on the team."

"Name?" Miss Ivey, clipboard in hand, was standing in front of Allison.

"Allison Blanchet."

"Year?"

"Freshman."

"What position are you interested in?"

"Quarterback."

Lillian snorted.

"Name?"

"Lillian Clark."

"Year?"

"Freshman."

"What position?"

"Wide receiver."

Miss Ivey moved on.

"If you're gonna be quarterback," Lillian said, looking at the goalpost, "you better get me the ball."

Allison took this as a positive development.

"Don't worry about me," she said. "You just get open."

In mid-October, Allison told Emma and Doug about Buddy. The difference between their ages had made her hesitate, but after a month, she'd had enough of sneaking around. She wasn't used to deceiving her parents; she didn't like it. Late one Saturday morning, and without devising much of a plan, she decided to tell them while they were all gathered in the kitchen.

"You remember Buddy from the theater?"

"Sure," Doug said. "You went to Warriner's with him to buy . . . mulch, was it?"

"Right. We're going out."

"Fine. Where to?"

"No, I mean we're going out. He's my boyfriend."

Doug, who was reading the sports section of the *Sunflower Enquirer*, put the paper down. Emma lowered the stack of dishes she was reaching up to put away in the cupboard onto the counter and turned to face her daughter.

"You're dating? Buddy?" She folded her arms, tightening her grip on the dish towel.

"Yes. I am." Allison hadn't thought she'd feel defensive so soon.

"Is this new?" her mother asked.

"Compared to what?" Allison thought making what seemed like a lively joke would help curb her defensiveness.

"Is this new?" Emma was not laughing.

"Not . . . exactly."

Emma and Doug looked at her, their brows furrowing in concert.

"For a month."

Doug drummed his fingers on the table.

"Any particular reason why you didn't tell us?"

"How could I tell you anything if I didn't know for sure?"

"What sort of . . . things . . . do you do . . . together?" Allison sensed that Emma was struggling not to sound too concerned.

"Just hang out with the kids at the State. Listen to music. Go dancing." She wished she hadn't added that last one. "We *all* go dancing, all of us together."

"So that's why you've been saying you've been out with the theater kids whenever you've come home late?"

"It's true. I have. With them and Buddy. Buddy's one of the theater people. He always brings me home before dark on weeknights. And by eleven on weekends."

"Well, yes, that's true," Emma conceded.

"It's no big deal."

"What's not?" Doug's fingers stopped drumming.

"I mean nobody cares."

"About what?"

"That he's five years older than me." She put it out there in a rush.

Allison met Doug's eyes and realized that she'd have to make a sale.

"He's not a teenager. He's mature."

The brown-and-gold starburst wall clock ticked. Emma's lower lip trembled.

"He has a responsible job. They wouldn't have promoted him to technical director if he wasn't a responsible person."

Emma was not sold. "What does a technical director do?"

"He's in charge of all the technical stuff. He makes sure the sets are built the way the designer designed them, that the lights are hung and focused according to the lighting plot, and safely, so that they don't fall on anyone's head." She was glad for the times in the past month Buddy had shown her exactly what he did—and that she'd been interested enough to re-member. She looked at Emma. "And he makes sure all the right material is bought for the costumes."

"He's responsible for all that?"

"For every show. And making sure that the props are made, or bought. Props are the things that actors handle. As opposed to what they wear. Which are costumes."

Doug seemed impressed, no less by Allison's strong attempt to make a sale than by Buddy's accomplishments at the theater.

"Would you excuse us? I think your mother and I should talk."

Allison went into the living room. She sat in Doug's arm-chair and looked out the picture window. She could see Bobby Sewell coming up the street on his bicycle. She wondered where he was going and, as he flew by, why he didn't stop to see if she wanted to come. He didn't even look at the house. He had stopped riding in the school carpool and was taking the bus. She never saw him at school. Or after. Or on weekends. As she said, she'd been hanging out with Buddy and the other kids from the theater. Who was Bobby hanging out with? What was going on with the boy she used to climb trees with, whom her mother feared might be a bad influence? He had been her friend. Now he was a mystery. As he rode by, she saw that he was growing his hair long.

"Allison?" Doug was calling her.

In the kitchen, Emma was now sitting beside Doug.

"We're glad you told us about Buddy," Doug said.

"Even if it did take a month."

"Great!" Allison was relieved. *That went well,* she thought. "He's really a good guy."

But something hung in the air that prevented Allison from thinking the discussion was over.

"Uhh. Can I go?"

Doug glanced at Emma. Emma looked at him. Whatever was hanging in the air got heavier.

"What?" Allison was determined to make the sale. She sensed they needed something else but didn't know what it was.

"Well . . ." Doug started to speak. And then he stopped. He seemed to be at a loss for words.

"Is he . . ." He looked at Emma again, who calmly looked back.

Doug cleared his throat.

"Is he . . . a gentleman?"

Emma rolled her eyes.

"Yeees . . ." Allison said, slowly realizing what she thought Doug was trying, through all the obliqueness he could muster, to ask. "Dad!"

He stopped again, embarrassed. Did he have something more to say? Emma continued to look at him. He looked at her. He lit a cigarette. He stood.

"I think I'm wanted on the golf course."

"Doug." Emma's voice stopped him.

He looked at her and tossed her the lifeline he thought she wanted. "And aren't they waiting for you at the bowling league?"

"Not on Saturday." But he was already on his way to the car.

Allison waited for Emma to say whatever it was that remained unsaid.

What she said was "He seems like a nice boy."

"He is."

"Has he tried to . . . ?"

"Mom! No!"

"I've given birth to five children," Emma said, trying to feel her way forward. She stopped, looking for the words. "I love them all."

Another pause. Allison waited.

"Oh," Emma finally continued, "that's not what I meant to say at all. I just want to say . . . I mean . . ." She stopped to light a cigarette. She took a drag. "Just don't go rushing into things."

She looked at the cigarette. "Well?" she said with a hint of impatience. "Off you go."

But Allison stayed where she was and watched Emma get up from the table and go downstairs. A moment later, she heard the vacuum cleaner running.

Yes, she was dating Buddy. The one damning thing she hadn't told her parents, and the one thing that would have put their minds at ease, was that he had yet to even kiss her. This confused and confounded her. He'd given her pecks on the cheek, but a real kiss? If, after one of those kisses meant more for siblings than grown-ups like her, she ever turned to look into his eyes, he would smile as one would at a child and kiss her forehead. It did make her feel good, and safe, to know that he respected her, but couldn't he see the question in her eyes? Still, he said nothing, and refused to act on what she meant to be an unmistakable invitation.

CHAPTER SIX

I t would be advisable to keep your children home from school
on January 15," said the letter from the Board of Education.
"Those African American students who nonetheless choose
to be present may wish to honor the Reverend King's memory
in their own way, and we think it appropriate to give them permission to do so."

By 1976, King's birthday was treated by some as an unof-
ficial holiday; others considered it a provocation. Many white
people in Sunflower regarded it as an imposition, an affront, or
an insult. There were others, Black and white, who thought it
an appropriate acknowledgment of a life of world significance
but which, because King was Black, was denied the same rec-
ognition as the Confederate war dead, who were remembered
each year on the fourth Monday in April, which the state
called Confederate Memorial Day.

The letter from the Board of Education, who had been
sending it out annually since 1970, was an attempt to mollify
both groups. It did not officially close the schools in honor of
King's memory; at the same time, it recognized the fact that

many students would make the board's action a moot point by not showing up.

Many Black students skipped school on January 15 to celebrate and march, so Braxton Bragg was largely empty. Since it was not an official holiday, teachers had to come to work, so those who didn't call in sick had the building to themselves with little to do besides wish that every day was as peaceful.

Allison, who, in the months since September, had gotten to know a few Black students at Braxton Bragg—mostly boys—felt an urge to march with them to city hall. But she was unsure whether she would be welcome. She decided to spend the day with Buddy instead.

"Something a bit different today," Buddy said over the blare of the pickup's radio. "A little business mixed with pleasure."

Allison wondered what he meant. As far as she knew, "business" was hanging out at the theater—either for rehearsals after school, when Buddy watched the staging, sketched a lighting plot, or supervised the building of scenery and props in the scene shop behind the stage—or standing in the rear of the auditorium watching a show on a Saturday afternoon. Today, however, was Thursday, and rehearsal (if there was one), wouldn't begin until four o'clock. It was not quite noon now.

Five miles outside of town, where the hills began, Buddy turned the truck onto a dirt path. He drove another two miles and then pulled off the road on the left side, into a small clearing, where Allison saw another pickup parked several yards ahead. It was smaller than Buddy's and older, and had seen better days.

Buddy reached beneath his seat and pulled out a briefcase of soft brown leather.

"Wait here," he said. "Won't be a minute."

He got out of the truck and walked to the driver's side of the other pickup. Allison watched as whoever was inside rolled down the window. Buddy smiled, said a few words, opened the briefcase, and pulled out a small package that he handed through the window. When he withdrew his hand, Allison saw a small wad of something that he slipped into the briefcase. He spoke with the unseen person for another moment, then came back to the Ford pickup. He knocked on Allison's window.

"Come on out and join us," he said, opening the door.

"What's going on?" Allison jumped down from the cab.

"A little party. In honor of your day off."

She followed him to the other pickup. Sitting in the cab was the Captain, putting the final touches on a joint.

"Well, hello there, young lady. Are you keeping time with this reprobate?" He laughed and passed the joint to Buddy who lit it, took a drag, and passed it back to his customer.

"Thank you, kind sir," the Captain said, offering it to Allison. "How about you? Or are you too young?"

"Hell no," she said, taking the joint and inhaling. It wasn't her first time getting high. She'd smoked many times with Buddy, never wondering about where he'd gotten the joint he'd produced on those occasions. They got high with the other theater kids, and cigarettes weren't the only things being lit under the smoking tree at Braxton Bragg. Pot was everywhere.

She returned the joint to the Captain, who took another toke.

"Well, I'd love to stay and chat, missy, but I mustn't linger."

"Are you headed to the pharmacy?" she asked.

"Nah. I'm taking the day off! Thank you again, kind sir," he said to Buddy as he rolled the window up. "Much obliged." He turned the engine on, steered the truck onto the path, and drove off, headed away from town.

It took Allison a moment to understand what she'd just witnessed.

"Do you sell pot?"

"I do. Indeed, I do." He put his arm around her. "That okay

with you?" Her body warmed to the feel of his arm around her waist.

"Sure. Not a problem."

"I didn't think it would be."

"Is the Captain a regular customer?"

"Now, that's the kind of question you'll have to learn not to ask. He was a little freaked out when I told him I'd brought someone with me, but when I told him it was you, he said, 'Right on. Bring the little missy over.'"

"So, was that the business? Or the pleasure?"

"That's a *good* question."

With his free hand he pulled another joint from the pocket of his flannel shirt, put it between his lips, lit it, took a deep toke, and exhaled a long stream of pot smoke.

"Best as I can tell, it was the business and *some* of the pleasure." He passed it to her. She followed suit.

When she exhaled, he took the joint from her and kissed her on the cheek. *Another one of those that don't count,* Allison thought. She turned toward him, saw the familiar half smile, looked him in his green eyes, and decided not to wait for them to invite her in. She drew his face toward her and kissed him. This time he didn't treat her like a favorite child.

They were back on the road headed for town. Allison leaned against Buddy as close as the bucket seats allowed. It wasn't the most comfortable position, but she didn't care. She had kissed him and he had kissed her back. Finally.

Queen's "I'm in Love with My Car" played on the radio. The anthem reverberated between them as Allison watched the street go by out the window.

"You're a disease, son," she said.

"And you've got me."

As they drove into town, they passed a group of perhaps fifty marchers headed toward city hall. Allison recognized several Braxton Bragg students. Some held signs that read "Make

Dr. King's Birthday a National Holiday" and "We Demand Decent Housing Now."

"Should we join them?" Allison asked. "Maybe we should join them."

"Maybe later," Buddy said as they drove past the protesters. He passed her the joint.

In the blur of faces, Allison thought she saw Lillian's, but couldn't be sure. Allison decided that if Lillian was there, she didn't want to be a part of it anyway.

"Never mind. Where to now?"

"To the State."

"The theater? What's going on this time of day?"

"You'll see."

It was just past one o'clock when they got there, and all the doors were locked. Buddy, however, had a fat ring of keys. He unlocked the stage door entrance and said, "Follow me."

Inside, it was dark. When they came to the entrance to stage right, Buddy unlocked that door. They stepped in. There was only a faint glow from the ghost light standing at center stage.

"That's not really there to frighten ghosts, is it?"

"Of course not. It's there for us. So that we won't trip and break our necks. Watch out," he said, taking her hand as he guided her around some set pieces for *Shenandoah*, a musical tale of a Virginia farmer who refuses to be drawn into the Civil War.

"Where are we going?"

"All will be revealed."

They made their way to the back wall of the stage. They stopped in front of another door, for which Buddy produced another key. They stepped through. He threw a switch; a line of fluorescent lights flickered on.

They were in a large room. The ceiling was thirty feet high; all around were more sets for *Shenandoah* and unfinished sets for the next show. There were power tools, paint cans, tables for the building of props.

Buddy swept an arm before them. "Here we are!"

"The shop?"

"What? All this glamour isn't enough for you? All right, then: the prop cage!" He swung his arm to his left toward a structure made of hard woven wire mesh, which was used to store the props for the current show.

"No one will be around for at least a couple of hours."

Although she was still pleasantly high, she felt her heart speed up. Buddy had brought her to a place where they were alone.

Another key unlocked the cage, and Buddy swung the door wide. About eight feet above their heads was a loft, reached by a metal ladder.

"Up we go," he said, and climbed, reaching a hand down to Allison. She didn't need help, but she took it anyway.

The loft was used to store curtains and drops. They settled into a pile of plush curtains.

"They don't call them soft goods for nothing," he said.

"Yep." She snuggled close to him. "Soft as can be."

"Cozy."

They kissed again and lay back.

"Soft goods," she said, running an index finger across his lips.

He turned toward her and laughed. "You're no radish. You're a rose."

"Oh God!" She laughed. "You're so lame!"

"You think so, do you?"

He shifted, and his whole weight came softly down on her, warm and enveloping. They both sighed. He cradled her head; she wrapped her arms around his waist.

She wasn't in a hurry to go anywhere else.

Is he . . . a gentleman?

Has he tried to . . . ?

Doug's and Emma's questions echoed in her mind.

Yes, he tried to, and yes, she said yes, and yes, she thought to herself, he'd been a gentleman, even though she had no other experience with which she could compare his manners. Of course, she had been in on it too; she'd not been passive. And he'd said he loved it.

It was three o'clock when they left the theater. In the pickup Allison shut her eyes and leaned against Buddy. Thoughts of everything else—of school, Lillian, her parents—were far away. She'd happily ride in the pickup with Buddy forever; no one else was necessary.

"One more stop," he said.

"Where? Why?"

"It'll just take a minute."

"Another sale?"

"Nope."

They pulled into the parking lot of a low cinderblock building. The neon sign in the big front window read "Sunflower Martial Arts."

"I want you to meet a friend of mine."

This was news to Allison.

"I thought I knew all your friends."

"Yeah?"

"Your friends are my friends, our friends from the theater."

He smiled. "Oh, so you know everything about me? You didn't know till this morning about my little pot-selling habit."

That was true. She suddenly wondered whether pot was all he sold. And whether whatever he sold had paid for the Ford pickup and the Vette.

"This is the dojo," he said as they got out of the truck.

"The what?"

"It's Japanese. It means 'school.'"

"Oooh—you know Japanese?"

"I do. *Aikido. Shotokan. Karate. Sake.*" He took her hand.

In a large room, a class of young twentysomethings was going through a routine, kicking and throwing punches. Every time they threw a punch, they made a sound that reminded Allison of an egg when it hit a sizzling pan. The class was conducted by a man who appeared to be slightly older than Buddy. Taller, more muscular, brown haired, and mustached. He had the clean-cut, authoritative look that belonged more to a television private eye than a teacher in a cinder block dojo in Sunflower, Georgia.

"Hey, Bud!" he walked across the room to where they stood near the doorway. He gave Buddy a particularly macho-looking handshake. "Long time no see."

"I've been busy."

"Who's your friend?"

Buddy, who had his arm around Allison's waist, pulled her closer.

"This is Allison."

"Hey, Allison." He extended his hand and Allison did the same, half expecting him to crush it. Instead, he was self-consciously gentle taking it, she thought, as if he wanted her to think that he might do her damage but would take the utmost care not to. As he shook her hand oh so gently, he looked her up and down. She stiffened and he moved his gaze to her eyes. "I'm Jon. I run this place."

She avoided his eyes and looked around. "Nice."

"How 'bout I give your friend a tour?"

"Sure," Buddy said. "Why not?"

Jon took them down the hall to another large classroom, similar to the first. The floor was covered with mats; around the perimeter were what Jon told her were training bags. Some hung from the ceiling, others were freestanding on the floor. Several had a model of a man's head and torso; others had simulated arms and legs as well. They weirded Allison out.

"The better to visualize your opponent when you practice punches and kicks," Jon said.

"Do you give them names?" Allison asked. "Like Ted or Billy?" She could see that he couldn't tell whether she was serious or joking.

"Nope. That'd make it harder to smack 'em." He gave one an openhanded punch in the face as they walked by. It wobbled backward, then righted itself. "But I'll make an exception in this case. I'll call him Buddy."

Against the wall were racks of what looked to Allison like pool cues.

"Bo staffs," Jon explained. "Made of bamboo. We use them in a style of combat called *bojutsu*, and *karate*."

The tour, which took them past a wall of plaques and photos and the pro shop where equipment and clothing were sold, ended in his office. He sat behind a walnut desk and put his feet up on it; Allison and Buddy sank into a leather couch. In the corner was a drum kit.

Allison looked at Buddy. "Do you do martial arts?"

"Used to. Until I got the promotion at State. And until I met you. Suddenly I was doing something I liked better."

"Aha!" Jon said. "So that's what you've been up to. You just dropped off the face of the earth."

"Like I said. I was doing something I liked better."

"I'll try not to be insulted on behalf of all your"—Jon paused, looking for a word—"former friends at Sunflower Martial Arts."

Buddy seemed about to respond but said nothing. He just looked at Jon, and his easygoing smile transformed into a grimmer straight line. Sensing the tension, Allison shifted on the couch.

"Do you play in a band?" Allison asked Jon, looking at the drum kit.

"Used to. Too busy now. Now I just play for fun. To work off energy. You should think about signing up for a course or two." Buddy, who had been holding Allison's hand since they entered the building, squeezed it tighter. "Girls need to know how to protect themselves. You can't be too careful these days with all those *miscreants* out there." He shot Buddy a look.

"Maybe I will. If I'm not too busy doing something I like better."

Jon laughed. "Pretty smart, this one."

"I think so. Let's go, Allison."

Buddy stood. Allison was only too glad to get out of there.

Jon walked closely behind them and followed them to the truck.

"Come on, Buddy. Since you've resurfaced, you better start coming around again." He gave Buddy a playful poke in the chest. "And bring your girlfriend."

Buddy opened the passenger door for her.

"Sure. See ya around."

Jon folded his arms on the bottom of the window frame. "Bye, Allison. Nice to meet you."

"Bye, Jon."

Through the side view mirror, she watched Jon watching them as they drove off.

"What was that about?"

"Nothing. Jon's okay."

"That's not how it felt."

"I used to hang out there, took a bunch of classes."

"You never said anything about it."

"Well, you know me. I'm not one to brag. *Hi-yah!*" He suddenly shot his right arm out as if he were about to deliver a punch to her shoulder.

"You're crazy." She snuggled as close as she could get. The visit to Sunflower Martial Arts had disturbed the wave of contentment she'd felt earlier.

"Why did we go there?"

"I wanted him to meet you."

"What took so long?"

"I wanted to wait till I knew we were good."

Allison was happy to know that Buddy thought that they were "good," but a part of her felt bothered. Did he mean that he wanted to wait until they'd had sex, when he could show her off as if she were a trophy? Despite Buddy's denial, the visit began to feel very much like a sale.

"Anyway, don't go back there for a class. Or for anything." That sounded like an order. The sharp edge to his voice was unfamiliar to Allison.

"You don't want me going back there?"

"Sorry. I didn't mean it like that. But Jon, all the guys there, really—and they're *all* guys—I just don't trust them with you."

"Okay then. I won't go back. I've got no reason to, anyway." She meant it, but for the first time, it sounded as if Buddy was giving her an order. She didn't like that so much either.

CHAPTER SEVEN

It was a Saturday afternoon. Mid-March. The flag football game between the seniors and the independent team took place on the Braxton Bragg football field before a surprisingly large and boisterous crowd. The seniors were resplendent in their professional-looking black-and-gold jerseys. The independents looked like the scrappy team they were, and they were proud of it. Their jerseys were constructed of thin red cotton, on which the team—during a raucous party the previous Saturday night hosted by Miss Ivey—had stenciled their own numbers in crude black numerals, starting with one thousand. They called themselves the Scrappy Cats.

Allison (number 1016) had prevailed as quarterback. In tryouts and practices, she'd proved to Miss Ivey that she was the fastest, the most agile, the most accurate passer, and the quickest to make decisions, even with the defense bearing down on her.

She was surprised at how much she wanted to be the quarterback. She discovered a delight not just in running the offense but in *wanting* to run it, in being the one to command the rhythm of the game, to decide in the moment who would get the ball if the plays (called by Miss Ivey) broke down—which in practice they often did. She was thrilled to discover her competitiveness.

She felt a release during physical activity that reminded her of riding her bicycle, which now sat in the garage, largely unused, since she'd taken up with Buddy. The kind of movement was different, but the burst of freedom and the release of energy from the cage of her body was somehow the same. When the ball came into her hands, so did power; her veins, arteries, and nerves came alive. As her responses quickened, her confidence grew. *Don't think,* an internal voice told her without waiting for Miss Ivey to give her the same advice, *just do.*

She was pleased, too, that the girls accepted her as their leader, even the sophomores and juniors. Now, with the Scrappy Cats, Black and white, she was all over the field, laughing, high-fiving, practicing, and memorizing the plays that Miss Ivey drew up.

Then there was Lillian. Allison had hoped that she and Lillian could get along, but Lillian showed no interest. When she caught one of Allison's passes, she just tossed the ball to Miss Ivey with no acknowledgment of who'd thrown it. Allison lost interest in cajoling her into even a bare-bones working relationship.

The other girls on the team defended her when Lillian threw random numbers or words into the cadence that Allison called at the line.

"What's with you, Lillian?" Tasha said to her during a break.

"I'm just having fun."

"You're just having fun for *you.* This is a team. If you've got a thing with Allison, deal with it with her."

"I am."

"Do it later. We want to play ball."

"She has to get me the ball."

"She *is* getting you the ball. I don't know how many times she's gotten you the ball today. I've lost count."

"Not me."

"You're not the only person on this team who wants the ball."

"Maybe I'm the only one who can score with it, though."

Allison and the Scrappy Cats trotted onto the field in a state of high confidence. They were going to have as much fun in this game with the seniors as they'd had for months in practice.

But the seniors soon disabused them of the notion that having fun would suffice as a winning strategy. On the opening possession, they marched down the field, hardly bothered by the Scrappy Cats' defense, and scored. Quickly, it was 7–0. Some senior members of the boys' football team, who had dressed as cheerleaders to root them on, now demonstrated their delight in their exuberant and clumsy way, insulated from the embarrassment of wearing skirts by the several six-packs of Coors they'd consumed before the game.

Then the Scrappy Cats offense took the field. The first play, which Miss Ivey called from the sideline huddle, was a pass to Lillian, who was to run straight up the right side. Allison took the snap from center, but before she could find Lillian streaking up the field, the seniors' defense penetrated the line. Forced to hold on to the ball, Allison was stopped for a yard. The tall senior who'd taken her flag threw it triumphantly to the ground.

"You're in for a long day."

"Don't you worry about me."

"You're the last thing I'm going to worry about."

Allison retrieved her flag and returned to the huddle.

"I was open," Lillian said.

"Sorry. They were in my face. I couldn't see you."

"It's okay," Tasha said. "Let's go get 'em."

The next two plays were just as unsuccessful, and the

two series after that resulted in six plays, two punts, and zero points. As Allison trudged to the sidelines, she heard Lillian say for anyone to hear, "We need another quarterback. I could do it better than her. I could throw the ball and still catch it myself." As she stood alone at the end of the bench, Allison could see Miss Ivey admonish Lillian.

Thanks to her success in practice, Allison had forgotten the fact that she'd never actually played in a game. She'd thrown the ball and caught passes with Will, but that backyard experience hadn't prepared her for the realities of a game any more than the Scrappy Cats' laid-back practices had. More than anything, the speed at which the seniors played surprised her.

If the Scrappy Cats called a run, the running back was at Allison's side to receive the ball before Allison herself had a firm grip on it. Even if she managed to get the ball cleanly into the running back's hands, the play would only go for a few yards before the defense, which had attacked the line ferociously, stopped the play. Receivers completed their routes before Allison could find them, while the offensive line broke down. Passes either fell incomplete or she got caught in the backfield and lost yardage.

Halfway through the first quarter, the Scrappy Cats trailed 10–0. Miss Ivey motioned Allison over as the offense again left the field.

"Take a deep breath. Breathe. I don't see you breathing out there."

"I think I've forgotten how."

"Relax. Pretend you're playing in the backyard with your brother. You don't have to force anything."

"Right, right."

"Just play and have fun. You can do this."

"Come on, Allison. We can do this!" Tasha patted her rump as she walked by. Behind her came Lillian. She stopped in front of Allison.

"I'm waiting. Not going to wait forever."

"I'll get you the ball."

Allison sat on the bench.

How am I going to do this? she asked herself. She closed her eyes and let a big breath escape. She was flooded with feelings of failure. Bleakness was followed by the sense that a chasm was opening beneath her feet, and then a flash of green the size of a pinprick. She took a breath—the first one she was conscious of since the game had begun. The green pinprick enlarged and became a bicycle, the green Schwinn Collegiate that Emma and Doug had given her when she turned twelve.

She was in the hills outside of town, riding fast, hair streaming behind her, shifting up and down through the gears, anticipating each curve, rise, and dip in the road. When a car came at her from the other direction, she'd glide smoothly to the right side of the lane, then back to the center in a single smooth motion. Instead of hesitancy and fear, she felt only joy as she picked up speed and she and the bike seemed to thin out, lose substance, and become wind. She heard Queen singing "I'm in Love with My Car."

"Let's go, Allison!" Tasha was standing in front of her. "We got them three and out. Where'd you go?"

"I'm here now."

As she took her place behind the center, she was half aware that she was still singing Queen's anthem.

Someone on the defense heard her and jumped offside for a five-yard penalty. Allison took a breath and released it. She felt some of the tension flow out of her body and thought she also felt the offensive line breathing with her. Maybe she imagined it, but that's how it seemed.

She called a running play. The ballcarrier appeared at Allison's side and took the ball in a smooth motion. She gained five yards before a senior pulled one of her flags.

"Way to go," Tasha said when she came back to the line.

Allison called another running play, to the opposite side, tossing Tasha the ball as she came up on her left from behind. Tasha found a gap in the line, ran to the outside, and cut up the field for six yards and a first down. A cheer arose from the Scrappy Cats' partisans in the crowd.

The Scrappy Cats gathered around Allison in the huddle.

"We're going to try a pass," she said, and called the play.

Lillian lined up on the right side, and after receiving the ball from the center, Allison dropped back. The play called for Lillian to run straight up the field for ten yards and then cut toward the middle. As if she were on her Schwinn anticipating a curve in the road, Allison looked to where Lillian would be in a second and threw the ball over the heads of the senior linebackers. In mid-stride, Lillian caught the pass, turned, and ran for another ten yards before a senior safety yanked out one of her flags. She tossed the ball to the referee and returned to the huddle.

"That's one," she said to Allison.

The Scrappy Cats were now on the seniors' thirty-six-yard line. A teammate came into the huddle with a play Miss Ivey had called on the sideline. Lillian lined up on the left side; Tasha stood a few yards behind Allison to her right, as if she might run a sweep. The center snapped the ball to Allison. Tasha ran to her left and Allison pitched her the ball. At the same time, Lillian ran to her right, behind the line and behind Tasha, who tossed her the ball. Then Lillian took off down the right sideline.

A senior linebacker yelled, "Reverse!" but by the time the other defenders reacted, Lillian had crossed the line of scrimmage and was headed for the end zone. The Scrappy Cats kicked the extra point, and the score was 10–7.

Then it began to rain.

The rain fell steadily but softly before the half, but during the twenty-minute halftime, it poured. When the teams returned for the second half, the field was soggy. In some places it had turned to mud streaked with green; yard lines were dissolving into dirty white smudges.

Miss Ivey told the team they would have to concentrate on running the ball. "It's too slippery and slow to pass, so we'll run it."

As the offense took the field, Allison looked at Lillian, who was glowering. Allison kept her mouth shut. She was determined to keep the high she'd felt when the half ended, and take the team with her.

Following Miss Ivey's plan, the Scrappy Cats pushed forward slowly on the increasingly wet and treacherous ground. Allison mixed handoffs with a few screen passes as the two teams slid down the field toward the seniors' goal post. The screens were to Lillian and Tasha, but Lillian wasn't mollified. Nevertheless, the Scrappy Cats got as far as the seniors' ten-yard line before their drive stalled in the mud. They kicked a field goal, and the score was tied at ten.

Determined not to be shown up by the upstart Scrappy Cats, the seniors then slogged in the opposite direction as the rain continued to fall. The Scrappy Cats stopped them at their twenty, and the seniors attempted a field goal. Their kicker slipped unceremoniously in the mud, but the kick was good, and they took back the lead, 13–10.

For the rest of the third quarter and much of the fourth, the two teams struggled over a small patch of muddy field, slipping and sliding a few yards first in one direction and then the other. By the middle of the fourth quarter, both teams were smeared with mud, and the Scrappy Cats' jerseys were so begrimed it was difficult to tell them from the seniors. Both teams began laughing at what felt like children playing in the mud, except for Lillian, who remained grim faced, and Allison, who enjoyed the absurdity of it but was still determined to win.

As the clock ran down to the final minute, the Scrappy

Cats still trailed by three. On a third down, they had moved the ball to the seniors' seven-yard line. Kicking a field goal would tie the game, and the Scrappy Cats could say they'd fought the seniors to a draw.

In a sideline huddle, Miss Ivey said to the team, "I leave it to you: Field goal and a tie, or do we go for the win?"

"Seven," Allison said.

"Yes!" the rest agreed.

"Let's do the reverse," Lillian said.

"That will take too long to set up in these conditions," Miss Ivey said. "But let's surprise them." She called the play.

Lillian lined up on the right side, Tasha between her and the center. A tailback and a fullback lined up behind Allison. The center hiked the ball and Allison dropped back to pass. The fullback, slipping in the mud, ran into Allison, knocking her off balance. In the second it took her to regain her footing, two seniors bore down on her from either side, the Scrappy Cats' two guards having fallen. Allison saw that the shortest path of evasion was straight ahead. She ran for the open space in front of her and located Lillian, who was just entering the end zone. She took a deep breath and hurled the ball. As she fell to the ground (she didn't know whether a defender had run into her or she had slipped), she saw Lillian come down with the ball. She threw her arms up in victory. The Scrappy Cats had won!

Then she heard the referee's whistle. She got to her feet, wiping mud and sweat from her eyes.

"There were two fouls on the play," the referee announced. "The quarterback passed the ball after stepping beyond the line of scrimmage. And offensive interference on the receiver, knocking the defender down. No score."

The seniors declined the penalties; the game was over. The seniors won, 13–10.

Lillian ran to the referee.

"I didn't push her! She fell!"

"That's not what I saw. Game's over." The referee walked away.

"I can't help what you saw. I didn't push her!"

The seniors were celebrating in the middle of the field as their cheerleaders, who had passed around a bottle of Captain Morgan at halftime, attempted a wobbly pyramid before tumbling, laughing hysterically, into the mud.

Lillian wasn't laughing as Miss Ivey took her gently by the arm and walked her to the locker room.

"She fell! She fell in the damn mud!"

"I know. The referee saw something else. We can't help that. You played a hell of a game."

"What's it matter if they say we lost?"

"Things don't always go our way."

Lillian shook Miss Ivey off and stalked to the locker room.

Allison walked across the field, scanning the crowd for Buddy. He said he'd be there if he didn't have to be at the theater. She didn't see him.

Raw and disappointed, she took pats on the back from Tasha and the rest of her teammates and a hug from Miss Ivey. In the locker room, she spotted Lillian sitting alone in front of her locker. She felt she should say something consoling to her, congratulate her for playing such a gritty, determined game—say the things that the others had said to her—but she couldn't make herself do it.

After showering, she took her time packing up her sodden jersey, pants, and shoes. As she walked down a hallway toward the exit near the parking lot, where some Scrappy Cats' parents were waiting to give the team rides home, she heard a voice.

"Yo—Lovey."

Lillian was standing in a doorway, waiting for her.

"Lillian. Good game." Allison squeezed it out.

"Hmmph."

"It sucks we lost."

"Yeah. It sucks."

"Not looking forward to seeing those seniors on Monday."

"Fuck 'em."

To Allison, this sounded like comradeship.

"Yeah. Fuck 'em."

They were walking side by side down the hall.

"You know what else?" Lillian asked. "I didn't lose us the game."

"I couldn't see. I was trying to get you the ball."

"*You* lost us the game."

Allison stopped.

"I was trying to get you the ball," she said again.

"You stepped over the line of scrimmage and lost us the game." She was standing too close. Allison took a step back.

"I couldn't even see the line—it was gone."

"You cost us the game."

"I wanted to win too, you know. A lot. But it's just a game." Allison was getting angry. "Get a life." She stepped to her right to walk away.

"You cost us the fucking *game*," Lillian said again, shoving Allison backward. Allison's head hit the wall, hard.

"I wonder where Wendell is," Lillian said. "I don't see him anywhere around here to save your ass, do you? Wendell!" she shouted. "Hey, Wendell! Come save this sorry girl's ass!"

Her head hurting, Allison shoved Lillian by the shoulders, and Lillian fell back a few steps.

"Well, well. Wanna get it on?" Lillian said, stepping back into Allison's space. They looked at each other. Allison tried not to breathe too hard. For a moment, nothing was said. Then, Lillian took a step back. "Nah. You're not worth the trouble."

She walked away.

Allison stood, trembling, unsure whether what she felt was anger, fear, pain, or adrenaline. Her head throbbed. She waited until she saw Lillian leave the building, then slowly followed.

In the parking lot, some Scrappy Cats were piling into a car. Not far from them was Doug's Cadillac DeVille, and Doug standing next to it. Allison hadn't known he'd been at the game. She threw her arms around him.

"Tough game, Radish."

"Oh, yeah."

"Want some Singleton Scramble?"

"That sounds good. I've got a headache."

On the way there Doug said, "I'm not sure about either of those penalties. That defender slipped in the mud; she didn't get knocked down. And I don't think you stepped over the line of scrimmage—you weren't that far forward."

"Thanks," she said, wondering if that's what he'd actually seen. She gingerly rubbed the back of her head. A bump was forming. She thought, *Something's going to change.*

After school on Monday, Buddy's orders be damned, Allison showed up at Sunflower Martial Arts.

CHAPTER EIGHT

Allison felt good in her white *gi* uniform, tied at the waist with the beginner's white belt. She quickly caught on to the training, and what she had learned about herself on the football field—the way that physical activity quickened her awareness, sharpened her responses, and gave her joy—was reaffirmed during her experience of the rigor and discipline of the dojo.

Buddy was right—all the teachers were male—but he was wrong about not trusting them. They saw the way that Allison attacked the work with seriousness and her approach to herself, which was humble, at least for a fifteen-year-old. They liked her and looked out for her.

Any vengeful intentions she might have felt toward Lillian faded as she absorbed the tenets of martial arts. The point was not to inflict injury, but to avoid it if attacked and gain time to escape the attacker. She believed the many motivational signs on the dojo's wall, including the one that read "To injure an opponent is to injure yourself. To control aggression without inflicting injury is the Art of Peace." One way to avoid injury was to avoid Lillian, and Allison did her best to stay out of her way.

After a little over a month, she knew that she wanted more

than just classes. She walked into the office one Friday after class.

"Hey, Jon."

He looked up from a book of diagrams and pictures he was putting together.

"What's going on, kid?"

She didn't like being called "kid," but this wasn't the moment to bring it up.

"I was just wondering, have you got anything around here that needs doing?"

"You mean like a job?"

"Like a job."

He put her on the phones for a couple of hours after class and drove her home afterward.

"I'm going to get my license in August," she said in the car one warm evening in mid-May. They had just left the dojo. "So, you won't have to drive me forever."

"Are you going to get a car?"

"I'm not sure how I'm going to swing that."

"Save your pennies."

"'Pennies' is right." She laughed.

"I beg your pardon, Miss Blanchet?"

She hadn't meant to ask for a raise so soon, and certainly not like that. It just came out.

"Sorry, I didn't mean it like that."

"Ask me again in a month. Meanwhile, you've still got Buddy to ferry you around, right? He can just drop you off; tell him he doesn't have to come inside."

Allison was silent. Buddy wasn't happy about her taking classes at the dojo, let alone spending time there when she wasn't. They'd had it out about it a couple of weeks before.

"I told you I didn't want you going back there," he'd said. They'd been sitting in his house, sharing a joint.

"I'm sorry, but I need to learn to defend myself."

"I can teach you that. Why didn't you ask me? I can show you now."

"You took a few lessons. I want to learn from the *sensei*."

"Oh, the '*sensei*.'" He fairly spat the word out.

"Don't say it like that."

"He's got you speaking Japanese now."

"That's what they call him. You know that."

"That's not what I call him."

To avoid looking at him, she glanced around the living room. She'd wondered about the house since the first time she visited, not long after she'd gone with him to the garden center. It was a ranch house built in the 1950s, one in a neighborhood of dozens near a park called Trillium Hill. The voices of parents and children still on the playgrounds and lake drifted through the twilight air.

Buddy lived alone in the house. When Allison would ask why that was, he'd say no more than that his parents were divorced, his mother had moved to Atlanta and was living with another man, and his father traveled a lot for work. Then he'd make a joke or change the subject. She'd never met his father or seen a car in the driveway that might be his.

She wondered why there wasn't more furniture in the house. A sofa, a couple of mismatched easy chairs, a pair of table lamps, and a new color television was all there was in the living room. A card table and four brown folding chairs comprised the furnishings in the dining room. A "vintage" (Buddy's word) linoleum-topped table and three metal chairs with worn red vinyl upholstery occupied the kitchen, along with a refrigerator with little in it other than orange juice, milk, and beer, and a gas range that looked as if the burners had never been turned on. There were miscellaneous dishes, cups, and glasses in the cupboards that might have been given away on the last day of a yard sale. A queen-size bed stood against a wall of the master bedroom without benefit of a foot- or headboard, its only company a maple bureau and mirror. The two smaller bedrooms had nothing in them but single beds and cheap dressers.

"Did your mother take all the furniture?" she asked.

"What are you talking about?"

"This place."

"I don't talk about my mother. You know that." His tone softened almost instantly, as if the subject of his mother hadn't come up. "Anyway, I'm not going to be here long."

"What do you mean?"

"I'm moving up."

"Moving up? Where?"

"Oh, let me have a little air of mystery for a while." He took her hands.

"You mean you're not going to tell me."

"Can't, not right now. But soon. I promise."

"You've got a lot of rules all of a sudden." She took her hands away.

"What's going on?" he asked.

"I told you. I want to know how to defend myself. I'm not going to get caught alone with Lillian again and not know how to fight back. I've got to at least give myself a chance to escape without getting my brains bashed in."

"I don't want to fight." He kissed her.

"I don't either. But you know me. I hate taking orders."

"There are other dojos in Sunflower. You don't have to go to Jon's."

"Well, the thing is, he's given me a job."

"A job?"

"Yeah, I know it's hard to believe, but I don't want to be handing out balloons to greasy little kids for the rest of my life."

"What's the job?"

"Answering phones. But Jon says that's just for now."

"I bet it is."

"What's your problem? What do you have against him?"

"We grew up together. Did everything together. Our parents were best friends. Then he got into martial arts. It took over his life. That's all he's about now."

"What's wrong with that?"

"It's boring as hell. Yeah, I took a few classes. They're fine for those who want them. I don't believe in all that discipline. You know me, I want to have fun."

"There's lots of discipline in the theater, isn't there?"

"I don't want you working there."

"You haven't said why."

"I did. I told you in the truck. Too many untrustworthy guys hang out around there."

"I haven't met any. Besides, you can trust *me*—right?"

Buddy got up from the sofa and walked to the kitchen.

"Want a beer?"

"Right?"

"Buddy's got to let you be the person you want to be," Jon said now, after Allison related the quarrel, "not who *he* wants you to be."

"What was going on with you and him that day we came? It felt weird, like you were holding something against him."

"He hadn't been around for a while—which is his business, not mine. When he was in class, there were days when he seemed very into it, and other days when his mind was somewhere else. Your mind can't be somewhere else when you're doing martial arts."

It was perhaps the most important lesson she'd learned at the dojo thus far: Where you put your mind was as important as where you put your hands and feet—concentration on the present moment and nothing else, not on the last movement or the next. *This* moment alone mattered.

"When I asked him what was going on, he brushed it off. Brushed me off. Then he stopped coming to class."

"Did he ever tell you why?"

"No, but this isn't a big town. I heard that he was selling drugs."

"Yeah, I know. He sells pot."

"We don't do drugs at the dojo. But we'd been friends all our lives, so I went to his place and asked him. He said, 'How is that your business?' So, I knew. I told him that if he wanted to do that, it *was* his business, but that the dojo was *my* business and that if he was selling drugs he couldn't come back. He said, 'What makes you think I'm coming back?' And he didn't, until he brought you around. I thought that maybe he'd turned over a new leaf. But I hear he's still at it. I feel bad. At heart he's a good guy. Or was, before he got into this."

"He still is. To me."

"We don't do drugs at the dojo," he said again. "And we keep the alcohol to a minimum." He looked at her. "Do you smoke pot?"

"I don't drink. I'm too young."

"Are you too young for pot?"

"I've smoked it."

"With Buddy?"

She didn't answer.

"If you're going to work with us and be in class, you have to give it up. You can't smoke pot and be in training for martial arts."

Allison wasn't ready to make any commitments.

"Isn't what I do on my own time my business?"

"Now you sound like Buddy. If you come to the dojo stoned, it concerns everyone. You could hurt somebody in class or, more likely, yourself. And what happens if you're high and find yourself in a fight? How will you be able to use what you've learned? Your reflexes will be slowed, your perception of what's happening around you will be distorted."

Allison thought about running into Lillian while high.

"Besides," Jon went on, "Buddy doesn't sell just pot."

"He doesn't?"

"Think about it. Do you think he could buy that truck *and* that Vette just selling pot around here?"

"What else does he sell?" Allison asked but wasn't sure she wanted to know.

They had arrived at the house on Huguenot Street. Jon pulled into the driveway.

"He sells hard drugs, Allison. Heroin. And pills—uppers, downers; you want it, he probably has it."

"Heroin?" It was a gut punch.

"Yes, I'm sorry to say." He thought a moment. "No, I'm not sorry. You need to know. He sells drugs. There's no way you won't become involved with it, one way or another. Do you smoke pot with him?"

"Yes."

"It won't be long before you'll be doing something else."

"How do you know? All he does is smoke pot—and sell it."

"You know that for sure? This can ruin your life."

She knew, as she walked to the house, that she couldn't tell her parents. She didn't want Buddy to go to jail, and even though she had never done anything but smoke pot with him, the police might think otherwise. And if Jon was right about the hard drugs, then what about the people Buddy had sold them to? Were their lives ruined? Was that Buddy's fault? If they were adults, wasn't doing heroin or pills their decision?

She didn't know any heroin or pill addicts. Their dilemmas, let alone their existence, were theoretical to her. But there was something else that wasn't, something that was as concrete, as real as it was possible to be. She would have to talk to Buddy.

The next day, Saturday, back in the almost empty house, she told him.

"I'm pregnant."

There was a long pause, during which she saw shock, panic, and dismay pass across Buddy's face.

"Are you sure?" he asked.

"I missed my period. So, I looked in *Our Bodies, Ourselves.*"

"What's *Our Bodies, Ourselves*?"

"It's a book about women's health. It said to wait two weeks and then get a test."

"You can get a test?"

"It's called an early-pregnancy test. They have it at Singleton's."

"You went in there and bought it?"

He sounded angry, as if buying the test in broad daylight somehow implicated him.

"No. I asked the Captain to get it for me. He did."

"That must have raised eyebrows, him buying that thing."

"I didn't ask how he got it. He gave it to me in the parking lot. I had to wait two hours for the results."

She expected him to say something. Or to hug her. He didn't, so she hugged him.

"What are you going to do with it?" He held her tightly.

It hadn't taken Allison long to answer that question for herself. She knew what would happen to an unwed mother in Sunflower: Goodbye to everything, including everything she was discovering about herself in martial arts. Goodbye to freedom. There would be stares, shunning, judgment. She wouldn't be able to go anywhere without whispered comments and sniggers in the air all around her. Life would become hell for her on Huguenot Street. And what about her parents? What would they want with an unwed mother for a daughter? She froze at the thought that they might throw her out. Where would she go? She was only fifteen, for God's sake.

"You're going to get rid of it, right?"

She pulled away and looked at Buddy. The green eyes that had made her feel so welcome, so at ease, were not welcoming her now. The door had been shut, the lock turned, and now she saw only fear and determination. Fear of having his life ruined by fatherhood? Determination not to be involved in this thing that was *her* problem?

"I know what I'm going to do," she said.

Back at home, Allison sat in her bedroom and did the deep breathing exercises she'd learned at the dojo. In through the nose. Down to the diaphragm. Out through the mouth. Again, and again, and again. After about twenty minutes, she felt calm, and hopeful that Emma and Doug would understand.

She went downstairs, found her mother in the kitchen, and told her. Emma, who had just finished washing her hands at the sink, at first could say nothing. She dropped the dish towel on the counter and hugged her daughter.

"My baby," she said.

They stood that way, between the sink and the table, for what felt to Allison like a long time before Emma spoke again.

"Your father must be on his way from the golf course; he'll be home soon." She stepped back, smoothing Allison's hair at the sides of her face. "We'll figure it out. The three of us." She hugged Allison again. "How are you feeling?"

"A little shaky."

"It will be all right. It will be all right." She released Allison. "Right now, I want to go pray."

Allison walked her upstairs to the master bedroom. At the door, Emma turned to her. "No matter what, we'll take care of you." Emma kissed Allison on the forehead and, leaving the door open, walked to the side of the bed. Allison watched as she kneeled, and then went back to her bedroom.

After a quiet, awkward dinner, the three of them sat on the sofa in the family room. Allison sat in the middle, her parents on either side, as if they were going to hold her up physically as well as emotionally.

"Of course, we wish this hadn't happened, but it has, and you'll have to learn from it. It was a mistake."

"Yes," Allison said.

"A serious mistake. The most . . ." Emma paused. Allison saw tears forming in her eyes. She found a Kleenex in the pocket of her jeans and gave it to her mother. Emma daubed her eyes. "The most serious," she went, "that a young woman can make. There was a time . . ." She paused again. "There was a time when parents in this situation"—she looked at Doug, who was grim faced but clearly going to let his wife take the lead—"when parents would simply tell their pregnant daughter what she was going to do. But that time is not now." She'd been holding Allison's right hand; now she squeezed it tighter. "You tell us. Do you know what you want to do?"

Allison looked first at her, then at Doug, who took her other hand. "I want . . . don't . . . I don't want it."

Silence. The air felt heavy to Allison as her parents said nothing.

Emma's eyes filled with tears again. She wiped them away. "I'm thinking about what I've always told all of you about religion. That the Bible's not a cookbook. That you have to think it through for yourself. But in this moment, I also understand that you must *feel* it for yourself." She looked at her husband. "Doug?"

Doug nodded and wiped his nose with the back of his hand.

"This mistake shouldn't dictate the rest of your life. No one mistake should dictate the rest of your life. Not in 1976."

"Thank you, Mom." It was all Allison could say.

"I also want you to know that this isn't easy. It isn't easy. But it seems that it's the right thing to do." She let out a long sigh.

Allison glanced at Doug, who looked worried.

Now that the decision was made, Emma sat up straight and put her other hand in Allison's. "We'll take care of it, don't worry. You'll take a few days off from school and work. We'll say you had the flu. You can still get the flu in May. That's all. I'll talk to Susan . . ."

"Does she have to know?" Allison was alarmed. She didn't think anyone else would need to know, including her sisters.

"She knows Atlanta. She'll find a good clinic there. There's no place here we'd trust."

Doug nodded.

"Besides, it's no one's business but ours, and there are too many nosy people in this town."

"Did you tell Will?"

"No, and I'm not going to. Unless you want him to know."

"No."

Doug finally spoke up.

"I want to talk to Buddy," he said.

The next evening, Buddy came over.

"I don't want to be in the same room when he comes," Allison had told Doug.

"It would be a good idea if you were. I don't particularly want him to feel comfortable. You don't have to say anything if you don't want to."

"Okay, Daddy. But I won't be happy about it."

"That's all right. Let him see you not being happy."

The three of them waited for Buddy in the family room, sitting as they had earlier—on the sofa, Allison flanked by Emma and Doug. She held both their hands until the doorbell rang. When Emma brought Buddy downstairs, Doug rose to meet him. As he stood in the center of the room, he looked to Allison like the assured vice president of sales she'd seen over the years at Britmar.

"Good evening, Mr. Blanchet." Buddy, looking pale and nervous, didn't so much as glance at Allison. He seemed far from the open, confident young man she knew.

"Good evening, Mrs. Blanchet," he said to Emma as she returned to her seat next to Allison. "Allison." He was weirdly formal. Allison looked him in the eyes and saw that he wasn't there.

"Hi, Buddy." She looked away.

"So, Buddy." The two men were still standing in the middle of the room. Allison remembered later that neither one had extended his hand. "Sit down." He gestured toward a recliner that sat at a ninety-degree angle to the sofa. "Please."

Buddy sat. Doug took his seat on the sofa, on Allison's other side. Allison stared at the blank television screen; Doug and Emma, like guardians, regarded Buddy, who spoke slowly and, it seemed to Allison, sincerely.

"I'm sorry about what happened. It shouldn't have happened, as I told Allison when she called me yesterday and asked me to come over." He looked to her for confirmation. She concentrated on the television. "I take full responsibility."

"There were—are—two of you involved. You don't bear the entire responsibility yourself," Doug said. "Still, you're a man, legally and morally. I'd have expected you to behave honorably, as I'd expect my own sons to do."

"Yes, sir."

"So, what are you prepared to do now?"

"I guess that depends on what Allison wants to do." There was an awkward pause. Allison finally looked up at him and thought she saw a plea to be set free from all this.

Doug was puzzled.

"Allison hasn't told you?"

"No, sir. When she called, she just asked me to come over and talk to you."

Doug looked at Allison, who shook her head minutely.

"Allison doesn't wish to speak. So, it's up to me to tell you."

"Yes, sir."

But Doug had stopped. As she watched Doug watching Buddy, Allison wondered if he was deliberately making him squirm.

"She does not want to keep this baby," Doug finally said.

Allison saw Buddy close his eyes and swallow. Relieved? For her? For himself?

"So, what are you prepared to do?"

"I'll pay," Buddy said. "For the . . . procedure."

"All right," Doug said. "I'm glad to hear you say that."

"How much do I . . . owe you?"

Doug named the price. Allison let out an unintended gasp.

"If you don't have a check with you now, you can bring one tomorrow," Doug said.

"I can give you cash right now." Now it was Emma's turn to gasp. Doug kept his response to himself as he stood. Allison wasn't so surprised.

Buddy took a large roll of cash from the pocket of his scarlet-and-blue satin baseball jacket and peeled off five one-hundred-dollar bills.

"Here you are, sir."

"All right, then," Doug said, and pocketed the money.

The clinic that Susan had located in Atlanta was pristine. The floors and glass surfaces shone as if the building had just opened for business that day. There was a lounge, where Emma and Doug were invited to watch television while Allison had the abortion. They tried watching *The Price Is Right*, but as Emma told Allison later, they had "all the concentration for television that a cat has for a dictionary."

As Allison was falling asleep on the table, she heard someone say, "Damn redheads. They're impossible to put out."

Another voice said, "Increase her 20 percent. And shut up."

That was the last thing she remembered.

They rode home in the station wagon that Doug had recently acquired as a trade-in for the DeVille. Emma had made the back comfortable with blankets, cushions, and pillows, and Allison drifted in and out of sleep. She stayed home the next day, and Emma, who brought her food and anything else she asked for, insisted that she remain in bed.

As Emma had suggested, Allison told her teachers, and

Jon, that she'd had a late case of the flu. At Doug's request, Dr. Wilson, the family's physician, provided a note to that effect.

Allison was certain that she'd hear from Buddy. He didn't call, not the evening of the abortion nor the day after.

"I was hoping he would be a gentleman," Emma said on the evening of the second day. "Or at least show some concern. But then, I was hoping he'd be a gentleman from the day you told us about him."

"He will," Allison said. "Maybe he's been busy."

"So busy at the theater? On weekdays? I know one thing: He's not welcome around here anymore."

Allison was surprised by how much she wanted to hear from Buddy and, as the days went by with no word, how worried she became. She decided to put aside what Jon had told her. At the end of the second week, she pulled her Schwinn out of the garage and rode the seven miles to Buddy's house.

The truck wasn't parked in the driveway. The garage door was shut and locked, so she couldn't tell whether the Vette was in there or not. No one answered the front doorbell. She wriggled her way between a low privet hedge and the picture window and peered in. She couldn't see Buddy, or any sign of life. She went to the back door and knocked. She called his name.

She thought that maybe he was out with one of the vehicles and that the other was in the shop. She seemed to remember him saying that one needed something fixed.

It was just past noon. She had no plans for the weekend, which Jon had given her off, so she sat on the treeless front lawn and waited as the sun moved overhead. The afternoon wore on; the house threw a shadow that slowly extended to the street. By four o'clock, a faint breeze was stirring when Allison got back on her bicycle and pedaled home. No one had come to the house.

Buddy was gone.

CHAPTER NINE

Buddy was gone, but Allison stayed on at the dojo. The energy with which she applied herself to her classes caught the notice of the core senior teachers. They began treating her as one of their own, stopping by class to follow her progress, seeing in her a junior version of themselves: not a full-fledged member of the Cadre, as they called themselves, but more than just a student.

Twice a week after classes, the Cadre met for fierce three-hour workouts. They practiced kicking and punching routines to keep sharp; in outings to the spaciousness of Montgomery Park, they honed their weapons skills in bo staff, nunchuck, and sword.

After her phone shift, Allison hung around to watch the workouts. One day, she asked Jon if she could join them.

He discussed it with the Cadre. They expressed concerns: On one hand, although she excelled as a student, she was still very much a beginner; she still wore a white belt. Martial arts etiquette required that all students be treated equally; still, the Cadre couldn't overlook her gumption and dedication and her hunger for learning. They all agreed to let her take part.

"It's not easy," Jon said to her when he gave her the news. "If it looks easy, that's because we've put in the work. You'll have to put in the work too. There are no shortcuts. You'll have to learn fast, stay alert, and not be afraid. And you'll have to get used to pain. My knees hurt all the time; sometimes I medicate in order to sleep. I'm telling you this so that you know what you're in for." He looked at her, trying to detect any sign of doubt. "You can change your mind. No honor lost."

At sixteen, Allison had touched only the fringes of pain. The falls from trees and her bicycle were distant memories. She'd told Emma that her abortion felt like the world's worst period. Serious pain was theoretical; chronic pain was still unimaginable.

"Don't worry about me," she said.

She worked alongside the Cadre in the kicking and punching routines, and on the bags that had once creeped her out. In aikido, she learned how to use an assailant's momentum against them with spiraling, circular movements that could be as beautiful as they were powerful. In judo, she learned to take an opponent down with maximum efficiency and minimum effort. She trained in the use of weapons, and she joined the Cadre in the knuckle pushups they did on the sidewalk outside the dojo. After seeing her do twenty-five, the Cadre made her an honorary member—the only female member.

When Allison was seventeen and had been training at the dojo for almost two years, Will came from Caracas to visit home.

"Who's this young woman?" he asked when he saw her for the first time at breakfast.

"That's your little sister growing up," Emma said as she passed around pancakes and bacon.

"Little no more," said Doug.

"I've grown over an inch in the last eighteen months."

"Yeah, you're heading into Amazonian territory, but that's not what I meant. Who is this mature young woman? What have you done with my sister?"

She had changed, but it was Will, who hadn't been home since before she began training, who noticed what had happened. After breakfast, as they walked in Montgomery Park, he saw the purpose with which she took in their surroundings.

"It's part of the training, to know what's going on around you," she said. "If a girl walks down an alley at midnight, she'd better be prepared."

"I guess that girl better be. But I don't see any girls here. I see my sister, who's turned into a formidable young woman. What did you do with my wiggly little sister?"

Allison raised an eyebrow. "And what about my brother Will? The one who didn't have flecks of gray in his hair. Where'd he go?"

"Traded him in for a newer model."

"Looks like an older model, if you ask me."

He gave her a joking elbow to the ribs.

"Watch it, or this new grown-up person's going to put you on the ground," she said.

"I promise to straighten up."

"If you promise to hang around, she promises to protect you from the hordes of women who'll throw themselves at you and your sexy graying temples."

"I'll hang around for a couple of weeks, maybe." The new grown-up person looked at him, disappointed. "You know me. Can't stay in one place too long. Especially this place. And as for those hordes of women, I've got all I can handle in that department, thank you very much."

That's all he would say about his life, love or otherwise, in Caracas and Saint John. But, as always, he'd discuss his practice of Buddhism, the philosophy of which, entwined as it was with aspects of martial arts training, was of great interest to the new grown-up person.

Two weeks later, Will was off again.

He wasn't the only one to leave. The Whitmore sisters both went off to college—Angel to DC and Amber to Murfreesboro, Tennessee. Bobby Sewell, who had begun receding from Allison's life in high school, came to the house on Huguenot Street one Saturday soon after graduation to announce that he was moving to New York City. He was vague when Allison asked him why, saying only that Sunflower was too small a place for him. She asked him to send her his address when he got one; he said he would. But he never did, and if he ever came back to Sunflower while she lived there, she never knew about it.

Allison herself wasn't interested in college right then; her life was increasingly taken up by activities at the dojo. Jon put her in charge of maintaining the book of drawings, diagrams, and photos that he'd been working on the day that she first asked him for a job. The book documented the forms and techniques that students had to master to advance through the ranks of belts, from beginner's white through yellow, green, brown, and finally up to black. The forms were called kata, and it was now Allison's responsibility to keep them clear and current as Jon added new techniques and skills to the dojo's offerings.

In her third year, Jon told her the time had come to enter tournaments. These were even more new experiences, and she loved to travel with the Cadre to states around the region. On the road, as at home, the Cadre now treated Allison as one of them. If they noticed the physical changes she went through between fifteen and nineteen (and how could they not?), they neither mentioned them nor let them limit the challenges and experiences that came with being a member of the Cadre.

She got a rush whenever she entered the huge gymnasiums in which the tournaments were held. As many as ten matches might be underway simultaneously on mats spread around the floor, men and women testing themselves against each other in kata forms competition.

What she found most rewarding, however, was the camaraderie that resulted from the pursuit of a common goal: In a two-minute match, how well could a person master her body and discipline her mind? How finely could she control her movements and reactions; how precisely could she focus on the present moment?

When she saw a side round kick coming toward her solar plexus or her head, or when she moved in on an opponent to deliver one herself, she learned about her courage and her limitations. Even though participants in a match were expected to pull their punches and never follow through fully on a kick, she never lost that visceral reaction when she saw that closed fist or that foot coming at her. She learned to counter, not flinch.

She also began learning about pain. Even a pulled punch or kick could hurt, and every now and then, an undisciplined or unscrupulous opponent wouldn't play by the rules. She was kicked in the face hard enough to loosen a couple of front teeth, in the back on both sides, and in the ribs. And she managed to hurt herself too, when an opponent was quick enough to evade her left side round kick and she hyperextended her left hip. Even as she learned to remain in the present moment, that hip with its shooting pain, the twisted knee, the broken ribs, the jolted spine, the torn posterior cruciate ligament, all would eventually serve as reminders of the past that came, unbidden, into the now. They would be reminders of the physical price she paid for the exhilaration and freedom she felt when she entered the dojo, worked out with the Cadre, or approached a match.

As for the emotional price of experience, it also wouldn't

be until later that she understood that at nineteen, she hadn't paid for very much beyond the pain of a disappearing boyfriend. Boyfriends, especially the ones who seemed to treat you well but kept significant parts of themselves secret—could be replaced.

Allison's attraction to Jon had been growing, even as, at first, she thought it was merely respect for the way he ran the dojo, the way the Cadre looked up to and emulated him, and, not least of all, his treatment of her.

"Around here, effort gets rewarded with more effort," he said. "You started behind, so I want to make sure you keep up." So, they worked on improving the skills she was learning in class, and she steadily moved up the ranks until she achieved a brown belt. During that time, he never took advantage of their relative positions in the dojo, nor asked any "favors" in return for his pedagogic attention.

He gave her a Saturday morning beginner's class to teach. Now, instead of handing kids balloons at Wendy's while their parents bought the burgers, fries, and milkshakes they'd consume in front of the television, she was giving them useful skills, the value of discipline and respect, as well as a workout to burn off all those calories.

By her fifth year, she had worked her way up to first-degree black belt. She received the belt in a bonfire ceremony that Jon and the Cadre organized on the banks of the Chattahoochee River. Ceremonial shots of sake were thrown back and, not for the first time, Allison was impressed by the balance the Cadre achieved between enjoying each other's company, a reverence for their practice, and an ability to not take themselves too seriously.

After she'd been presented with her belt, Jon said, "This is a real achievement. If you'd told me that the girl who walked into the dojo one day five years ago with no previous interest in martial arts would be standing here now in a black belt, I would not have believed it."

The Cadre cheered.

"Remember, though, that tonight you are *Shodan*—the first *dan*, the first degree of black belt. That means that you have mastered the very basic skills of our art. You have a long way to go if you want to achieve the sixth *dan*, when your skills will be truly superb." He paused. "So don't get a swelled head."

He and the Cadre bowed to her; she bowed in return. He gave her a hug, and the Cadre cheered again.

Was it the hug? Or maybe the bonfire, the companion-ability of the Cadre, the sake? Each dispensed its own degree of warmth. Whatever the cause, at that moment, something in Allison turned over and she realized that she was in love with Jon.

This was entirely different from her feelings for Buddy. She'd been fifteen then; five years later, she'd learned a few things about who she was. When she looked at her body, in-juries and all, when her students acknowledged her expertise with bows before and after class and she returned the respect, when the Cadre made her one of their own because she'd earned her place among them, and when she moved in with Jon, she knew who she was.

CHAPTER TEN

Jon lived in a one-story brick cottage with a steeply pitched roof and a large front porch. Four tall posts supported an oversize wood-and-stucco pediment with a fake coat of arms glued to the center, and the porch was further obscured by a balustrade, also wood, painted to look like marble.

Allison didn't mind the pretentious additions someone had made to the porch before Jon moved in; sitting there with him was her favorite way to spend the evenings when they weren't at the dojo. The cottage, at the northern tip of Montgomery Park, was a short drive from Huguenot Street, which sat at the southern end, but Allison rarely found the ten minutes required to make the trip to her parents' house.

Her life was with Jon and at the dojo, but it had been two years since she'd taken a class in anything other than martial arts, and she'd gotten restless with curiosity. She realized that she missed the world of books her mother and Mrs. Maye had opened for her, albeit selectively, in high school.

She enrolled at Sunflower College, part-time so as not to disrupt her life at the dojo, taking business, accounting, and history classes. She thought that the accounting course would provide her with a new set of skills that she could use at the dojo, but discovered that she had an aptitude for it, as she did, likewise, for business. The excitement around the television miniseries *Shōgun* was responsible for her taking a course in Japanese history. Jon brought a television into one of the studios, and for five nights the Cadre watched in awe and fascination the daring of Richard Chamberlain, the intrigues of Toshirō Mifune, and the doomed heroism of Yōko Shimada.

Doug and Emma weren't thrilled about Allison's choice of school or her enrollment status, but she pointed out to them that Will hadn't gone to college at all, and while Susan had gotten a BA in English and Sarah one in biology, they were hardly using them in their current occupations as Atlanta housewives. In any case, since Allison was no longer living at home, she didn't have to face her parents' disappointment on a regular basis.

Allison and Jon had been living and working together for a couple of years. One night following a workout, the Cadre adjourned to the House of Swing, a bar that featured a juke box that played jazz from the 1920s into the 1970s. Some of the Cadre headed for the pool table, while Jon and Allison took seats at the bar.

"I think maybe we should start a fight," Jon said, nursing a seltzer and lime.

"What do you mean? About what?"

"Not us. Or not us alone. I mean a good old-fashioned bar fight."

She shook her head, as if, with some help, the words might rearrange themselves into some sensible order.

"As a test. For you."

"You're going to have to explain yourself."

"Nobody doubts your abilities in anything you put your

mind to. Or your heart. You start strong when you come into a match, but . . ."

"But . . . what?"

"You reach a certain intensity—and then you stop. You don't fully commit."

"You've never said anything like that to me before. No one has." She was hurt. She covered. "You're talking to a first-degree black belt. Watch it, or I might put you under that barstool."

"After all, the stakes in a tournament are hypothetical."

"Countering a flying foot to the face is not hypothetical. Not in my book." She was trying not to get angry.

"I just think that if you found yourself in an uncontrolled, real-life situation like a bar fight, you'd have to decide whether you've got what it takes to finish someone off. That's all."

"'That's all'? I can't believe you want me to get in a fight. *In a bar.* And since when is what we do about finishing somebody off?"

"I'll be here if things get out of control. And so will all the other guys."

"Oh, and so you also think I'm going to need you to come to my rescue? Fuck that."

"Okay, okay. It was just an idea."

"You know what you can do with it."

But Jon's attention had been drawn to the television hanging behind the bar. The eleven o'clock news had come on, and the story suddenly absorbing his attention was about a murder. A young Sunflower woman had been strangled to death in her bed by an intruder. The murder had occurred just a couple of hours earlier; not much else was known.

The next day, further reporting revealed that the victim, a twenty-eight-year-old woman named Andrea Rice, had been strangled with one of her own stockings. At about nine o'clock, the murderer had used an object that might have been a crowbar to break the lock on the rear door of the house—where she lived alone—surprised the victim in her bed, raped and strangled her, and then escaped the way he entered. No property seemed to have been taken.

A week later, another young woman who lived alone was raped and strangled in her bed. After forcing open a rear window, the intruder attacked his victim with one of her own stockings, which it seemed he'd taken from a drawer the police found open. Joanna Robbins, twenty-five, had just begun what she'd hoped would be a long career as a high school science teacher at Sunflower High in Montgomery Park, not far from where she'd lived.

The police reported that in the drawer from which the stocking had been taken, they found an envelope containing $200. The killer had left the money behind, so they confidently asserted that robbery wasn't a motive.

A week later, a third attack occurred. Toni DiVincenzo was thirty years old and worked in an optical store in one of the malls on the outskirts of town. The murderer had broken in through the rear door of her rented town house near Singleton Pharmacy and attacked this victim in the same way as he had the first two.

By now, the alarm and fear in Sunflower were palpable. The police began staking out the neighborhoods where the victims lived. Many single women, fearful of being alone at night, went to stay with friends and did their best not to walk by themselves.

Allison said to Jon, "We've got to do something."

She drew up flyers that read "Self-Defense Classes for Women. Free. Taught by a Black Belt in Martial Arts" and posted them in Montgomery Park and other places around town.

Immediately, the dojo was flooded with calls. Thirty women turned up on the first day of class, ready to learn how to defend themselves.

When Allison took her place at the front of the studio, there was a rustling among the crowd.

"A woman?" someone whispered.

"A kid," another woman said under her breath but loud enough for Allison to hear.

"Isn't a man going to teach us?"

"Hush. We haven't even started. Give her a chance."

"Good morning, ladies," Allison said. "I've got a question for you." She made sure that the women in the back could hear her. "Did a man save Andrea Rice or Joanna Robbins? Which man was it who rescued Toni DiVincenzo when she was attacked?"

No one replied.

"As the flyer says, I have a black belt in martial arts. Here it is." She pointed to the belt around her waist. "There aren't a lot of men in this town who can say that. I doubt there are many cops in this town who could say that. What I *don't* doubt is that they could probably use a few lessons from me. Shall we get started?" She knew Doug would have been proud.

"We'll cover a lot of important principles in these classes. The first one is that self-defense is just that: defense. What we want is to avoid injury if attacked and gain time to escape. It's not about beating someone up or being a hero. It's about taking care of yourself should you be attacked."

To start, she taught them some simple moves.

"This is Travis," she said, pointing to one of the bags she'd brought to the front of the studio. It was shaped like a man's head and torso. "He's going to assist me today."

"The heel of the palm to the nose can be most effective when it comes to pushing the nose into the brain. That gets an attacker's attention." The women laughed. "And there's no risk of breaking one of the twenty-seven bones in your hand, as there is with a punch." She demonstrated on Travis. "We call that a palm strike. It can be combined with another one to the throat. The first strike, to the nose, pushes the head back, exposing the throat."

She assaulted Travis again. "Lethal."

In subsequent classes she taught them other techniques.

"This one is to keep the attacker further away from you. The idea is to attack his kneecap." She demonstrated a side kick to the knee. "Right out of Bruce Lee," she said. Some of the women didn't know who Bruce Lee was, but to Allison, all that mattered was that they learned the kick.

"You can break his kneecap with this one, but a good sprain will work too—the pain and shock will slow him down and give you a chance to get away. But if he still comes after you, what can you do?"

"Push his nose into his brain!" someone said, and the women laughed.

She had them bring in brooms and showed how they could be used as bo staffs to create space between themselves and the attacker, and how to use them as a spear to strike a forceful jab to the abdomen.

"What about the balls?" one of them wanted to know.

"Excellent question. Don't go for the balls, ladies. I know it may be tempting, but you'll have too much adrenaline pumping through you to hit such a tiny target. And believe me, men who attack women have the tiniest balls. Once you've jabbed him in the belly, don't wait to see his reaction. Strike him on the side of the head, then on the other side, and then get the hell out of there."

She showed them how even a cane or a walking stick could be used as a lever, using the assailant's momentum to throw him out of range of their bodies. She took them outside for a mace and pepper spray drill, and on walks around Sunflower to heighten their awareness of their surroundings.

"We're not out for the fresh air, ladies. Be aware of your environment, where you are and who's there with you."

In coffee shops and on bus rides they practiced looking at people.

"Pick one person. Look carefully. Then close your eyes and describe what you saw in as much detail as you can. Male or female? Color of eyes, of hair. What kind of hair? Long, short? Curly, straight? Are they wearing a hat? Describe that. What were they doing? Where are their hands? Then open your eyes and see how accurate you were. Then choose another person." When one woman saw a man in a blue pinstriped shirt and another saw the shirt as solid blue, she made a point of discussing it.

"It's hard, isn't it? But if you practice, before you know it, it will be second nature, every time you go out."

She drilled them on sounds: Was that car door opening or closing? Was that a laugh or a shout, what direction did it come from, and was it a man or woman? How close or far away were those footsteps behind you and how quickly were they approaching?

"Reducing your risk through awareness of your surroundings is 90 percent of self-defense."

She visited their homes. She made sure there was a broomstick, cane, or baseball bat within reach to be used the way she'd taught them. She helped them identify an exit route. A few had barred all their windows.

"That might keep him from getting in," she warned, "but suppose he gets in through the back door? And if he's standing between you and the door, how will you get out?"

The course was so successful that immediately after it ended, Allison offered another one, and another thirty women enrolled.

It was difficult to feel fulfilled, however, with the killer still at large. During the two months in which Allison was teaching the women of Sunflower self-defense, he had killed two more victims in his usual fashion. The *Sunflower Enquirer* dubbed him the Sunflower Strangler, and the name was taken up by the rest of the local media.

Even Allison was on edge. She put a bo staff in the bedroom and wouldn't go to bed until Jon came home. She called Emma every evening or stopped by to check up on her, even though Doug was also there.

"If there's one good thing to come of this—not that there is—it's that now I get to see your face," Emma said one night.

All the murdered women lived alone, which suggested to Allison that the Strangler had cased each residence before choosing his victims. She and Jon walked the perimeter of her parents' house, but one night when Jon suggested doing the same at theirs, Allison balked.

"If you do it, I'll be here alone," she said to Jon. "But if we both do it, he might get in."

"That doesn't seem very likely to me," he said, "but okay, we'll stay in."

"That's good."

She put on a white cotton nightgown to ward off a late-night chill; they lit candles and got into bed. Jon had taken his chloral hydrate to help him sleep.

She said, "I think we should make self-defense classes for women a permanent thing."

"I was thinking the same thing. Maybe some of the Cadre can help out."

"I'd like to keep doing it myself. But that might mean someone would have to take my Saturday kids' class."

"We can figure it out." He held her hand.

"They hurt tonight?" she asked, touching his knees.

"Like a son of a bitch." In a few minutes, the drug did its work and he was asleep.

Allison put out the candles. She was thinking about the classes when, as she drifted toward sleep, Lillian's image floated into view. She was certainly one woman who, at first glance, anyway, didn't need lessons in martial arts; someone would have to be a fool to take her on. Still, she might benefit, as Allison herself had, from the discipline and the positive outlet for energy that might otherwise be self-destructive. She wondered where Lillian was. She had her to thank, after all, for the good place she found herself in now.

A noise brought her back to consciousness. Or perhaps it was something that occurred before a noise, or alongside it. Suddenly, she was alert. She took a breath, smelled the air. Something was wrong. Then she definitely heard a sound, as if someone had brushed against a wind chime. But she and Jon didn't have a wind chime.

"Jon!" She shook his shoulder, but he didn't respond. He was already deep into his chloral hydrate–induced sleep.

"Jon!" She shook him again. He mumbled something softly but didn't move.

She would have to do this without him.

She felt for the bo staff she kept beneath the bed. Taking it in both hands, she stepped cautiously into the dark living room. They should have left a lamp on, she thought. Stupid. And why hadn't she done any classes in the dark, since the Strangler always attacked at night? She stood still and listened.

Did she hear someone move? She thought she made out a shape standing near the back door that led to the yard; against the darkness of the room, a deeper layer of black was moving. And here she was, she thought, a target in her white cotton nightgown.

He was standing not five feet away. Maybe four. As her eyes adjusted—so slowly—she thought, *This is him.* She had the bo staff. If she could stop him, she'd put an end to the dread that all the women of Sunflower had been feeling for months.

"Hold it!" she said. He stood there, seemingly uncertain. She thought if she attacked his solar plexus, he'd buckle, lower his head and hands. Where were his hands? All she could see was a large, vague dark shape.

She thrust the bo staff toward his belly. He might have seen it coming against the white of her nightgown because he stepped back and dodged to his left. The blow was a glancing one, but enough to elicit a grunt. Until that moment, she still couldn't see his arms or hands; suddenly they were in front of him, and in his right hand he was lifting a crowbar.

She shouted, "Jon!"

The figure swung the crowbar down to shatter the bo staff, which Allison was drawing back for another strike. It caught the bo staff and knocked Allison back on her right foot, off balance, exposing her body; she swung and felt the staff slam his neck, again not squarely, but enough to push him back toward the door.

As the figure staggered back, the overhead light came on, blinding Allison. Jon, still drugged, stumbled into the room.

"He's got a crowbar!" she shouted. "I can't see!"

The moment's blindness had given the figure the second he needed to escape through the rear door he'd forced open. As he disappeared into the night, he kicked a cymbal from Jon's disassembled drum kit. He'd brought it home from the dojo months ago, and it had been sitting nearby since. The Strangler had brushed against it when he entered, making the wind chime sound that had alerted Allison.

She dropped the bo staff and stood shaking in the middle of the room.

"I did it wrong!" She turned to Jon and started to sob. "I did every goddamn thing wrong!"

PART THREE

CHAPTER ELEVEN

On a normal day, the trip north on Highway 1 from Santa Cruz to Gualala would have taken four hours, thanks to the low speed limit and drivers' natural inclination to slow down even further to take in the wonders of one of the most beautiful stretches of coast on the continent. The two-lane road wound along dunes, hugged cliffs, slipped among cypress and redwood groves, threaded through vineyards and wineries and small white- and red-roofed towns.

However, on this clear Friday in mid-March 2020, the road was eerily quiet. Allison couldn't remember an afternoon when there were so few cars on the road.

The towns were empty too. Driving through Pescadero, Half Moon Bay, and Pacifica, Allison and Tom counted exactly eight vehicles. San Francisco, where negotiating the ten miles of traffic between Nineteenth Avenue at the city's southern end and the Golden Gate Bridge at the northern tip might usually take an hour, was a ghost town. Braving the wind swirling in from the bay, a few bundled-up souls jogged across the bridge—almost the only traffic on this magnificent, lonely span. The comfortable folks of Marin

County were holed up in their hillside homes. San Rafael, Petaluma, Bodega Bay, Fort Ross, Stewarts Point, all were shut down.

They had left Santa Cruz at noon; when they pulled into the little market a mile from the house in Gualala to pick up a few things for dinner, it was not even three o'clock. Theirs was the only car in the parking lot.

With an effort, Allison turned and planted her feet on the ground before prying herself out of the Prius's driver's seat. Tom came around from the passenger's side to help.

"You know," he said for the tenth or possibly the hundredth time, "it would be easier on you if I drove."

"I know, I know," she said, taking his hand and hoisting herself up. "My back and hips would appreciate it. My nervous system, not so much."

"You'd think I was a lousy driver."

"You're a great driver. I'm a lousy passenger." She put on a gray-and-apricot plaid mask. "You know me and control when it comes to driving."

"Oh, I do." He put on an N95.

A cold wind was blowing in from the west off the ocean as Allison put one foot stiffly in front of the other, and they walked slowly toward the entrance of the store, where, for some reason, the lights were out. She regretted that she wouldn't have time to limber up before they got back into the car.

The store manager for at least the last twenty years, Celia—sixty-five, tall and straight, with iron-gray hair gathered into a chignon—was standing behind the counter, looking grim. She wasn't wearing a mask, but Allison, who just wanted to get back to the house and stretch her body, wasn't going to get into it.

"What's going on?" She stood a safe distance away.

"Power's out," Celia said. "All the cold and frozen stuff's going to be ruined if it doesn't come back on soon."

"How long has it been out?" Tom picked up a basket and headed down an aisle.

"An hour, so far."

"Do they know why?" Not wanting to offend Celia, even if she was annoyed by her seeming refusal to wear a mask, Allison pretended to browse through a crate of apples at the far end of the counter.

"A grass fire out by the airport took out some power lines. Or maybe the power lines started it. Wouldn't be the first time. The fire department's out there now."

Once, Allison might have commented on how it was much too early in the year for a grass fire. Thanks, however, to the twenty-year megadrought, there was no longer such a thing as a fire season. Or rather, the entire year was fire season.

"And," Celia added, "now there's wind too."

Celia launched into another topic, but Allison no longer heard her. Her mind began racing: The wind was blowing fiercely; a fire was burning near the airport. For a moment, she thought she saw black smoke rising above rugged hills and felt as if she were about to scream.

She forced her mind back to the basket of apples in the darkened store and discovered that she was squeezing one tightly in her right hand.

Celia was finishing saying whatever it was she'd been saying. "And you're the first people to come in today."

"Really?" Allison said.

"Highway 1 was empty, all the way from Santa Cruz," Tom said, coming up to the counter with his basket that held a box of pasta, a jar of pasta sauce, and a loaf of rustic bread. He grabbed half a dozen apples from the crate where Allison was standing, including the one she was still squeezing tightly, put a few dollars on the counter, and stepped back.

Celia sighed as she rang up the small sale.

"Visiting your grandkids?"

"No," he said. "We're not doing that now. Too risky. We were checking on the house. We were going to put it up for sale, but it looks like that'll have to wait."

"Anything else?" Celia asked.

"No, that'll do for now," he said. "We were going to make a stew, but I don't think chopping in the dark is a good idea. So, just pasta tonight."

"Well, come back if you need anything else. It's not like there'll be a line."

"We will," Allison said as she headed for the door.

Since they hadn't eaten lunch, they decided to fix an early meal while it was still light enough in the kitchen to see what they were doing. After a simple pasta dinner cooked on the gas range and a bottle of red from the local winery, they went up to the bedroom. Sitting side by side on the bed, they held hands as, through the wide windows, they watched an osprey as it hunted for its own dinner in the fading light. First, it hovered, then, feetfirst, it plunged fifteen feet to the water below, snagged a large fish, and then awkwardly lumbered skyward again. It flew to its nest, which Allison knew was close by, atop a cypress tree one property over.

Every day she looked for the osprey. Should it fail to catch its prey the first time, the sight of it rising heavily upward, patiently circling, plunging, and rising again, filled her with hope. Up in the air, flying, in motion.

SPRING 1985

From a helicopter flying over Olympia, Georgia, Allison could see that the parcel of land below her fit all her client's requirements. Adjacent to another parcel, on which a strip mall would soon break ground, the property's ingress and egress were more than adequate; all she had to do was lay it all out for the client sitting next to her. It was the perfect location for the McDonald's that he wanted to build.

The day was bright, the sky was clear other than for a few puffy white clouds, and the breeze was light and warm. The client seemed to be on his way to being satisfied (perhaps the martini at lunch had helped; Allison had abstained). It was in moments like these that she realized how lucky she was, or rather, how lucky she continued to be.

At twenty-five, she was vice president of commercial sales for one of the leading real estate firms in the southeast corner of Georgia. The helicopter was a perk of her position, but also necessary: Her portfolio consisted of large tracts of land that needed to be shown from the air to developers of apartment complexes, strip malls, and the fast-food restaurants with which she'd been dotting the landscape since the early eighties. She might be known around the office as the Queen of the Fast-Food Franchises, but she didn't mind. In fact, she embraced the title. It was a far cry from standing in a Wendy's on weekends, handing out balloons for five dollars an hour. Now her hands were grease-free, and she was the proud occupant of a corner office.

Best of all, however—and even better than the corner office, the many commissions she'd been ringing up, the Datsun 280Z two-seater, the one-bedroom condo overlooking the Back and Mackay Rivers and Blue Heron Island, and her monarchial title—was the time she spent in the air. Once again, she found a place to feel free and unburdened, safe from whatever might tether her to the ground.

By the early eighties, it had become necessary to untether herself from Sunflower and everything that held her there, including those people and things she loved. For a long time, the memory of the night when she confronted the Sunflower Strangler weighed on her. It wasn't so much that she'd failed to catch him as that, in that moment of crisis, all her training—which should have responded without hesitation or the need for thought—deserted her. How could she expect the women she'd trained to defend themselves when she, their teacher, had failed so miserably? Yes, it was dark, and yes, he had a weapon, but everyone knew his modus operandi, and still she couldn't prevent him from escaping. The fact that martial arts (as it had been taught to her and as she preached to her students), was about self-defense and was not meant to be used as an offensive weapon did not clarify matters for her.

Something in her snapped that night. Her faith in her training began to ebb away, and she felt diminished as a teacher and competitor. A month later, in Atlanta, her mind went blank one minute into a tournament match, just long enough to take a powerful kick that broke two ribs. The pain was bad enough, but even more debilitating was the fear that she might lose focus like that again.

When she said she couldn't face her classes, Jon made it clear that it was all right to stay away from the dojo for as long as she needed to. The Cadre, too, did their best to be supportive. They taught her classes, brought meals to the house, went on bike rides with her. They reminded her that after she confronted him, the Sunflower Strangler had ceased his attacks on women. The police had yet to catch him, but she could take credit, they told her, for scaring him into disappearing. This was no small thing, and the women of Sunflower were in her debt for showing him that women could fight back.

It didn't feel that way to Allison.

She began spending time at the house on Huguenot Street. She'd sit for hours in the wing chair in her old bedroom, watching the nuthatches and orioles in the magnolia tree. She looked through her old books, including the one about the little girl who flies the airplane, which had been her favorite.

Doug and Emma thought that a professional change of

scene might do her good. Doug remembered her declaration, years ago in his office, that she wanted to be a salesman, so he suggested she contact an old friend of his in the real estate business. He knew that she'd done well in her business classes at Sunflower College, and a real estate job, he figured, would get her outside, traveling the county, and widen her range of acquaintances.

Allison was intrigued. She enrolled in a real estate course at Sunflower and, as she spent more time pursuing what she was starting to sense was a new career, was startled to find herself understanding what Buddy had meant when he said that the dojo had taken over Jon's life. Jon's life *was* all about the dojo. And hers was too.

And while that was an admirable thing that had led, as Will had noticed, to her transformation into a powerful, mature woman, Allison was now learning, or relearning, that the world was a larger place than the four walls of the dojo.

Things with Jon began foundering. She never blamed him for turning on the light and blinding her at the crucial moment, but neither could she let him comfort her, and in the weeks and months that followed, he felt that. There was no explosion, no big scene, just a gradual fading away of need and pleasure until the day when Allison told him that she was moving out.

As she talked to him, she twisted the ring on her finger. It wasn't an official engagement ring—it didn't have a diamond—but Jon had given it to her the day that she had moved in, offering it as an "understanding" that they were both serious about their future together.

Jon still wanted to make things work, tried to convince her to stay.

Allison listened, her voice steady yet tinged with uncertainty. "Too much has changed," she said after giving it a final thought. "For better or worse, the confrontation with the

Strangler put me on a path I never expected. I'm not saying I'm giving up on what we talked about . . . I just need to see things from a different perspective."

Six months later, the police arrested a suspect in the Sunflower Strangler killings. The case hinged on two eye-witnesses and some personal item found at the scene of Toni DiVincenzo's murder—a ring or necklace or something that the police were convinced belonged to the killer.

The eyewitnesses were Allison and Jon—but Allison had been blinded by the sudden glare of the living room lights, after Jon, groggy and stumbling, had flipped the switch.

At the Sunflower jail, the two stood behind a plate glass window as the suspects shuffled in one by one. Allison's breath caught at the sight of the lineup, her fingers clutching the edge of the counter.

"Do you see someone you recognize?" the police captain asked, his voice low and measured.

Allison's eyes widened. "Yes," she whispered, her words trembling in the air. "But . . . it can't be him."

"Which person?" The captain leaned closer, his expression unreadable.

She hesitated. "Him. But it's not possible."

The captain's brow furrowed. "Why not?"

Allison shook her head, her voice firmer now. "I know his face. Not from that night, though—from high school. He would never be the man who did this."

Jon, standing quietly beside her, spoke for the first time. "She's right. I can't identify anyone from that night either." His tone was heavy, tinged with frustration.

The captain sighed, scribbling notes on his pad. "Not him, then."

Allison's gaze lingered on the man she'd pointed out, her heart heavy with doubt and certainty colliding in equal measure.

Despite her testimony to the contrary, the police eventually charged the man with multiple crimes—three counts of rape, three counts of murder, one count of breaking and entering, and one count of assault with a deadly weapon. After hearing the news, Allison sat for hours in her bedroom chair, staring out at her magnolia tree, distraught. Had they actually caught the right guy? Her uncertainty ate at her. She thought back to her high school classmate, the one she saw in the lineup. She never talked to him much then but knew well enough he was friends with everyone, the kind of guy who volunteered at the soup kitchen and helped grandmas cross the street. Then again, how could anyone ever really know another's true nature? Even Buddy wasn't the guy she'd thought he was, after all. Yet still, that guy in the lineup, her old classmate—he wasn't the same height as the guy who stormed in and attacked her, didn't have the build.

She kept watch on the magnolia tree until the sun set that evening. She expected to see birds, but there were no birds that day.

Within a few months, she'd finished her real estate course and gotten her license. Ellis Davis, Doug's real estate friend, took her on, putting her in residential properties, at first as a favor to Doug. Before long, however, he saw that Allison, like her father, had a knack for talking to people on their level, for listening, and for matching what they wanted with properties that the firm was selling.

After she surprised him by closing several deals, Davis moved her from residential sales to commercial, and a few months later, called her into his office.

"I need someone to run the commercial division with Randall in Olympia."

Randall was vice president of commercial sales and Ellis's son; Olympia was a town of fifteen thousand on the other side of the state. It was much smaller than Sunflower but growing, and the chance to put 250 miles between her and her home-town held a surprising appeal.

"Think it over," the elder Mr. Davis said.

Allison said, "I'll go."

"Really?" Jon said when she came by the dojo to tell him. "You're moving to Olympia?"

"Something is telling me to go."

"Isn't anything telling you to stay?"

"A lot. But with everything that's happened, I can't. You know why."

"I thought that we could get through this."

"Maybe we can. But right now I have to be somewhere else."

Jon said nothing. He fiddled with a pencil.

"Maybe my attention span is getting shorter," Allison said. "I like seeing different people every day. I like helping them solve their problems. I like being on the move."

None of this was new to Jon.

"The ring?"

"I want to keep it," she said.

But she knew that by leaving Sunflower, she would be leaving Jon too.

And with that, she left both.

"We're right over it now," she said to the man from McDonald's. On the map she held, she showed him the location and pointed to the site over which they were hovering.

"There it is." She spoke loudly, above the racket made by the helicopter's rotors. "There's the causeway." She pointed to-ward the elevated road that carried traffic to and from Blue Heron Island and Sea Island. "It's less than a mile from the site. Once they finish widening it, it will carry double the traffic it does now."

He nodded approvingly.

She signaled to the pilot to circle around the parcel to give the man from McDonald's a closer look.

"There's space for a hundred cars," she said.

"Got it," he said, and nodded again. Then he gave her the thumbs-up, indicating that he'd seen what he'd hoped to see.

"Okay," Allison said to the pilot. "Take us home."

This would be her third sale this year. It felt good to be the Queen. But as the helicopter headed for the landing pad, she felt increasingly anxious.

It had nothing to do with the sale, which she was certain she'd make. It was about the figure she knew she would see any moment.

And there he was, a speck on the pad, growing larger as the helicopter descended. She could see him clearly (she was certain it was a man even though she'd never seen any defining features). As the helicopter approached the ground, the dark figure looked up at her, as he always did.

She looked at the pilot and the man from McDonald's. Neither gave any sign of seeing him. No one ever saw him but her. When she looked back at the ground after scanning their faces, he was gone. This was also true to form. The figure always vanished before the copter touched down, and she never saw him leave.

Perhaps it was just an illusion, a momentary hallucination, but if so, it was one that had been occurring for well over a year, closer to two, ever since the Strangler visited her. She had read somewhere that these phantoms weren't uncommon with victims of assault, but she'd hoped they would go away after the Strangler's conviction and imprisonment. They hadn't. But now she had a job to do, so she pushed the thought from her mind.

"That's a good-looking site," said the man from McDonald's once they were on the ground and heading for her car. "It has definite possibilities."

"Possibilities?" Allison asked, giving him her best professional smile.

People in Sunflower would have recognized the smile. They might not have recognized the rest of her, which she had refashioned for her new life in Olympia. Gone were the sweats and T-shirts she wore at Sunflower Martial Arts; now she wore business suits. The ponytail that had tamed her long red hair was gone, replaced with a short cut that didn't require much maintenance—and didn't blow in her face when she flew in a helicopter.

"Well, let's say definite 'probabilities,' then," he said with a laugh. "No sense keeping you in *too much* suspense."

"Have you got a few minutes to talk about it back at the office?"

He looked at his watch. It was three o'clock.

"Oh, I just might. And by the way, I told a friend of mine to stop by today. He might have some business for you too."

CHAPTER TWELVE

This boy's got some money. Big money," the man from McDonald's said as Allison drove him back to the Ellis Davis Real Estate office in her Z car. "And he's looking for land."

"Well, I've got land. What's it for?"

"To build a factory on."

Meaning, Allison knew, at least five acres, maybe more.

"What's he going to make?"

"He'll tell you about it. After we finish *our* business."

"Then let's get to it."

As Allison pulled into the parking lot, she noticed a fire engine–red Porsche Carrera with Ohio plates. She hadn't seen it in the lot before and wondered if it belonged to the friend of the man from McDonald's. That might mean that he had money to spend on real estate. It also might mean that he put more of his money into cars and less into land. Either way, her interest was piqued.

It was piqued further when she saw the man himself taking up a fair amount of real estate in a leather club chair in the waiting room. He stood when she and the man from McDonald's came through the door.

He was tall. He held out a large hand that looked like it had done its share of manual labor, not the hand of a wealthy man. She wondered if she didn't catch a glimpse of axle grease under the fingernails.

"Eric Eagan," he said, shaking her hand. While he and the man from McDonald's exchanged hellos, she gleaned what she could from his appearance. Mid-thirties, she guessed. Aviator glasses—everybody was wearing those these days. Over a white turtleneck, a blue-and-white racing jacket with sponsor decals from makers of tires, lubricants, and spark plugs. Jeans and tennis shoes. Not the wardrobe she was used to seeing on Ellis Davis clients.

The pleasantries between them were brief. Then Allison invited Eric Eagan to sit for a few minutes while she met with his fast-food friend.

"I'll be right here," he said, sitting down. He crossed his legs, folded his hands in his lap, and smiled at her.

The meeting was short and to the point. The man from McDonald's was interested in the property. The price was within the range he'd specified a few weeks earlier, before seeing it from the air. Allison promised to draw up a contract for his attorneys to review.

Eric was still sitting, hands in his lap, when they emerged. It occurred to Allison that he looked like a little boy waiting for his mother at the doctor's office. After seeing the man from McDonald's out, she caught the eye of the receptionist.

In a low voice, the receptionist said, "It's good to be the Queen!"

Allison never knew whether a subtle nod of the monarchial head, a deep bow, or a middle finger was the proper response to this good-natured ribbing. She settled for the nod, ushered Eric into her office, and shut the door.

Eric took a seat across from her desk, pushing the chair back a foot or two to accommodate his long legs.

"I understand you're looking for some land for a manufacturing facility."

The Allison who lived in Sunflower would never have said "manufacturing facility"; she would have said "factory." However, in Olympia, working in a field dominated by men, she chose to be as precise and unambiguous in her speech as the most formal, old-school veterans who surrounded her. It minimized the potential for misunderstanding and said to her male colleagues, *I'm as professional as you.* She sent the same message with her wardrobe.

"You've done your homework."

"Not really. A little birdie told me. We were at about three hundred feet at the time." She still left room for a little charm; she didn't have to be formal all the time.

"The little birdie's right on the money."

"And what will you be manufacturing in this facility?"

"Small kitchen appliances: toasters, toaster ovens, coffeemakers. And our newest thing, immersion blenders. Stuff like that."

He looked like an odd fit for a manufacturer of immersion blenders, with his large-boned, broad-shouldered, athletic body, strong jaw and prominent chin, those unpampered hands, and windswept brown hair that would always look windswept, whether there was a wind or not.

Allison realized she had stopped listening.

". . . been in the business for a hundred years," he was saying. "About five years ago, we branched out into radio stations, and now we're exploring the financial industry."

"You're certainly covering the bases," she said, hoping that her neutral statement didn't sound asinine.

"I've got a lot of brothers, and we're all in the business with my father, so no base is uncovered."

"And you're covering the kitchen appliance base."

He grimaced slightly.

"That's me."

She hoped he hadn't noticed the small breath she took and expelled to recover her concentration. Concentrating came easier if she adjusted her focus every now and then on the Lucite globe she kept on its transparent pillar on her desk. Its miniature patches of land and sea were within her line of vision, so she could glance at it briefly while barely losing eye contact. Doug had taught her that eye contact was as important as listening, but Allison knew that if she didn't break away for a moment, the eye contact would become staring, and the staring, in turn, would cut off her hearing. Sometimes, the eye was the enemy of the ear.

For twenty-five minutes they discussed the square footage of the factory and the acreage required, not just for the building, but for parking, the maneuvering of trucks on and off the property, sewer and utility lines, all the infrastructure details she needed.

"I've got a couple of properties that might suit you," she said. "One is about twenty miles south of here in St. Marys near a Trident submarine base. Why don't I schedule a time for us to visit?"

"I'm free tomorrow. And the day after that. Also, the day after that. Actually, I'm pretty available until I head home next week."

"And where's home?"

"Ohio. Outside Cincinnati."

Yes. The Porsche.

"Then why don't we meet back here tomorrow morning at ten and we'll drive down?"

"How about this evening at seven and we'll have dinner?"

This was something new. And dangerous: She had never been tempted to cross the line between work and her personal life, and she was determined to be professional.

"Are you asking me out?"

"A business meeting. Strictly for business."

She looked at the Porsche.

"I accept." The other truth was that if he hadn't asked her, she would have been sorely tempted to ask him. "Strictly for business."

She walked him to the parking lot.

"Make a reservation at the most expensive place in town. It's on me."

He got into the Porsche and drove off.

When Allison came back to the office, Randall Ellis was waiting by her door.

"Eric Eagan?" he asked.

"Know him?"

"Slightly. They own homes on the island and have looked at commercial property here before—with other firms."

"The island" was Blue Heron Island. Anyone who lived there had money.

"Now he's found the right one. And he's looking to build a manufacturing facility," she said. "I'm going to take him down to St. Marys to look at that parcel. I think he'll be interested."

"Good for us. And might you be interested in *him*?"

"Why do you ask?" She knew why. To Randall, she wasn't just an employee (and a particularly high-performing one). She was a fellow Sunflower native and the daughter of a friend of the family, in other words, someone whose welfare he felt duty bound to protect. His touch was unobtrusive, however; he watched over her without fuss, and Allison appreciated what she knew to be thoughtfulness.

"Well, with good reason, the Queen might take a gander at a wealthy consort."

"I *know* that's not what you think of me."

"It's not. Just a word of advice. Be careful. He's a bad boy."

"*Now* you've interested me. Bad how?"

"He likes his cars fast, his airplanes faster, and he takes

too many chances in both. You need someone more sedate and predictable. Like a nice doctor or lawyer."

The waiter had cleared away the entrée plates and served sambuca and espresso.

The candle in the votive holder still burned, the reflection of its flame elongated in the empty wineglasses. Allison and Eric had talked—but not for too long—about real estate; he was intrigued by the parcel near the submarine station.

"Maybe we should be making parts for them," he said. "Who'd be more interested in immersion blenders than sub commanders?"

Then, the talk turned to the two people sitting across from each other on the leather banquettes, who had emptied their wineglasses.

Allison was proud of the parents who raised her after bringing up four much older children, and how they carried on despite Doug's business reverses. She told him about her life in martial arts but couldn't bring herself to mention the night that she came face-to-face with the Sunflower Strangler. She said that she'd given up the sport because it had gotten to be too hard on her body, which was true. She had nothing but good things to say about the support she'd received from her family, and credited Doug for the lofty position—the Queen of the Fast-Food Franchises—that she had since attained.

"I wish I could say the same about my family," Eric said.

"Tell me more."

He ran down the history. Born to a prosperous, old family in southern Ohio, who had started out in the nineteenth century as peddlers (a part of the story long since erased from the official corporate history), then they'd opened a dry goods store, then another, over time expanding as far north as Cleveland and as far east as Pittsburgh. By the twentieth century, the Eagan Corporation was manufacturing eggbeaters, strainers, melon scoops, and other kitchen tools. From there, it was a natural evolution into electrical appliances.

"We make a hell of a microwave. Best one manufactured in America. The *only* one manufactured in America, actually. We're proud of that."

"But?" Allison ventured.

"I don't know why any of this should interest you. It sure as hell doesn't interest me."

"What doesn't?"

"This. What I do. What I come from. I know I'm lucky to have everything I have—or, I should say, share, seeing how it's all owned by the family: the horse farm in Virginia, the beach house in Nags Head, the co-op on Madison Avenue. Did I mention that we kids were flown to private school in our private plane?"

"No. Did I mention that my dad drove us to the integrated school across town so that we wouldn't have to take the bus?"

"That sounds like real life. I'll trade you."

"I'll take the beach house and the horse farm."

"I'll teach you to ride."

"Teach me to fly." The desire revealed itself unpremeditated.

Eric smiled. "That can be arranged. My brother is an instructor, a damned good one. I could show you the ropes in my twin engine, but you would need to start in something appropriate for beginners. Not that it's all that hard. First, you go up"—he moved the candle along a line between their faces, adding a loop-de-loop as he went—"and then you come down." He put the candle back on the table. "Nothing to it. You try it."

She picked up the candle and held it between them.

"First, you go up," she said.

"But it's not a helicopter. Fly—live a little."

She drew it left to right between their faces.

"And then you come down." She laughed. "I think I'd like it very much."

He wrapped his hand around hers and gently brought the candle down to the table.

"Hand-eye coordination is key," he said. "Your martial arts experience will serve you well."

"I also want to learn how to drive fast cars."

"You want the whole package, do you?"

"Why not? My first boyfriend had a '65 Corvette Sting Ray, but he never let me drive it."

"Shame on him."

"I *was* fifteen."

"Was that your Z car in the parking lot?"

"Yep. But I mean *really* fast cars."

"And what's this?" He pointed to the ring that Jon had given her, which she had never taken off.

"My second boyfriend—the one after the Sting Ray—gave it to me, years ago. We had an understanding then."

"Oh, no," Eric said, gently pulling the ring from her finger. "You're not going to marry anybody but me."

She withdrew her hand lightly and looked at him, eyes narrowing just slightly. How seriously should she take this?

"What happened to our business meeting?"

"Oh, this is very serious business."

CHAPTER THIRTEEN

C ome with me," Eric said two months later, after dinner at the same restaurant. "I know a house on an island."

The island on the other end of the long causeway from Olympia was called Blue Heron. A large barrier island, it was a place of beaches, shops, and hotels, but also of estuaries, marshes, and maritime forests that shared space with a middle-class population and a small enclave of the very well off. Eric's family had built a few houses they'd hoped to sell to the latter population; when Eric first took Allison to the island, one still hadn't sold.

"But only," he told Allison as he showed her around, "because it's the biggest and most beautiful."

It was on a point. To the east, at the back of the house, fifty yards from a stone terrace, a finger of the ocean called Alexander Inlet intruded. To the west, beyond the front door, was marshland; beyond that lay the intracoastal waterway, down which one could travel in a small boat as far south as Jacksonville.

"How about I buy it for us?"

It was larger than any house Allison had ever lived in and

larger than they needed. *Or rather,* she thought to herself when, a few weeks later, she unpacked her things, *larger than we need now.* There would be plenty of room in it for children.

The rooms were large and high ceilinged. Even on the warmest day, a breeze would flow through the wide windows and the French doors that opened onto the terrace.

As Allison sat cross-legged near the marsh's edge, the island taught her about the complexities of silence, which could be absorbed only in stillness. Emerging from the quiet, at first indistinguishable from it, the low murmur of the breeze rustled through the marsh's green mantle. Then the rasping call of a marsh hen might surface, or the gabbling chatter of a roseate spoonbill, or the soft croak of the island's namesake. She breathed it all in, inhaling the sounds as well as the scents, and with the exhale came peace.

From the house, a long path, shaded on both sides by live oaks, led to a boathouse that sat on the waterway. Spanish moss, hanging from the limbs of the oak, glinted gold at sunset; at night, moths rested in the branches and fluttered their velvet wings.

At high tide, Eric and Allison would set out from the boathouse on their small outboard fishing boat. Eric had studied the tides and learned the locations of the sandbars; he enjoyed the slow speeds they necessitated and the concentration required to navigate the narrow channels without running aground.

"We're not flying today," he'd say. "We're gliding."

In those moments near the marsh or on the waterway, Allison couldn't remember when she was less interested in speed. The outboard motor *put-putted* as it nudged the boat along, she and Eric leaning comfortably together in the stern. She felt like a teenager on a date, as if she didn't quite know what would come next, as if each moment was new and each nerve was tingling. Wrapping her arm around his waist, she would nestle closer, and as she was no teenager, she knew what would come later, at home, in bed. During those days on the island, time came as close to standing still as she'd ever known, and it was surprisingly all right.

In the winter, they would head out early on a Saturday to catch kingfish. Dolphins escorted them in the waterway, the sun glinting on their undulating backs as they swam around the boat, asking the couple for nothing but the pleasure of their company. They stayed out until they lost the light in the early evening and then headed for shore. After grilling their catch with friends, they drank beer and danced to Michael Jackson or Whitney Houston until late into the night.

"We treat everyone we encounter with kindness. With grace. It doesn't matter who they are: a client, a prospective client, a colleague, or a competitor. Whether you're talking to me, to Mr. Davis, or to the gardener or his second assistant, we treat each one as we would like to be treated: with kindness, generosity, and respect. We put ourselves in their shoes and see what the world looks like from where they stand."

Stuart Owen, senior vice president, was speaking at the weekly prayer meeting.

Allison went reluctantly. She hadn't been to church on a regular basis since her awe of Reverend Hewett had been overcome by her interest in boys. She felt put off by the unstated but strongly insinuated suggestion that, while attendance was not required, as vice president of commercial sales, she was expected to set an example. So, every Wednesday morning at eight thirty, she sat in a folding chair in a conference room, where the large polished oak table had been pushed aside and the faithful gathered, coffee cups in hand.

Stuart—a contemporary of Ellis Davis and an early partner in the firm—always included a Bible verse in his talk. These were of little interest to Allison, who still believed in Emma's image of the Bible as an inspirational document, not a recipe book. However, she found herself attracted to his bigger message: that kindness was a quality not only *wanted* in business, but necessary.

She also discovered that it worked.

She channeled the energy that she didn't expend on cutthroat competition into listening to her clients. When the client didn't know what they wanted, her careful questions teased the answer out of them. Stuart's approach harmonized with Doug's: Discover the client's problem and try to solve it. The satisfaction she derived from making a sale was like the satisfaction she felt on Blue Heron, that she was one with what surrounded her. On the island, it was the water, the birds, the sound of the wind, living with Eric. At the office, it was responding to the needs of her clients and satisfying the expectations of Randall Davis.

Amid her growing success, she realized, for the first time, how difficult the years following his dismissal from Britmar must have been on Doug. He'd been a successful salesman all his life, until he started selling a new idea, hydroponics, in a territory that didn't embrace thinking outside the deep, familiar furrows. The business had finally died not long before Allison moved to Olympia.

"I've put it out of my misery," Doug told her. Since then, he spent much of his time "degrading my game," as he put it, on the fairways of the public golf course. He and Emma still played cards with friends, but life was slowing down for both of them.

Allison tried to get back to Sunflower once a month, hoping it made up for the few years she'd shared the cottage with Jon and couldn't find the time to drive ten minutes to the Huguenot Street house.

"I know you'll like Eric," she told them before bringing him with her for the first time.

They did.

"You've moved up," Emma said to her as they cleared away breakfast the morning after she and Eric arrived.

"I didn't think that sort of thing mattered to you."

"When it comes to my children, it does. He seems mature and stable and knows where his next meal is coming from, and there's nothing wrong with a little security." Allison wondered what Emma would think when she told her about the cars and planes. "Plus, having someone in the family from outside the South is good. It adds variety to the gene pool."

"We haven't decided whether to jump into that pool."

Emma put down the dish towel after drying her hands at the sink.

"Well, the water looks fine. Put on your skimpiest bathing suit and dive in."

It was golf that united Doug and Eric. Allison had told Eric to bring his clubs, and he and Doug headed for the course first thing after breakfast.

"I could have played another eighteen," Doug said when they got home that afternoon, "but I didn't want to use up all the joy in one day. Better save some joy for tomorrow."

That night, Eric said to Allison, "You've got a good thing going here with Emma and Doug. I'm not sure I'd have ever moved away."

"They're good people. But if I never moved away, you'd have bought the land for the business from Stuart Owen. Then where would you be?"

There was one place on the island where Eric and Allison gave themselves permission to go fast: on the tarmac of the small airport two miles from the house.

"Okay," he said. They were sitting in the Porsche on an empty stretch of the airstrip. "We're going to learn how to do 180-degree turns."

"When in racing do you need to do a 180-degree turn?"

"Never. It's just fun. Now, watch."

He put the car in reverse. "I'm going to put some speed on it."

Allison jolted as the car, moving backward, picked up speed.

"Fun, huh?"

"Woo!" she shouted, putting her hands on the roof for support.

"As I take my foot off the gas, I'm turning the wheel to the left." The rear of the car spun right as the front pulled left.

"Now I brake."

As he did, the car turned more quickly.

"That adds some snap to it."

As the car came out of the turn, he shifted to second gear, and then to third, and the Porsche took off down the tarmac.

"Woo-eee!" Allison shouted. It was the rush she'd dreamed of since the days spent riding in Buddy's Vette.

At the end of the tarmac, Eric executed another 180.

"Ready to try?"

"Try and stop me."

After three tries, it felt as natural as if she'd been doing this turn since the summer she got her driver's license (and learned the truth about Buddy).

Eric also taught her hand-brake turns, which were handy when making tight corners, and how to weave quickly in and out of traffic. To master weaving, they moved to the part of the tarmac where the small private planes were tied down. Since they didn't move, the tutorial didn't exactly duplicate real-life racing conditions.

"But you're not going to be a race car driver," he said to her, "so this will do fine."

"What makes you so sure?" Allison said.

But Eric also had to attend to business. He worked conscientiously with the contractors to get the factory built; once it was up and running, the family gave him permission to bring in the assistant manager from one of the Ohio plants to run it. He knew that this man, Roberts, was good at his job and—at least as importantly—had the confidence of the family. So, Eric left the day-to-day operations in his hands and tended to the affairs he really cared about. He would check in with Roberts once a week, in person when possible, and report the news back to his father, Ben.

What he cared about was racing. He had driven endurance races through the streets of Miami and St. Petersburg; he'd raced once at Le Mans. This "hobby," as his father called it, was a point of friction within the family. His father and the three brothers who were in the business disapproved of the time, energy, and money that he devoted to it. His oldest brother, Gerry, who had escaped the orbit of the Eagan Corporation and had become a successful artist out around San Francisco, was all for Eric's leading the life he wanted, and rarely missed an opportunity to say so. His mother, Rina, who generally supported the family position, once told Eric on the sly that she didn't care what he did with his life if he obeyed the law and didn't take foolish chances.

"I told her," he said to Allison one evening as they meandered down the waterway, "that I promised to obey most laws, and would take as few foolish chances as I could while driving over a hundred miles an hour."

"I'm with you," Allison said. "Wherever you go, whatever you want."

"What I want is to marry you."

He never said what he'd done with the ring he'd slipped off her finger that first night in Olympia. Or rather, he gave her alternative stories at different times:

"I dropped it down the garbage disposal by mistake."

"I gave it to the paperboy to give to his girlfriend, should he ever get one."

"I left it in my jacket pocket and someone at the dry cleaners must have made off with it."

"I accidentally tossed it out the window of the Porsche."

She never knew whether any of these stories were true, only that she never saw that ring again. In the boat, he produced a replacement: a diamond, not ostentatious, but large enough to be noticed. He slipped it onto her finger and waited for her answer. In the quiet, they heard a gentle *glub, glub* in the water and caught a glimpse of a river otter swimming near the boat before it dove under.

"She must have found the old ring. Keep it!" he shouted to the otter.

Allison said yes.

The wedding was to take place in Sunflower. Emma made Allison's dress, and Allison, unlike her teenage self would have been, was proud to wear it.

As Emma made a few last-minute alterations to it a week before the wedding, Allison thought of Mrs. Maye, and the photo she, as a five-year-old, saw in the *World Book Encyclopedia* of a Japanese woman wearing an *uchikake*.

"I told her I wanted one," Allison said to Emma, "and she told me I'd have to marry a samurai."

"And have you?"

"I think maybe I have."

The day before the wedding, she and Eric met Gerry, who had flown in from San Francisco, at the airport. He was unmistakable in violet shorts; a flaming orange, pink, and lilac paisley shirt; and Birkenstocks.

"Try looking a little more conspicuous," Eric said, wrapping his arms around his oldest brother.

"When are you joining the rebellion?"

"One of these days."

"Watch out. 'One of these days' becomes 'I never got around to it' if you don't watch out."

"Gerry's from California," Eric explained.

"You ought to be too," Gerry said, looking at Allison. "You'd fit right in."

"I'll take that as a compliment. But right now, we love our life on the island."

"We've got plenty of islands near Sausalito."

Eric rolled his eyes. "Really?"

"Belvedere. Angel Island. And the Farallons are only thirty miles off the coast of San Francisco."

"No one lives on Angel Island, or the Farallons."

"Tell that to the cormorants and seals."

"I'll leave that to you, Doctor Dolittle."

The brothers laughed, and Allison noticed how much easier it was between them than it was between Eric and the rest of the family.

They had reached the rental car in the parking lot and stowed Gerry's luggage in the trunk.

"Are the rest of the happy family here?" he asked.

"They're all at the hotel."

"Unless," Gerry said, "they're scouting properties for another ten factories from which they'll bury the world in toaster ovens."

"Or immersion blenders."

Everyone, however, was on good behavior at the rehearsal dinner, and the Eagans and the Blanchets ate and drank cordially. Afterward, Mrs. Eagan took Allison aside.

"I have a little something for you." Mrs. Eagan opened a box she'd brought from the hotel and, from beneath a carefully arranged mound of tissue paper, drew a large wedding veil. It resembled a lace mantilla, constructed to rest directly on the bride's head and extend down to her wrists.

"I know that Eric's told you that it's a family tradition for every girl who marries into the Eagan clan to wear this veil. It was made in 1870, or so the tradition goes."

"It will be beautiful."

"Yes, it always is, no matter who wears it. Not that you aren't beautiful already, of course."

The weather the next day, a June day in 1987, was perfect Sunflower: a high blue sky, a bit of haze, and a few clouds lazily floating by. St. George's Episcopal Church was festooned with roses imported from Venezuela by the Eagans, and as the organist played "Bridal Chorus," Doug escorted Allison down the aisle.

As she approached the altar, where Eric and Gerry, as best man, stood waiting, she might have thought of Buddy disappearing on her, or of Jon vanishing into his work at the dojo, or for that matter, of leaving him for a new life in a new city, or of the couple of men in Olympia who had come and gone before Eric. Instead, she thought of Emma and Doug. She thought of how they raised her, having already brought up the four Old Ones (all on the bride's side, looking radiant and happy, Will looking especially tanned and handsome), with all the care they could muster. She thought of them to the extent that she could think of anything besides putting one foot in front of the other, bringing the other foot next to it and stepping forward again, holding Doug's arm, until she was standing next to Eric in front of Reverend Hewett. His hair was silver now, but his pastoral presence was as warm and his voice as commanding as ever. She heard him ask if she would take Eric Eagan's hand in marriage, in sickness and in health, until they were parted by death.

The couple spent a few days in Sunflower before heading back to the island. She took Eric to Montgomery Park, where she had ridden her bicycle fast beneath the laurel oaks, red maples, and loblolly pines; they ate at the lunch counter at Singleton Pharmacy, where the chili was fine but not as good as when it was made by the Captain, who had retired and was said to be living just across the border in Alabama. She didn't take him to the State Theater or to Sunflower Martial Arts.

On the morning of their departure, Allison sat down at the kitchen table with Will and picked up that day's *Enquirer.* "Exonerated: Man Released in Sunflower Strangler Case" read the banner headline across the front page. She caught her breath and put down her coffee cup. The paper reported that her old high school classmate had been set free after a lengthy appeal, with help from a group of advocate lawyers who had proved that police and prosecutors had intentionally withheld exculpatory evidence during the original trial—evidence that completely dismantled their case.

She felt Will's hand on her shoulder. "Try to let it go," he said.

"Let it go?" She rolled the paper in her hand as she stood. "Do you know what this means? It means the real Strangler is still out there."

Allison fled to her childhood bedroom, her sanctuary, and found herself searching for the birds in the magnolia again, the *Enquirer* crumpling in her grip. She thought to call Jon and get his take on the news, but no—she'd shut the door on that part of her life. Besides, the dojo had shuttered, the last she'd heard, and Jon had skipped town.

She unfolded the newspaper, read the headline again, and slumped at the photo of her old high school classmate in a bright prison jumpsuit. What to make of all this? A part of her was relieved he'd found justice, another part of her regretful she herself hadn't helped him achieve it, given she was never fully convinced of his guilt. Still another part of her felt a new fear surfacing now that she was back here in Sunflower without the real Strangler behind bars.

She said little the rest of the day. The family came to the airport to see them off; she hugged her parents, Will, and the other Old Ones goodbye.

Eric was at the controls of his two-engine plane. As they rose from the runway, Allison looked down, surrendering herself to what she knew she would see, especially now, after the news that the Strangler was still at large: the dark figure looking up at her, arms at his sides. There was no need to acknowledge him, she told herself; he knew that she saw him.

See you at home, he might have been saying.

She had told Eric about the figure one evening as they sat in the backyard, watching the water in Alexander Inlet turn from blue to gold to gray.

He listened, put his arm around her, and said, "I don't know what that means or who he is, but you're safe with me."

The flight east to the island, which took an hour, went smoothly until they were passing over Olympia, when Eric turned to her. At first, she didn't know why he was looking at her, and then she realized that there was less noise in the cabin than there had been for the last forty-five minutes. She suddenly had a queasy feeling as she felt the plane slipping downward through the air.

"We've lost an engine," Eric said over the headset.

Allison grabbed her seat. It was the only thing she could think to do.

"Yep. The right engine's out." He could have said "Pass the beans," for all the urgency his voice expressed. "Don't worry."

He pressed a button, releasing the oil pressure in the dead engine, which allowed the propeller's leading edge to sit parallel to the air flow, reducing the drag on the plane. Allison tried to watch, but the flick of a switch meant nothing to her, and she felt the plane slip farther toward the ground. She felt helpless; there was nothing she could do but grip her seat tighter.

Eric banked the plane three degrees toward the left engine and pushed ever so slightly on the left rudder pedal, deflecting the rudder in the same direction. Allison saw the plane tilt slightly to the left and, a moment later, felt it stabilize. It was holding its altitude.

Eric, unperturbed, turned to her.

"Just like I said, nothing to worry about."

A flushed and amazed Allison regained her breath and said, "You hardly did anything!"

"There isn't much to do if you know what you're doing. You'll learn."

Allison said nothing for a moment.

Then, "What? You mean I'll have to lose an engine?"

"You have to if you're going to learn how to recover."

The thought was distinctly unappealing. She closed her eyes for the last few minutes of the flight, so if the dark figure was on the runway to greet her, she didn't see him.

CHAPTER FOURTEEN

It was a hazy Saturday morning in March on the racetrack at Sebring. Allison had spent the better part of Friday in the timing stand, stopwatch in hand, timing Eric's practice and qualifying runs for the twelve-hour endurance race that would begin shortly, just after ten o'clock.

Since he and Allison were married in Sunflower three years earlier, Eric had averaged ten races a year, and she flew with him in the plane to most of them. She often did the flying as well, now that she was licensed. Seeing the earth gliding below gave her a different sense of freedom than riding her bicycle or driving the Porsche; breaking free from gravity provided a fresh kind of exhilaration.

They had flown down to Central Florida from Blue Heron on Wednesday. That night, they partied with the three drivers and the Circus, Allison's term for the teams that supported the racing series: the pit crew, which might include as many as ten men; the mechanics; the sponsor of the team; the owner of the car; and the massage therapist. The wives and girlfriends had come too. They weren't accessories—they timed the qualifying rounds, made sure the drivers had food and clean clothes during the race, and held the team, and each other, up. That night, they drank and laughed; the next three days would be hard work.

Eric's team's lap times in the Porsche prototype 3.0-liter flat-six engine were competitive in its division, but not stellar. Of the sixty-five cars entered, the Porsche was positioned right in the middle of the pack, at thirty-second.

The team was led by its sponsor, a thirty-year-old television action star and heartthrob, Billy Paul Keener, who, in addition to paying all the bills, was also one of the team's three drivers. Everyone agreed that he was a nice enough fellow for a star whose acting experience consisted of riding motorcycles and then throwing a smoldering look toward the camera while tossing his hair back. He was usually considerate of those around him, as long as they didn't come between him and a mirror. He did have, however, a habit of crashing cars into walls, which alarmed Allison the first time she witnessed this at the Grand Prix of St. Petersburg, Florida.

"Don't worry about him," Eric said. "He does it all the time. But, to his credit, he always pays for the repairs—if the car can be repaired."

In fact, everyone agreed that Billy Paul was a good person at heart, and generous with money, if a bit dangerous around cars.

The third driver was the car's owner. JD Grover's family owned a famous brewery in Milwaukee. They were rich. Racing car owners are, almost by definition, wealthy. The average driver might be lucky to break even over the course of a year, and drivers, of course, believe they know more about driving, and cars, than owners. But JD, who started out as a driver, understood the pressures not only of driving but also of being a son whose passions lay outside the venerable family business in which it was assumed he would one day take his place. He and Eric got along fine.

Two years before arriving in Sebring, Allison had been with Eric at Daytona, so she understood the grueling nature of endurance races. Like most of the team, she was awake for all twenty-four hours of Daytona, but Sebring, although only half as long, was more brutal. Its track, shared partly with the regional airport, was rough and uneven. It jolted every inch of a driver, from the moment he drove onto it until he climbed out of the car after his two-hour leg, his body soaked in sweat and reduced to jelly.

Allison would spend most of Saturday in the team's trailer parked near the pits and the paddocks. What had been a party atmosphere on Wednesday night was something else now. Nerves were on edge. The unbroken stretch of twelve hours was about to begin; whomever had the stamina, skill, and luck would win the trophy and the purse, while those down at the other end would get little more than plane fare home. There would be many obstacles to overcome—sixty-four of them, not including the road, the walls, the different speeds of each division's cars, and the Porsche itself, which would have to withstand all twelve hours of the race's determination to wear it down. No one spoke about the danger of driving a car to its limit on a track where everyone, all wanting to win by racking up the most laps over the course of half a day, was doing the same.

Each driver would take two two-hour legs; Billy Paul took the first one. Eric, who would take the second, left the trailer along with him at nine o'clock. Allison knew that Eric would be talking with the other drivers about the condition of the track, listening over the radio to the discussions between Billy Paul and the pit crew as Billy Paul drove, or hearing from Billy Paul himself about how well the car was performing. There was no downtime for the drivers except for brief rests between legs. It was exhilarating and exciting, but it was a job.

Allison watched the race on the trailer's television with

Tammy Spaulding, a veteran massage therapist she'd met on Blue Heron, who now traveled with the Circus.

"Try to relax, honey," Tammy said. "Your shoulders haven't moved for ten minutes."

"I could use a drink," Allison joked, "but nothing we've got has alcohol, and everything has caffeine."

"Gatorade doesn't have caffeine."

"Not what I had in mind."

Shortly past noon, after finishing the first leg, Billy Paul came into the trailer. His cool suit, worn under his fire suit, had kept the temperature down in his torso, but his head, neck, and legs were soaked in perspiration.

"Damn this Florida humidity," he said, tossing his helmet onto the sofa and throwing himself down next to it.

"How'd it go, sweetheart?" Brenda, his wife, a young actress hoping to make it in Hollywood, wrapped her arms around him and kissed him.

"Hot as hell. And I think my spine's been permanently displaced two inches to the right." He held up a hand. "Look at that. Trembling. Damn this Sebring track."

"How about a massage?" Tammy said.

"Sure thing, Miss Steel Fingers. After a shower."

He loosened the top of his bright-red fire suit, stretching his long legs in front of him.

"I thought I was going to cramp up in that little can."

"You're sweltering," Brenda said. "I told you to wear the white suit."

"Allison," he said, "do you see Eric on TV yet? Did they show me?"

"No, not yet. And occasionally."

"Just occasionally?"

"You were in the middle of the pack. You know they like to concentrate on the leaders."

"Rub it in, please. I had trouble finding an opening."

"Shower," Brenda said. "Then, massage. Then, something to eat. Then, rest." With her long feathered and highlighted brunette hair and toned body, Brenda might have looked like another Hollywood actress on the make. But she was smart and knew how to take her husband in hand when he needed taking.

"Yes, ma'am, sir." Billy Paul dragged himself off the sofa. "I've got a good feeling about this race!" he suddenly shouted, taking Brenda's hand and disappearing behind a partition.

Tammy shook her head.

"Ten hours to go," she said.

"Ten beautiful, terrible hours."

Allison had come to love the life of racers: the painstaking work on the cars in the paddocks before the race; the trials, when the drivers pit their cars and skills against each other, each vying for the pole position; the roaring sound of up to sixty-five engines revving at once that must, Allison thought, be what life was like inside a runaway cement mixer. The choreographed movements of the pit crew when the car came in for new tires and fuel filled her with awe: the car airjacked off the ground, four tires replaced, the car lowered to the ground, eighteen gallons of fuel pumped into the tank, and the car back in the race, all in eight seconds. The sight of all that speed and the determination shown by every driver and team member—each race was a chance to change the trajectory of a life.

She watched the television, looking for the orange-and-white Porsche numbered 62. Catching up to the bigger, more-powerful GTs at the turns and then hitting the gas on the straightaways was Eric's specialty, and she knew that Eric would be looking for places to pass.

Adrenaline coursed through her; she tried to control it by staying still. The air in the trailer was sticky. Billy Paul was singing in the shower, but a feeling of anxiety was enveloping the metal and chrome interior.

She couldn't relax when she watched Eric race. It was easier to watch the other drivers, and today, the cameras were obliging. She caught sight of him just once, as he made a move and passed two cars in the big bend and stayed tight to the inside at turn seven.

The cars leading the race continued to get most of the cameras' attention. The drivers were the familiar names, the ones who had a habit of winning. They were among the best drivers, sponsored by the big companies, or had the wealthiest owners who could spend freely on the best chassis, engines, and other parts and equipment, and could easily pay the $50,000 or $60,000 it cost to enter ten races a year.

On the other hand, support from his own wealthy family for what they called Eric's "hobby" had never been unqualified. In Indianapolis, the spring that he entered the 500, his parents and brothers were happy to cheer him on from the coveted seats near turn one that Eric had bought for them. He had made it through two qualifying rounds, but with the slowest time, he was "on the bubble," meaning that he could get bumped from the field if another car surpassed his speed in the next round. In the third round, fourth gear in his Eagle-Cosworth failed, and he didn't make the cut.

After that, perhaps coincidentally, the family enthusiasm began to wane. His mother, at least, feared for his safety and hoped he would give the sport up. The men (save Gerry) objected to all the money he was spending, not to mention the time away from his responsibilities to the Eagan Corporation.

"They're just envious because you're doing something you actually want to do," Gerry counseled after one tense Christmas family gathering where the subject had been raised again. "You don't hear any complaints about the money they're spending on their planes, hang gliders, boats, homes, and travel to fill the holes in their empty lives."

Gerry had told Eric and Allison that the family had hoped

their marriage would cool Eric's desire to race, but they were disappointed; he had his best year after marrying Allison. She cheered for the team in the mid-eighties, when it came in second in its division at 24 Hours of Daytona; a couple of months later, they drove the Porsche to a win at Sebring, and again in May at the Miami Grand Prix. Even winning the Porsche Cup, as Eric did in that decade, failed to impress the family.

"I can afford your being away only so long," his father told him a few weeks before this most recent trip to Sebring. "I get the idea from Roberts that you can be impossible to reach on the phone, and that even when you're at the plant, your mind is somewhere else, you're not paying attention. What am I paying you a salary for?"

"Do you think he's threatening me?" Eric asked Allison.

"That you would even need to ask tells you the answer."

Her mind had wandered away from the race. As she thought back on his family's wish to control Eric's future, his defiance reminded her of Will, who had always lived his life by his own lights. The difference was that Emma and Doug had never tried to stop Will or even talk any sense into him. They were proud of his independence, his competence, his bravery. Allison felt the same way about Eric.

Somewhere, distantly, someone was shouting, "Fire!"

Her mind snapped back to the television. One of the announcers was saying something about a fire.

"In car 62 on turn sixteen. The rear has just burst into flame."

For an instant, Allison saw the white-and-orange Porsche with flames shooting out amid thick black smoke pouring from its rear, just as it drove off the television screen.

"My God!" she heard herself shout as the announcer said "More as we know it" and the cameras cut back to the leaders.

Brenda picked up the phone that connected the trailer to

the team's pit box. She reached for Allison's hand as she tried to hear someone on the other end above the grinding noise of the race. Meanwhile, she looked at the television and said, "They're waving a yellow flag."

Allison couldn't look. She closed her eyes and automatically thought of Emma reacting to the news of Will's disappearance at sea. Although, with the exception of her wedding, she hadn't seen the inside of a church for a couple of decades, she silently prayed.

"What's happening?" she asked Brenda, eyes shut.

"They don't know. They can't get Eric on the radio. It happened at turn sixteen. They said they'd call back." She put the phone down. "If it was really bad, it'd be on the TV, right?" She squeezed Allison's hand.

Allison tried to control the tears that were coming. She told herself, *Calm down. You don't know anything yet.*

Billy Paul, stripped to his shorts, appeared from behind the partition, Tammy behind him.

"What's happening?" he asked. "Is he okay?"

"Waiting to hear," Brenda said.

She and Billy Paul stood, eyes on the television. Tammy sat down next to Allison and took her hand.

She had tried to prepare herself for a moment like this. There had been other accidents. Eric might joke about Billy Paul's car-crashing habits, but between his love of speed and the urge to push a car as far as it could go, he'd also had his share of crack-ups. There was a reason that one racing journalist had called him "one of the bravest drivers around to push Porsches to their limit."

One year in Miami, he started in the pole position, hit the guardrail on the twentieth lap, and still managed to keep the car in the race. He suffered a concussion, but he won.

During an earlier race at Sebring, his cool suit failed, sending hot water flowing through it instead of cool. He was in a groove, though, and refused to leave the car until he finished his leg. He wound up with heatstroke, but this time no trophy.

In a pounding rain during the Sports Car Challenge at Mid-Ohio, a car attempting to pass threw so much spray onto his windshield that he couldn't see the road. Coming out of turn thirteen onto the straightaway, he was driving blind.

"All I could do," he told Allison, "was count to ten and guess that the next turn was coming. So, I backed off, but now the car that had tried to pass me was behind me. He slammed into me and sent the car into the air. It landed on the guardrail. The car was a write-off, but all I got was a twisted knee and a bruised foot."

"Haven't any of these accidents made you afraid of what might happen?" she asked him once.

"Of serious injury? Death? I know what can happen when I'm driving 160 miles an hour, but I don't think about it. I don't have time. Don't worry about me. I know what I'm doing."

He had been racing since he discovered go-karts at age ten. His father had bought him one that achieved a top speed of nine miles an hour, thinking that his son would soon become bored with it and move on to normal preadolescent pursuits, like football. But driving laps around an indoor track awoke something in his blood, and for the next four years, he could be found on weekends learning the rudiments of driving, from weaving between cars to how to come out of a turn into a straightaway while losing as little time as possible.

Boarding school slowed his progress, but he took up dirt bikes and motorcycles when he graduated. Then, a family-mandated detour to business school took him off the road again. Undeterred, he squeezed motocross races into his first foray as an Eagan Corporation rookie, even under his father's vigilant eye at the company's home plant in Ohio.

A year into his Eagan employment came a timely inheritance from a maternal aunt, and he announced that he intended to put part of it toward tuition at a racing school in Florida. By this point, another family might have gotten the idea that he wasn't about to give up racing, but this clue eluded the Eagans.

For his part, Eric saw that he had to live, at least for the time being, in both worlds. The decision was pragmatic. The latest in kitchen appliances provided the funds that enabled him to race professionally, even if part-time. So, he weaved his way between the Eagan Corporation and the gasoline smell of the pits and paddocks, the thrill of entering a turn late and leaving it early and then barreling into the straightaway, leaving the other drivers behind.

"It's not just the speed," he explained once to Allison. "It's the awareness of everything around you. You'd think it would all be a blur, but different things catch your eye each time you pass the same point. By the time I've finished the race, I feel as though I've seen everything, on the track and off. I've never felt anything close to that when I'm not racing."

Allison understood. She had tried to teach that total awareness to her martial arts students in Sunflower, and it's what she felt herself when she was in a match. You're flying, time has stopped, and nothing escapes your field of vision.

She had no idea how long her mind had been wandering, chased by the fear of the worst away from the television. Now she was suspended in the timelessness of helpless waiting.

The phone rang. Brenda picked it up before the ring ended, listened for a moment, and then gave Allison a thumbs-up.

Eric was all right. He had stayed calm and driven the burning car off the course past the pit to turn one, where a fire truck waited to douse the flames. He leaped out, skipping away from the car. The engine was fried to cinders. The intense heat had peeled away the paint on the chassis and raised blisters on the back of his helmet. The fire suit had saved him.

When he got back to the trailer, Eric gave Allison a hug.

"Do I smell like barbecue?"

"You smell fried. I'll take you fried, basted, braised, you name it."

"Fried is what I am. I am one fried driver."

"But," Allison said, "you're alive."

"Yep. To race another day."

PART FOUR

CHAPTER FIFTEEN

Allison is in a forest at night. She watches four men in ragged jumpsuits fling a fifth man into the air. Like a top, he spins himself around, picks up speed, gains altitude, and then disappears upward through a stand of pine trees.

A young woman, dressed as a butterfly whose diaphanous, billowing monarch wings float her above the vapor rising from the forest floor, acknowledges another woman below her, spinning on the back wheel of a bicycle.

At the base of a pine, a third young woman, with four narrow fins growing out of her lower back, waves the upper pair. Like a mistress of ceremonies, she glides to one side, presenting a group of young people, perhaps college students, sitting around the tree in a circle. Despite a chill in the air, they are dressed in shorts and T-shirts. They are passing around a bottle of bourbon in one direction, and a joint in the other.

They offer both to Allison, who is standing off to the side and who, with a smile of thanks, shakes her head as she watches six more good-looking young people in parti-colored tights climb up and down six pine trees. One woman is climbing upward upside down. Applause drifts up from below.

Allison is now standing in a field of chaparral. Somewhere close by, something is burning. It's raining, and in her light cotton shift and espadrille wedges, she realizes she's not dressed for the damp any more than those young people partying beneath the tree are. In the middle distance she sees five giants, each with three revolving arms. Wiping the rain from her face, she watches them resolve into wind turbines.

Walking uphill, she struggles to keep her footing on the rocky, muddy ground. She wishes she had brought her hiking sticks.

She realizes she is looking for Eric, and has been doing so for a long time. The sounds of the party, or festival, now at a distance, fade away. There is only the low sound of wind and the rain falling softly around her, slowly soaking her.

There, about fifty feet away and on higher ground, stands Eric. Allison shouts his name. He raises his right arm, in which he holds a large orb.

Allison makes her way toward him, negotiating the slippery, sticky upward slope, and sees that the orb is his racing helmet. She notices that the paint on the back is charred and peeling.

"Where have you been?" She is out of both breath and patience. If he senses her mood, he doesn't appear bothered.

"I'm here, waiting for you. Let's go." He turns away, and through the smoke, she sees the red Porsche Carrera with Ohio plates.

He is in the driver's seat; she's next to him. He pushes a button that releases the oil pressure in the dead engine. He steps lightly on the left rudder pedal. The car begins to sink in the mud. The engine turns over and Allison notices how warm it's getting.

"Nothing to worry about; I can handle it," Eric, now in his fire suit, says, as the sky glows red around them.

She woke up alone in the house in Gualala.

She'd been having this same dream for many years. She'd tried pushing it away when she woke, but over time she learned that the harder she tried to dismiss it, the more stubbornly it clung to her throughout the day. She let it linger as she got out of bed, and the dream walked with her as she put on a robe and went to the kitchen, until it dissolved without so much as a goodbye.

Tom had risen early and, once again, slipped out, sparing her the worrying sight of his leaving. It was a clear day, a good morning for a hike to take her mind off Tom's work. A long hike if she could manage it and if there weren't many people about.

After breakfast, she began the routine: First, she rubbed the THC cream onto her left hip. This was the nearest she came now to her pot-smoking youth. Next, she applied a strip of the kinesiology tape to her right glute, then one on her lower back. Then on her right shoulder. Her left elbow. Her left hip. When she finished taping herself up, the figure she saw in the mirror looked like a battered doll that had been dragged up and down a flight of concrete steps and patched up with Band-Aids.

Twenty minutes of stretches followed: legs, arms, shoulders, back, sides, hips, neck, ankles; anything that could be stretched, she stretched. There were days when it felt like the preparation took longer than the hike.

She worried about Tom. She didn't have to see him leave to know that he was performing Covid tests again. Long lines of cars would be waiting at what had once been a drive-in movie theater, and a staff of doctors and nurses would administer the tests to the people inside their vehicles. There would be countless opportunities for exposure to the virus; the state had recorded almost five thousand cases so far. The risk to the staff was lower when they conducted the tests outside. Supposedly. But how much lower?

Standing on the terrace, she heard the osprey's quick, sharp cries before she spotted it circling above her. The air was warming, although a slight chill still clung to the bluffs and hills. Hiking sticks in hand, she set out.

SPRING 1991

Allison wheeled the twin-engine Baron over the foothills of the Santa Cruz Mountains.

"Right down there"—Eric pointed out the passenger window—"is the new place."

They were flying east over Saratoga, California, toward San Jose. The new place was on the edge of downtown, with views of both the mountains and the city.

"Would you like to parachute in and make a grand entrance?" Allison asked.

"No, let's just take it to the airport."

A year had passed since Eric escaped the burning Porsche at Sebring. Although he made light of it at the time, over the next few weeks, the reality of his dance with death sank in. He thought again about his divided life, and if once he had succeeded in justifying it to himself, he now found that the trick no longer worked.

"I know what the right thing to do is," he said to Allison one evening as they drifted down the waterway at Blue Heron a month after the incident. "I should settle down and accept my life as a small moon circling planet Eagan, earn a dependable living, and content myself with this house, the marshes, the ocean, and everything we love."

"But?"

"But already we spend a third of our lives asleep. Why spend another third doing something that means nothing to us?"

"These days, you don't spend a third of your life at the factory."

"Okay, a sixth. Even so. If I don't break free, I'll die for certain."

"So how do we break free?"

Eric took her hand. "Leave the East Coast. That's where the company is concentrated."

Allison looked at the sky. The winter constellations were just beginning to appear in the clear air.

"I'll miss it here," she said. "But there are stars in other places."

"In California?"

"Let's ask Gerry if there are stars in California."

Eric called Gerry the following night.

"Hold on a minute," Gerry said. "I can't hear you."

Eric heard what sounded like Tom Petty singing "Free Fallin'." It was hard to tell, given the loud conversations covering the music, as well as what sounded like a bag of ice being poured into a tin tub near the phone.

The sounds subsided.

"You caught me mid-party," Gerry said. "That's better. I'm out on my deck now."

"A party? On a Tuesday?"

"Is it Tuesday? I've lost track."

"If you're having a party, why isn't it on your deck?"

"Spoken like an Easterner. It gets chilly in Sausalito once the sun sets. But I'm out here looking at the bay and the Golden Gate Bridge. You ought to see it. California's not fallen into the ocean yet. We're holding on by our fingertips, waiting for you to get your butt out here."

"That doesn't sound too safe."

"'Safe'? Coming from you? I'm telling you, you need to put some space between yourself and planet Eagan. Then you'll be safe. They didn't put the West Coast three thousand miles from the East Coast for nothing."

"So, where in California?" Allison asked Eric the next night.

"Are you really willing to give up Ellis Davis? Blue Heron?"

"I know it doesn't make much sense, leaving all this to give you more chances to catch on fire. But I'm willing to risk it. And maybe I need to see some place in the world other than Georgia."

"When you put it like that . . . You'd do that for me?"

"I want you alive, but I want you happy too. Besides, you won't be racing cars forever."

"Look at this," Allison said the following night, handing Eric one of the California guidebooks she'd picked up in town. "In 1970, the population of San Jose was 445,000. Last year, it was 783,000. That says growth. That says people are buying real estate. I think I could do okay there."

Eric took the book from her and read.

"It says that before it was known as Silicon Valley, they called it the Valley of Heart's Delight, for all the fruit trees and grapevines, oranges, cherries, and figs." He laid the book in his lap. "Now it's all computers and computer chips."

"And corporate offices, office parks, and manufacturing facilities. The Queen of the Fast-Food Franchises is about the become the Queen of the Computer Kingdom."

"And a few orange groves."

The next evening, Eric called his father to tell him he was resigning.

"You're letting the family down," his father said. "I can't say I'm surprised."

"By my resigning? Or letting the family down?"

"Both."

"I'm giving you a break. You've wondered for a long time why you've been paying me a salary. Now you can find the right person to run the place and not have to wonder. Hire Roberts. No one knows the operation better. Including me."

"You're not in a position to tell me what to do."

"Okay. It's just a suggestion. Hire whoever you want."

Another pause.

"My heart's not been in it for a long time," Eric said. "You know that."

"Yes, you've made that very clear. Well, I've never believed there's any sense in trying to talk someone into doing something he obviously doesn't want to do."

There were murmurs on the other end.

"Your mother wants to speak with you."

"Eric?"

"Mom."

"Dear, you know we're very disappointed."

"I'm sorry."

"You know how much it hurts us when someone in the family leaves the business. It says they don't value what we value."

"That's not how I think about it."

"How are we supposed to think about what you think about it?"

"I don't know, Mom. But there are different ways of expressing values."

"I don't want to have a philosophical conversation."

"I'm not leaving the family. The business has gotten by fine without Gerry and it will get by fine without me."

"Time will tell. Now, I want to ask you a favor."

"Sure, Mom."

"Just please be safe."

Allison gave up her job at Ellis Davis. She told herself there was no better time to strike out for new territory. By 1991, she had developed a large clientele and a larger network. Few in Olympia knew the market, the land, or the landowners better, and she had been Randall Davis's leading agent for several years. More important to her, he had looked after what he'd considered to be her best interests, as if they were brother and sister.

"Hate to see you go," Randall said to her at the party he threw for her at the same place she'd had her first dinner with Eric.

"In a few months, you'll forget all about me."

"Never. What's your name again?"

At the end of the evening, he said, "I'll miss you, Your Queenliness," and gave her a tight hug. "If you crash and burn in California, there will always be a desk for you here, and a phone—if we can spare one."

"I'm not going to crash and burn. When it comes to figuring out what they need, people are the same everywhere. In a year, you'll be working for me."

Doug and Emma came over from Sunflower for the farewell dinner party and stayed the week with Allison and Eric on Blue Heron. They had rarely visited, but it wasn't for want of invitations. Allison suspected that they felt awkward in the big house that, with gorgeous views and every modern convenience (and every appliance made by Eagan), spoke of wealth. She was glad they had come this last time, before everything was packed, before she and Eric were gone from it, from Georgia, and from the East, for good.

On Saturday, while Eric and Doug were playing golf, Allison and Emma took a walk along the inlet. Allison mentioned her one regret about the big house: that they had not had children to fill it with noise and life.

"Noise can be overrated," Emma said as they walked along the shore. "No one's figured out how to make silent children, and after raising five of you, I think that would be a very good idea. At least on some days."

"But you don't regret having kids, do you?"

"Not for a minute." She looked across the inlet as a flock of black skimmers landed on the opposite shore. "But it's not for everybody."

Allison waited. Was there more to this?

"Are you saying it's not for me?"

"Not . . . necessarily. You have such a wonderful life as it is." She swept her arm, taking in the inlet and the marsh. "Look at those birds."

It didn't take them long to find a place in Saratoga, a small town nestled between San Jose to the east and the Santa Cruz Mountains to the west, near the southern end of Silicon Valley, forty miles south of San Francisco.

It wasn't like the house on Blue Heron. It wasn't a house at all. A landlocked duplex two-bedroom condominium with a screened-in balcony and views of the mountains and town replaced the large, airy sanctuary with the ocean inlet at the back and the marshes and waterway at the front. It was meant to be a prudent choice: Eric still had family money from a trust, but for his own income, he was dependent on finishing high on the leaderboard, and while Allison had passed the California real estate exam and gotten her license, she had yet to find a brokerage with an opening for a supersaleswoman from the Southeast.

"One bedroom for us, one for visitors," Eric said when they saw it for the first time. "Cozy."

And for children? Allison thought.

"And for children?" she said when they walked through it again as the new owners.

"Yes, definitely children," Eric said, sounding none too definitive. "But now? Before we're settled and we know how things will work out?"

"I know I'm past thirty."

"You're all of thirty-one."

"Thirty-one today, forty tomorrow. I don't want to be like Emma, having a kid when I'm over forty and tired all the time."

"Well, then we won't have five kids."

"How about two?"

Now they were outside, walking behind the condominium. The grounds were extensive, shaded with crepe myrtle and eucalyptus. A swimming pool glared a blinding blue in the sunlight.

"I'm afraid," he said. This was not something Allison was used to hearing him say. "I don't want to be a father who tells his kids what he expects them to do with their lives. Who puts the family business before their happiness. I always thought that the idea of turning into your parents was a joke. But when I stop and think about what I might do to a kid—it's not so funny."

"Then teach them to be like you."

"A guy who hangs out at racetracks and once in a while wins something?" He laughed.

"No, Mr. Porsche Cup. A guy who knows what he wants and goes and gets it. Despite what his family thinks."

He took her hand as they walked to the far side of the pool and stopped beneath a eucalyptus.

"Is that the sort of father you'd want?"

"You'll make a great father."

"Someday. Maybe."

Allison sat on the balcony looking toward the mountains. A barely perceptible breeze brushed her face. Was Emma right? Was her life with Eric too good to disrupt with children? "Disruptive" described her accurately enough when she was growing up. But she'd learn from that when it was time to raise her own children. She was sure that she and Eric would know when to let their kids run wild and when to instill some discipline. Or try to.

A Central California guidebook lay on the white wicker table next to her. She found the pages about the Hakone Gardens, located a few miles away. The collection of Japanese gardens had been established after World War I by a wealthy philanthropist who had been so affected by the gardens she'd seen in Japan that she created her own version on eighteen acres in Saratoga. Allison thought they'd be worth a visit.

"I got you a little something."

Eric came onto the terrace with a box.

"It just came on the market. I thought it would come in handy once your real estate empire cranks up."

She opened the box, which was white, trim, and stylish. Inside sat a computer, like the one she'd used at her desk at Ellis Davis. But this one didn't need a desk.

"It's called a laptop," Eric said. "Totally portable. Doesn't even need a mouse. It has a trackball—whatever that is."

"This is cool!" *Anyway,* she thought, *unlike a kid, I won't have to worry about where it goes at night.*

CHAPTER SIXTEEN

Three months had gone by since Allison and Eric had moved into the condo in Saratoga: for her, three months of scanning ads for real estate jobs and sending out résumés, races at Willow Springs and Laguna Seca for him. She had yet to land a single interview, and Eric finished out of the running in both races.

Allison had been right about the housing market: It was booming as business in Silicon Valley continued to expand. She was wrong, however, about her chances of breaking into it. No matter her sales record in Georgia—without contacts, all doors seemed closed to her.

Sitting on the terrace on a warm June day, she was perusing the ads yet again when one caught her eye that wasn't for a real estate agent. A computer manufacturer one town to the north was seeking a project manager to oversee the construction of a new campus. The company's name was familiar; its logo was emblazoned on the cover of her laptop.

She had never overseen the construction of a campus (or anything else) on a parcel of land she'd sold, but in order to find her clients the right property, she'd learned a lot about what was required to build any number of different projects. It would take no more time to submit a résumé and cover letter to this company than to any of the dozens of real estate firms she'd contacted, and the return could hardly be less.

So, she was pleased with herself when she received a call the following Tuesday from a young-sounding manager who introduced himself as Bruce and suggested she stop by in two days for what he called a "convo." She'd planned to go up to Sears Point in Sonoma County with Eric for qualifying rounds that day for that weekend's race, but she was intrigued about the job and about the company that made the laptop she could take with her, should she ever have anywhere to go.

That Thursday she presented herself at the company's offices, which occupied a blazing-white building in a part of town dominated by tech companies. She was wearing one of her best business suits, a double-breasted jacket and straight skirt, a white blouse with a high collar and a white scarf tied in a floppy bow. The suit and her business pumps were light pink, which accented her still-short auburn hair: a friendly power look meant to impress, rather than intimidate, a colleague, especially a man.

The cavernous lobby, lit by a large skylight, was empty, excepting a receptionist who sat behind an oak desk. Allison gave her name, and a few moments later, a slim young man stepped out of an elevator and walked toward her.

"Hey, Allison! I'm Bruce."

The informal greeting was nothing compared to Bruce himself, who wore a T-shirt with the yellow visage of Bart Simpson, cutoff shorts, and a pair of formerly white, now gray, tennis shoes.

"Good to meet you," Allison said.

"Come with me!" He spoke as if he were inviting her to the company picnic rather than a job interview. As he led her to the elevator, Allison got a view of him from the rear. She was pretty sure that the back of his T-shirt read "COWABUNGA!," also in yellow, but she couldn't see the word in its entirety, thanks to the long brown ponytail that hung down almost as far as Bruce's waist.

She followed him to a muted white conference room on the third floor, where three other young men waited. They, too, were dressed in T-shirts and shorts, looking as if their next appointment was at the beach for some serious surfing. Allison suddenly felt out of place, overdressed, exposed as a fraud. She clutched her black leather shoulder bag to her lap.

"This is Ron and Randy. Allison's here for a cultural interview," Bruce said, addressing the other two men. This term was new to Allison; on the phone, Bruce had said nothing about a "cultural interview." She noticed that neither Ron nor Randy had a copy of her résumé on the table before them, or any other paper on which to take notes. It didn't matter, since none of them seemed to have pen or pencil either. There were, however, four small bottles of water.

"I brought copies of my résumé," Allison said, passing them out. The three men barely glanced at them.

"So, Allison," Bruce said, clasping his hands behind his head and slumping in his chair, "what kind of things do you like to do when you're not working?"

She wasn't expecting that question, at least not until they had covered her work history, qualifications, and the nature of the job for which she'd come to interview.

"My husband and I are new to the area. In Georgia—where I lived all my life before coming out here—we boated and fished and spent a lot of time outdoors. We lived on Georgia's eastern coast, so we were always on the water. Once upon a time I did competitive martial arts."

"Whoa!" said Randy.

"Neat," said Ron.

"We're still learning about Saratoga. I like the Hakone

Gardens." She'd visited once and was seduced by the calm beauty of the tea garden, the wisteria arbor, and the azalea and camellia groves.

"Hakone Gardens! Excellent!" That was Randy. "I love that new bamboo forest. And the multicolored koi are way cool."

"Way cool," Allison agreed.

"What's your husband do?" Bruce asked.

"He's a race car driver."

"No way! Does he race at Indy?"

"Once, before I met him. He's done Sebring and Daytona. And he's won the Porsche Cup."

"Wow. My dad watches Indy."

"He's up at Sears Point now, for the race this weekend."

"Has he won anything lately?" Randy asked.

"He's in a bit of a dry spell. It happens to every driver."

"Bummer."

"Could you tell me a little about the job? It sounds like a terrific challenge."

"Oh yeah," Bruce said. "Eight buildings. And—how many square feet?" He looked at Ron.

"About nine hundred thousand?"

"Sounds about right."

"That's a huge undertaking," she said. "I'd love to hear more."

"Allison," Randy said, "do you have, like, a philosophy?"

"For work and life," Ron clarified.

"It's all one, right?" asked Bruce.

"Right." Allison quickly gathered her thoughts for yet another unexpected question. "For one thing, I believe that, in work and life, listening is more important than talking."

The three men nodded.

"I try to lead with kindness and grace."

"Kindness and grace," repeated Randy, as if auditioning the words for a mantra.

"I've found that kindness, grace, and respect matter as much as what you know about your territory or product. Dealing with people the right way gets you better results than assuming a big master-of-the-universe persona, throwing your weight around, and plowing through people as if they were obstacles rather than partners." Was she sounding too earnest? It was only what she'd learned from her father and Stuart Owen.

There was silence. Randy's eyes seemed to have glazed over. Then, "Right on!"

"Positation," added Ron.

"What's that?" Allison asked, making sure to smile. "It's not a word I came across growing up in Georgia."

"'Positation' means saying yes to everything that life offers. 'Yes' opens up the future; 'no' is death."

"No shit," said Bruce. "Cool!"

"My dad taught me that. He's an old hippy." Ron beamed, proud of the fact.

Allison had lost track of where the interview was going.

"I have one of your laptops," she said. "I love it!"

"Cool," Randy said. "Does it work?" He laughed.

"It makes my life a lot easier."

Bruce gave her a thumbs-up. "So, I think that's it."

Allison tried not to show surprise. "Aren't we going to talk about the job at all?" She wasn't sure whether she was disappointed, angry, or just completely flummoxed, but she tried to stay neutral.

"We'll be in touch," Bruce said, standing.

Allison stood. "Great. I look forward to it."

As Bruce escorted her from the room, he said, "I hope your husband wins the race."

Was that as simple a wish as it sounded? Or was it his way of saying "You didn't make the cut"?

"I hope so too."

By the time she'd gotten home, she knew how she felt: She was angry.

"I've never had an experience like that," Allison said to Eric over the phone that night. "It seemed like we were talking different languages. Is 'positation' English?"

"It is in California."

"I don't think they took me seriously for a second. Am I just too old for them? For their . . . culture? And what the hell is a 'cultural interview'?"

"Have another glass of wine. I am."

"It was supposed to be a job interview, but it was more like a pot party at Alpha Kappa Karma."

"Will you go back if they call you?"

She thought about it. "I'm still curious about the job. And it's not like anyone else is knocking down our door for my services. So, yes."

"Well, maybe this will help. I met someone at the track yesterday. He sells refurbished planes. He's looking for a partner. Maybe I'm the guy."

"You mean alongside racing?"

For a moment, Eric was silent. "We'll see how it goes this weekend."

That didn't sound right to her.

"How'd the qualifying round go?"

"In the middle."

"How does it look for Sunday?"

"I'll give it my best shot."

She sensed discouragement in his voice.

"How much of a buy-in does the guy want from his partner?"

Eric told her the figure. She did a few quick calculations in her head. The Eagan Family Trust provided them with a decent base income, which was especially welcome during these lean months, but withdrawing a large amount would significantly reduce that cushion.

"Wow."

"Is that a positive 'Wow, I can't believe this great opportunity has fallen in your lap' or 'Wow, you've got to be out of your mind'?"

"I'm just trying to figure out how we'd make it work."

"We'll see what happens this weekend. I'm seriously thinking about getting out of racing."

"Say that again?"

"I'm thinking of getting out. Let's face facts: I haven't won or placed high for almost a year. And everything's getting more expensive: transportation, tires, entrance fees. I don't know how people who aren't millionaires do it in this state. It costs more and . . ."

He stopped talking.

"And?" Allison coaxed him.

"It's less fun. A lot less fun."

Allison felt something go out of her—not for herself, but for him. It had been his life, and sharing his joy in it had become part of hers.

"In that case, who is this guy?"

"His name is Paul Wyman. He's a friend of JD's. JD asked him to come in on buying a new car, and since he has no experience in racing, he started coming around a month ago. We got to talking, and he told me he buys used planes, refurbishes them, and sells them."

"People buy used planes?"

"Just like used cars."

"'She only flew it to church on Sundays'?"

"Something like that."

"And you like this used-plane salesman?"

"I do."

Apparently, he'd caught Eric just when the doubts appeared. A good salesman, Allison knew, could sense when a customer was serious about buying.

"So, what do you think?" Eric asked.

"I think that since you're looking forty in the eye, if you get out now, you'll never go back."

"That's the idea."

"Think it over. Don't decide based on what happens this weekend. At least wait until you get home and we can talk it through."

Eric sighed. "It's been a good run, I guess. I did what I wanted to do and wasn't too bad at it. I just wish I could have been better."

He sounded as if he'd made up his mind, and she wondered if he had heard her. "You were—you are—absolutely great."

Allison wished this wasn't happening over the phone. She wanted to hug him tightly.

"Oh, there are a few guys who won more races. And a few million more dollars."

"Winning isn't just about winning."

"I'll ponder that from the middle of the pack."

"I wish I was there with you."

"Me too."

Rina called the next day—for Allison, not Eric.

"I know that things are still slow for you on the job-hunting front."

"I'm not worried," Allison said, lying. "I've always found work when I wanted to."

"I know, dear. I imagine you want to now. That's why I'm calling. I've heard about a job in California. Well, *Ben* heard about it, and he told me."

"Really?" A part of her was ready to jump at any opportunity, even before knowing what it was. She had to force herself to seem noncommittal. "Tell me about it."

"I understand it's not far from you. In Palo Alto. Ben's joined the board of a company there that makes computers."

"Oh? Which one?" Allison pictured Rina arriving in a Liz

Claiborne dress and a triple strand of pearls for an interview at the place Allison had started calling the Casual Computer Corporation and coming face-to-face with Bruce, Ron, and Randy.

"It's called Stanton, for the man who started it. They make mainframe computers. I'm not sure what they are, but apparently, they're big business. Ben heard they're reorganizing their customer briefing center—I guess that's where they brief customers—and they have openings. Since we've been following your . . . situation, Ben, who has a lot of respect for you, you know, suggested that he knows someone who, with a little training, would be just perfect."

Allison knew that Ben was aware of how successful her real estate career had been, but he'd never mentioned that he respected her for it.

"Well, what can I say? Thanks, Rina."

"Are you interested?"

"Sure."

"We thought you would be. Let me give you the name and number of the person to contact."

"And please thank Ben for me."

"It's our pleasure, dear. All we want is for you to be successful. And happy."

Allison put the name and phone number in a drawer, intending to forget about it. Accepting help from the Eagans after Eric had freed himself from servitude but had yet to find his footing in California held little appeal. Besides, she'd just read in a computer business magazine, which she'd picked up to prepare for her interview, that mainframe computers were on their way out. A leading industry analyst had predicted that the last one would be unplugged five years from now, on March 15, 1996. Why board a sinking ship?

Four days later, she got the call from Bruce for a follow-up interview. She considered wearing jeans and a polo shirt, although she'd still risk being overdressed. But Bruce didn't say who would be there, and people up the food chain might be present. *Someone at that company must wear a suit,* she thought. In any case, she couldn't pretend to be someone she wasn't. She picked a white suit, the jacket with long collars and a single button at the waist, a straight white skirt, black-and-white pumps, and a loose-fitting dark-pink blouse.

When he met her in the lobby, Bruce was dressed as before, his T-shirt reading "Give Me Some Space," alongside a photo of Captain Picard from *Star Trek: The Next Generation.*

Walking to a conference room on the second floor, she realized that she had not seen any women in the hallways. None sat in the informal meeting areas scattered here and there, none in the cubicles in the middle of the floor or in the offices, and none in the green conference room she entered with Bruce.

Today, there were six men around the table. All were dressed like Bruce, Ron, and Randy (who were present too), although some had given in to the adult ethos and wore long pants. No last names or titles were mentioned. Were any of them executives? It was impossible to know. Everyone was glad to meet Allison, and this time one of the men even asked her about her work experience. Again, no one offered any information about the job.

Afterward, Bruce walked her to the elevator.

"I'm just curious," Allison said. "I don't mean to tell you your business, but will we ever talk about the job?"

"Oh, yeah—probably at the next interview."

"I have one other question; I hope you don't mind: Do you employ many women?"

"We're working on it!" The elevator doors closed.

A third interview followed. Allison learned that the position would start in early September, but she left with no more information about the nature, responsibilities, or duration of the job; how it fit within the company's overall plans; or how much it would pay. And still she saw no women other than the one at the reception desk.

Every day, she looked at the name and number that Rina had given her. The pressure to find work was growing because by the time he came home from Sonoma, Eric had decided to become a partner in Paul Wyman's refurbished-plane business. More than that, she had learned that she wasn't the sort of person who could sit at home and wait for the phone to ring. She needed to be out in the world, moving through it, doing something.

In her spare time, she'd pick up the Lucite globe that had once sat on Doug's desk. He'd given it to her as a good luck charm when she moved to California. She would turn it in her hand, looking at its brown continents, and wonder, as she had as a child, what countries they were and where she might go.

She spent a day at the library reading up on mainframes, which, she learned, were large computers with vast amounts of computing power and memory that could complete millions of calculations at high speed and were used for data and transaction processing—everything from satellite imaging to airline reservations to medical research. They could run different operating systems at once (she read up on those too), meaning that a new mainframe could do the job of multiple older models and could run twenty-four hours a day with no downtime.

However, they required enormous rooms to house them, and large amounts of electricity to power and cool them. Now smaller computers, even personal computers, like the ones made by the Casual Computer Corporation, were becoming more powerful and could be linked via networks, meaning that they were beginning to do some of the work that mainframes did, hence the warning that the behemoths would soon find themselves next to the abacuses in exhibits about the way people once performed calculations.

She also looked up customer briefing centers in a slew of computer and information technology magazines and understood their purpose immediately.

When she got home, she picked up the phone and called Stanton.

CHAPTER SEVENTEEN

Eric settled into his new life. He thought he would miss the adrenaline rush he experienced every time he walked into the paddock. Where would he discharge the nervous excitement he'd felt since the day he drove his first go-kart back in Ohio?

To his surprise, he felt no unmanageable energy requiring an outlet.

"It's all fallen away, like . . . what? A Datsun with a dirty carburetor," he said to Allison one evening on the terrace a month into his new job. "I loved racing, but something was wrong."

"What was wrong?" Allison poured another round of a Russian River California white into their wineglasses.

"If you're going to be successful in that business, you have to want to win more than anything else. And I wanted to win—but not more than anything. That was never me. I never admitted that to myself. I did it because I had fun. That's really it. I wanted to have a good time. And I did."

He paused, sipped his wine, and looked toward the mountains, which were edging into purple as the sun set. "Was I wrong to lead people on?"

"What people?"

"The people who paid me, who trusted me to race their cars to win? Billy Paul, JD, all the ones before them?"

"Did they complain that you didn't take winning seriously enough, or that you didn't drive hard enough or smart enough? Or that you risked your life so they'd make more money than you did?"

"Still . . . that reminds me, you know what else I don't miss? Risking my life."

He had rarely talked about this during his racing days, and Allison had done her best not to think about it. They both knew that every time he drove a car onto the track he might be killed, so why talk about it?

"Now I get paid to sell planes, and I'm not concerned about winning, or whether my cool suit will work, or how to approach a curve, or what the guy who wants to pass me is going to do. I'm a partner in a good business. As long as we're selling planes, I've got it made."

He was flying more now that he was working with Paul Wyman. He'd fly with customers who wanted a test run before buying a plane; he or Paul would ferry a plane they'd bought elsewhere to their hanger showroom, or to a distant repair outfit if an issue arose with a plane that their own team couldn't address, or to a customer who lived a distance away.

"I get to spend every evening on this terrace with you and the mountains and the sunset." He examined his wineglass. "And the lovely California wines."

"How about a little red?"

"Why not?"

Allison poured from a new bottle of Santa Cruz Mountains Pinot Noir.

"Look at me. I can relax now that I'm not putting my body on the line to earn a buck." He took her hand. "I'm safe. I've got you. What else is there?"

"You're happy, you're safe, we have a regular income," Allison said. Taking a breath, she dove in. "And . . . children?"

This was the first time she had brought the subject up since they had inspected the condo before moving in.

"Well . . . now that you're working, you won't have time, will you? I mean, you want to establish yourself at Stanton first, before disappearing on maternity leave, right?" He lifted his glass. "Cheers."

The Casual Computer Corporation invited Allison for a fourth interview. She turned them down. After exactly two interviews at Stanton, they offered her the briefing center job, and she accepted.

The atmosphere at the office, which was painted in pale shades of gray, matching the suits that most of the men wore, was about as far removed from the Casual Computer Corporation as she could imagine. In fact, everyone wore suits—which meant that Allison could feel at home wearing hers. The men spoke in low tones; there was no hint of the boisterousness that always seemed on the verge of exploding at the CCC. Stanton had formed a partnership with a Japanese mainframe firm, whose executives were often around the office and who added to the formal feeling of the place. The Japanese were unfailingly polite; after meeting her, they'd give a deferential nod. Allison liked them for their courtliness, which reminded her of Doug. She liked less their habit of then transferring their attention to the men in the room, even as she realized that this behavior was no different from the Americans at Stanton. And, as at the CCC, there were few women to be seen at Stanton, and those that were had to fight for attention. Had her youth blinded her in the past to this male habit? Had the men she'd worked for in Georgia only appreciated the aspects she offered other than her talent? Surely, that couldn't be said of Ellis or Randall Davis, or of Stuart Owen. The Cadre at Sunflower Martial Arts had given her the respect she'd earned; it'd had nothing to do with her relationship with Jon. She'd always worked with men and liked it fine. Still, while the men at Stanton were polite enough, she had yet to sense, in her first few months, that they saw her the way she'd been seen in Georgia.

Her role in the customer briefing center—to match clients' needs to Stanton's products—suited her perfectly. As she mastered the range of mainframes, software, and services, she applied Doug's lesson about listening. The old saw about sales was true: If you could sell women's self-defense training, or real estate, you could sell computers the size of a living room.

"Oh yeah—I can sell anything."

Allison was at lunch in the company cafeteria listening to a project manager she'd met in the briefing center that morning.

"I don't think there's anything I can't sell. If it's legal, I can sell it. If it's illegal, I can still sell it. Not that I would."

"Of course not."

"Depending on what it was."

Allison looked closely at him. He resembled the other men of Stanton: hair (dark), medium length, parted casually just off the center of his head, styled to look as if it weren't; white shirt, dark-blue tie with gold links to match his dark-blue suit. The suit was his way, Allison surmised, of standing out, just enough, in this staid company. No rings.

"So, what's your story, if I may be so bold?" he asked.

She gave him the short version: real estate, marriage, move.

"Welcome to Stanton. A decent place to start." He leaned closer. "Take it from me, though, it's not the place to spend your entire career."

"Why not?"

"Nice people. Not a lot of balls. Sorry," he stage-whispered. "Listen, I'm going to build—with some partners at a chipmaker that shall remain anonymous—a huge parallel supercomputer with several thousand processors. It's going to be the fastest supercomputer in the world. One hundred and twenty-eight gigabytes of memory."

"One hundred and twenty-eight gigs? That'll set you apart."

"Sure will. I don't mean to brag, but I'm going to be a big name in this business before these dinosaurs sink in the West."

It was an odd metaphor, but she took his point.

"I didn't catch your name this morning."

"Marty Schliemann." He held out his hand. She shook it; he held on.

"How about a drink tonight?"

"Husband," she said. "I mentioned him, remember? Former race car driver?"

"Right. Now a used-plane salesman." He let go. "It's an open invitation."

"I'll remember that."

Her halibut fillet finished, Allison stood and picked up her tray.

He stood too. "Someday you'll be working for me."

"Marty, I look forward to the day."

"And you didn't take him up on his offer of a drink?"

"I did not."

"Maybe you should have. What's a '128 gigabytes'?"

They were driving up to Sausalito, where Gerry was throwing a party.

"A byte is a unit of information used by a computer. The computer stores it and then retrieves it to run, say, a calculation, for example. A gigabyte is equal to a million bytes, so that's 128 million pieces of information."

"How can anyone begin to fathom how much that is?"

"If a computer has the capacity to store that much information and can recall and calculate it super fast, then it would be the most powerful computer in the world."

"So, it would be a tempting target for Goldfinger, and James Bond would have to come to the rescue of the civilized world."

"Let's not get ahead of ourselves."

"I'm glad you explained that. I'll stick to airplanes."

Gerry had rented a large portion of a park near the marina and across the street from an old warehouse where he lived and worked. Scattered across the lawn were several tents in which he'd placed picnic tables for his guests to eat, drink, and shelter from the August sun. Under the largest tent was a stage on which a band was playing; Allison could see, at a distance, an outdoor stage as well.

"Some bash," Eric said, embracing his brother.

"It's been a great year so far, so why not celebrate?" Gerry was feeling expansive. "A bunch of pricey commissions, and in a few weeks, I'll be lighting my first rock concert."

"Rock concerts?"

"Yep. Working in three dimensions is a whole new challenge. A hell of a lot of fun—and you wouldn't believe how much they pay."

"No kidding? Who's the band?"

Gerry mentioned the name: a famous band. "They're a hoot! You wouldn't believe!"

"Maybe I would."

"They're playing today," he gestured toward the big tent. "You'll see them later. Come over to the studio first, have a look around at some of the stuff that's paying for this shindig."

They followed him across a gravel road to the warehouse on the water's edge. The entrance opened onto the second floor. Canvases in assorted sizes in various stages of completion were scattered around on easels. Sawhorse tables, spattered from years of work, were covered with tubes of paint, pastel sticks, pigment pots, mineral spirits, rags, pencils, palette knives, rolls of tape. There was also a television, a VCR, and stacks of video cassettes, which Gerry explained were recordings of band concerts he was studying. Allison, though, was attracted to the balcony. The view of the bay, of Angel Island, and, in the distance, the skyline and hills of San Francisco, reminded her of Blue Heron and how cares fell away in the salt air and bird-song. She missed the water.

"I live on the third floor. This is the studio. Have a look around," Gerry was saying as she reentered the workspace. There were group portraits and single portraits, all painted flat against the canvas, the figures emerging from strong, visible brush strokes and wide swaths of color. This blunt approach was mitigated, or complemented, by detailed attention to highlights and shadows, especially on exposed flesh, which, depending on the picture, emphasized or undercut Gerry's nonnaturalistic style.

"Who's this?"

Allison was standing in front of the portrait of a man in a maroon robe. He wasn't tall, but his strong arms, folded over a mustard-yellow sash; shaved head; and deep-brown eyes gave him a look of serene and powerful determination. Here was a man at peace, but also at attention.

"That's Lama Thokmay, a Tibetan priest. I met him in Nepal. He runs a school there for children who are shunned from other schools because they have a physical deformity, like a cleft palate."

"Is he as magnetic in life as he is here?"

"Charm for days. You should see him raise money when he comes to San Francisco. He knows how to work a room."

"So, he's a salesman."

Gerry looked at them both. "Who isn't?"

They walked back to the park as the sun reached the top of the sky. Young and old people strolled the lawn. One man stood out from the crowd, most of whom were dressed in shorts, T-shirts, and sneakers or sandals. He was dressed in a

well-fitting powder-blue suit, crisp white shirt, oxblood loaf-
ers, and a snazzy white fedora.

"Who's that?" Allison asked.

"That's Willie Brown. Speaker of the state assembly and
the most powerful man in California. And a good friend. Want
to meet him?"

The Speaker, surrounded by a gaggle of young women, was
schmoozing and clearly having the time of his life.

"Maybe another time. He looks busy."

"Sure. Listen, I'm going to stroll and check up on my other
guests. Have a bite to eat and a drink; I'll catch you later." He
stopped to whisper something in Willie's ear that made the
Speaker laugh, and strolled away.

Allison and Eric grabbed a couple of beers and two plates of
crab cakes (Gerry wasn't stinting on the food) and sat at a table
under the big tent where the famous band was in the middle of
a jam session. They had been around for years and attracted a
huge and extraordinarily dedicated following, many of whom
accompanied them from show to show, blissing out on a very
California mix of bluegrass and driving rock.

Two leisurely but well-dressed couples in their thirties
asked if they could join them. One of the men, who'd introduced himself as Jeff and said that he specialized in intellectual property at a large law firm in San Francisco, produced a
quart baggie containing a small amount of white powder.

"Would you folks like to partake?" he asked Allison and
Eric.

"What is it?" Allison asked.

All four newcomers looked at her as if she'd spoken in
some rare dialect.

"It's coke," the lawyer said. "Everything goes better with it."

"Did you think it was heroin?" the woman he was with
asked, laughing. "Can't help you there."

Allison blushed.

"No thanks," said Eric. "I fly planes for a living and can't do drugs. But feel free."

"I'm also a pilot," Allison added, not mentioning that for her, flying was only an avocation.

"Copilots in life too?" the woman asked.

"We share a cockpit," Allison said.

"Cool."

The lawyer laid out the powder in neat lines on the table, and the two couples helped themselves with a designer straw that the woman, Anne Marie, produced from her purse. Then they all chatted about the usual things: the weather, the traffic, how they each knew Gerry. The other three were lawyers too, and they were all employed at the firm that represented Gerry's intellectual property interests.

"You must know his work pretty well," Allison said.

"Well enough to tell one painting from another, usually," Anne Marie said.

"And now he's going into rock concerts," Eric added.

"We don't handle that."

Gradually, it became clear that the four attorneys were more interested in each other than in Gerry's relatives or rock concerts, and Allison and Eric found themselves excluded from the conversation. Eric looked at her and shrugged. They stood.

"Enjoy," he said to the four, and he and Allison left the tent, the band still jamming.

A Ferris wheel stood close by the tent, and the line to ride it wasn't long. As they took their place, Allison noticed for the first time that there were children present along with the adults who were helping themselves to alcohol, coke, and, she could tell from the aroma wafting around them, pot.

"I wonder if Gerry told his guests who planned to bring drugs that children might be here?" she said as they were seated in one of the white metal cars and the locking bar brought down.

"The invitation said kids were invited. I suppose he expected people to use their judgment."

When they reached the top of the wheel, she could see the Golden Gate Bridge, its graceful span resting on either side of the bay. In the distance beyond the bay, she could see the fog slowly rolling in.

They joined a crowd of people sitting on the ground in front of the open-air stage. A bottle of bourbon, passed hand to hand, approached them from the left. This time, Allison and Eric each allowed themselves a swig and then passed the bottle on as a joint came toward them from the right. Eric passed the joint to Allison; she admired the aroma and sent it on its way.

On the stage, acrobats performed to a band's accompaniment. They danced and spun and flung one another skyward, and Allison was mesmerized. Eventually they fitted tall poles into slots and climbed upside down before stopping and balancing themselves parallel with the stage. In one motion, they jackknifed their legs and, as easily as she had climbed trees when she was eight, shimmied upward before sliding headfirst to the stage. Soon afterward a young woman spun around on the back wheel of a bicycle; another ran in place on a treadmill hidden in the floor, while giant monarch butterfly wings fluttered from her back. A third woman, also outfitted with wings—slender, diaphanous ones this time—weaved a sinuous dance around the poles before the climbers lifted her aloft and carried her away like a fairy queen. In the gathering dusk, the effect was magical.

The music, the beers and bourbon, the sun, and possibly a contact high, combined to give the show the quality of a hallucination. Allison and Eric stayed, rapt, longer than they'd intended.

Finally, a little unsteadily, they rose and moved on.

"I'm going to lean on you," Eric said.

"No fair. I was going to lean on you."

"It's time we started back."

"I guess."

"I wonder where Gerry is."

Under the big tent, the famous band had at last finished jamming, their place taken by another popular group from Berkeley. They found Gerry at a table with several other people who were helping themselves to lines of coke.

"Gerry, we're taking off," Eric said, laying his hands on his brother's shoulders.

Gerry turned and looked up. His eyes were a bit glassy. "Already? Stay awhile and visit with my friends here."

"I think we've partied enough for one day. We should start back."

In the near distance, the slow-moving fog had started to turn the brightly dressed acrobats into pastel smudges hanging in the sky; surely they'd have to stop.

"Will you be able to make it home?"

"We'll be fine," Eric said. "I'm licensed to drive in all weathers just by the instrument panel."

"The fog will burn off once you're south of the city." He walked them to their car. He was still animated after a long day that was far from over. "I'm so glad that you two are out here now. I want to see more of you. Come whenever you want; there's plenty of room in the warehouse on the third floor." It was his turn to take Eric by the shoulders. "Listen, little brother. You came out here to race cars. Now you're selling planes. That's good; that's excellent. If that's what you want, I support you 100 percent. One hundred percent." He gave each of them a fierce hug. "Now, fly away, lovebirds. And be safe."

CHAPTER EIGHTEEN

Mr. Hyousuke Nakamura, a visiting executive from Stanton's Japanese partner firm, Sakasama, looked on, amazed at the scene unfolding in the briefing room. Allison was about to give a pitch to potential clients from a large San Jose bank when a sales manager named Johnny Schmidt stood up from his table a few feet away. He was a big man, and his imposing bulk drew all attention to him.

"That's all right, Allison," he said. "I'll handle this. Why don't you take notes?"

There was a barely audible intake of breath around the room as the clients and Mr. Nakamura sensed that something unrehearsed was happening.

Allison was cool. She looked down at the waiting pile of handouts, and then up at Johnny.

"No need," she said. "I've got it, thanks. I don't need notes, but you can take them if you like."

The men in the room—there were only men in the room, as usual—shifted uncomfortably in their seats. Beneath his thinning tufts of brown hair, Johnny Schmidt's round face turned red, making him look more beet-like than usual. His chins wobbled in disbelieving indignation, and when Allison wouldn't budge, he sat down. Mr. Nakamura sucked his teeth in disapproval, but his eyes registered a different reaction. Allison did her presentation undeterred and, judging from the client's response, made the sale.

"I admit I am not used to witnessing such behavior," Mr. Nakamura said to her a few days later. "This is not how we do things in Japan."

They were drinking sake in a Japanese restaurant in Palo Alto at a table near the sushi bar. It was December, and the holiday lights were strung across the streets of the business district.

"I was out of line. But my father taught me to do my job whatever the obstacles, and I was facing a large obstacle."

Mr. Nakamura tried not to smile. "I should admonish you for your lack of loyalty to your superior. But he was arrogant and rude, and showed you disrespect. That was equally dishonorable."

"Martial arts taught me to stand my ground."

"Martial arts! You American women!" He smiled with approval.

They were not strangers. Since he'd first arrived that summer, they had gotten to know each other. When she took him to Hakone Gardens, she could tell that he not only approved, he was moved as they walked through the bamboo garden.

"It makes me a little homesick," he said.

He was a trim man, probably in his early fifties, although his abundant, well-coiffed hair was silver. His smile was kind, although Allison knew that he'd not risen through the ranks of the Japanese tech industry on kindness alone.

From their table, Allison could see a woman in a dark-blue suit at the sushi bar. From the rear, she seemed familiar. She turned her attention back to Mr. Nakamura.

"Someday, you must come to Japan. Work in our office. Your expertise at selling would be most welcome."

"How would your colleagues react to a woman running a meeting?"

"Much like Johnny, I'm afraid. But you handled that, and together, we could deal with my colleagues. What they like are results, and you get results. Not that it would be easy. We Japanese tend to be set in our ways."

"Nothing at all like here. I would love to see Japan." She told him how she'd first discovered Japan in Mrs. Maye's *World Book*, and how the teacher had told her she would have to marry a samurai if she wanted to wear an *uchikake*.

"I'm not sure I can arrange *that*."

"That's okay. I'm married to my own samurai now."

They finished their sake and Mr. Nakamura stood.

"I must go. I have a dinner meeting. But you stay. Have another cup of sake."

"I think maybe I will."

Mr. Nakamura left. As dusk fell, Allison watched the holiday lights wink on. She thought about ordering another sake but decided against it. Eric would be getting home, and she looked forward to sitting with him in the early evening on the terrace, a bottle of wine and two glasses between them, looking out at the darkening hills and talking about their day.

The familiar-looking woman was still at the sushi bar, and Allison saw that the dark-blue suit she wore was a uniform. On her way out she walked closer so that she might recognize her.

She gasped. She was certain her mouth had fallen open, and in the moment it took to recover, the woman had turned and seen her.

"Lovey?"

The name froze Allison in place. All the words she'd thought she'd say to Lillian over the years should they ever meet again went out of her head. "Lillian."

Between the two names, a bad movie unspooled in Allison's mind in which she always played the loser: a young Black girl with a tennis racket, a powerful forehand, and a rude way of refusing Allison's congratulations after a win; a teenager banging her into lockers at Braxton Bragg, facing off in the hallway before Wendell stepped between them; the Scrappy Cats on the sodden football field, and another deserted hallway after the game. Then that movie was replaced by the one that came after.

"I have something to thank you for," Allison said.

"You do? I'm glad to hear it."

"Thanks to you, I got into martial arts. Changed my life."

Lillian, still seated, considered this and regarded Allison.

"Well, from the look of it, congratulations."

She stood. Instinctively, Allison stepped back.

"Peace," Lillian said.

Allison noticed the wings pinned above Lillian's left breast.

"Air force?"

"Yes, ma'am."

"Operation Desert Storm?"

"I was stateside for that." She extended her hand.

Allison had resented this woman, whose hatred of her she could never penetrate. She had nursed that resentment into a fine, sharp instrument that goaded her into becoming a woman who no longer feared Lillian. Once accomplished, time transformed that resentment into cool indifference and, finally, dismissal. Trust? That had yet to arrive.

Still, she reached out her hand.

"Peace," she said.

Forgetting her desire to get home to Eric, Allison sat down at the sushi bar and they talked. Lillian told her she'd joined the air force after high school, in 1978. Her first job was as an aircraft maintenance officer; after a few years she attended Squadron Officer School, did a four-year tour overseas in Germany, and spent several years on the headquarters staff at Wright-Patterson Air Force Base near Dayton. In the past year she'd become a recruiter.

"And this is where they sent me," she said.

When Allison told her of her confrontation with the Sunflower Strangler, Lillian stared into her empty sake cup.

"That's why I left Sunflower—to get away from all that bullshit."

Now she was in the second year of a three-year assignment as a recruiter, based in San Jose. "I go into a lot of schools. Who'd have thought I'd like that?" She laughed.

"So, you've made a career of it?"

"I'm a lifer. Have to be, to be a recruiter. They treat me well. It's not perfect. But it's no worse than the outside. I haven't seen anyone get lynched." She paused and looked around the restaurant, which was beginning to fill up with dinner customers. "I like the order, and the discipline." She turned her gaze back to Allison. "Surprised to hear that? I've changed, Lovey. Like you."

They'd finished their sake some time ago. When they stood to leave, having agreed to stay in touch, Allison asked, "So, what do I call you now?"

"You can call me Airman Clark."

"Really?"

"No, just call me Lillian. And I'll call you . . . Allison."

"I'm getting a little itch for something," Eric said one morning as they loaded the dishwasher after breakfast.

"What sort of something?"

"Something fast."

"Uh-oh."

"And nimble. And sure footed."

"No cougars running around the house. Sorry."

"Not a cougar. Not even a Jaguar."

"And so . . . ?"

"A new Porsche 911 Carrera. Like the one I taught you to drive. But better."

They'd sold the Porsche when they made the move to California. Now it seemed that Eric had enough confidence in the future to buy a new one.

"The new big thing is that it has all-wheel drive."

"We'll certainly need that here. I mean, with all that snow we get."

"Who says we won't be taking a trip to Tahoe? I'd like to do that next winter. And we've had fourteen inches of rain since November."

"Now it's March. How much more are we likely to get?"

"We just had two full days of it. And you know what lousy drivers people are in the rain. I'm not putting our lives in their incompetent hands."

Allison got serious. "Things are looking that good?"

"The numbers are going up and up. That plane we bought last month that's been in the shop in Columbia? Paul and I are flying up there today in the Cessna to ferry it back. We'll have the next payment on it tomorrow." Columbia was 130 miles northeast, in the Sierra Nevada foothills.

"There's still rain in the forecast," Allison said.

"Yes, but not till late tonight. We'll be home before then."

"Be careful, please."

"It's just the usual. Nothing to worry about."

"Even so." She didn't know why she felt uneasy.

"Is there any coffee left? I'd like another mug."

When Allison walked into the office at 8:30 a.m., Johnny Schmidt was standing in the lobby. She didn't expect he was waiting for her, as they'd barely spoken since the day she'd told him he was welcome to take his own notes. She still wasn't sure what had rankled him more: that she refused to be put down, or that she'd made the sale.

"Come to my office," he said, by way of greeting, "before we meet those people from Australia."

"Those people from Australia" sold bull semen. They were

looking to expand and modernize, meaning they'd need to carefully track each movement, meal, moment of sexual congress, and every resultant newborn calf of an increasingly large herd. The meeting was an hour away. There went a good portion of her final prep time, she thought, trying not to show her annoyance.

A young man was sitting in Johnny's office pretending to read *The Wall Street Journal* but clearly nervous and preoccupied. Gray suit, white shirt, blue tie, hair styled to look like it wasn't.

"This is Josh," Johnny said, easing his bulk into his chair.

The young man stood.

"Josh Power."

"Josh is going to run the meeting. You. Take. Notes."

"The meeting with the Australians?" She was so surprised by Johnny's first statement that she barely registered the second.

"Take him to your office and bring him up to speed."

Allison had made this meeting happen, done all the work to bring the Australians nine thousand miles to Saratoga. Who the hell was this Josh Power? What rock had he crawled out from under?

She smiled, steaming, as she led him to her office.

"New?"

"I worked for Johnny—Mr. Schmidt—as an intern a couple of summers ago, before I took a job at Dynamotion."

She knew Dynamotion. They developed video games. "And now you're here." The rock, of course, was Johnny Schmidt.

"Mr. Schmidt says there's no better experience than being thrown into the deep end."

With cement overshoes, she thought. There was no way this kid was going to master the material in what would now be under fifty minutes. She quickly summarized the pitch, showed him the handouts, and in the briefing center before the Australians arrived, ran through the slides outlining the hardware, software, and service options she thought would best match their needs.

Josh did his best, which wasn't good. He'd had no time to understand what he was selling, let alone its context and the Australians' needs. He had no real confidence, therefore, in himself or in what Stanton could offer, and this was what he communicated to the visiting ranchers. He stammered, hemmed and hawed, read from the slides and handouts. Allison was embarrassed for him; Johnny stared angrily at her, as if Josh's failure was her fault. She knew very well that Johnny didn't think much of women and liked to promote young men whom he could control. But he couldn't have sabotaged himself more thoroughly if he'd gamed it out for a month, which, possibly, he had.

The jetlagged Australians were, at best, unconvinced and, at worst, questioning why they had come all the way to Saratoga. Grim faced, they sat in the briefing center while Johnny tried earnestly to encourage them to return the next day for a follow-up. Allison sat, hands folded, mouth shut. She would have come to his aid had he asked, but he didn't ask.

"Here are your notes," she said after the Australians had left, and dropped them on the table in front of him.

She sat for a while, talking to Mr. Nakamura on the phone, trying to not shake with rage as he calmly reiterated his invitation to come to Japan. "It will at least be a change of scenery. And there is much scenery like Hakone Gardens there."

By the time she got home that evening, the weather had changed to match her dark mood. By dusk, the sky had turned gray and large raindrops had begun to fall.

All right, she thought, watching the sky, *maybe we should get that all-wheel Carrera.* The thought had less to do with slick roads than what the Carrera promised: speed. She could sure use a way to get out of Stanton fast. But that thought was erased by another: It had taken months to get this job.

If Johnny Schmidt was aiming to make her quit, why should she give him the satisfaction? And if she were fired, how long would it take her to find another? She wasn't going to rely on Eric's income alone to pay for an expensive car they really didn't need.

At six, Eric called. She was in the bedroom.

"I thought you'd be home by now," she said, looking out of the east-facing windows. Watching the rain come down.

"We're still at the airport in Columbia. Eagle Peak, a little airline that flies out of here, is having a barbecue. We stayed later than we expected."

"It's raining here now. Pretty heavily. Please don't ferry the plane tonight."

"We've decided to stay over. There's a motel a few miles away; one of the guys from Eagle Peak will drive us over. We'll ferry it back tomorrow. It's supposed to be clear by morning."

"Good. I won't worry, then."

"Nothing to worry about."

The receiver jostled on his end. "Thanks," he said to someone. "They just handed me another beer. How was your day?"

"Peachy." She told him about the switch that Johnny had pulled that morning that had left her steaming all day.

"I tossed the notes under his fat nose after the Australians left."

"I would have punched him in the nose instead. I admire your restraint."

"I need my job. Especially if we want that Carrera."

"Don't worry about that. I've got it covered. We've got sales lined up like buses. They'll be rolling in. I promise."

She knew how much this new business's success meant to him. It would prove to his family that he could succeed at something he loved without them, and in a language they would understand: profits.

"Okay. I've made a note of that. You stay put tonight."

"We will."

"I love you."

"Back at ya."

She felt relieved when she hung up the phone. She had a glass of wine with dinner and was in bed by ten.

It was sometime past 11:00 p.m. when the phone rang.

"Is this Mrs. Eagan?" the voice asked.

"Yes. Who is this?"

"My name's Maxine Clement. I'm with Eagle Peak Aviation. I'm calling from the Columbia Airport."

Allison fumbled with the light switch on the table lamp next to her.

"Yes? Oh, the airline throwing the barbecue. Is my husband all right?" *What could be wrong? Too many beers? Did he party too much?*

"I got a call from the tower. The air traffic control tower."

Allison wondered what that had to do with Eric.

"Your husband and Paul Wyman took off about an hour ago in a Cessna 172."

"That can't be . . ." Allison sat up in bed. "Eric told me they were staying the night in a motel."

"The tower called me because one of my pilots is flying the plane."

"Wait—wait. What?"

"One of my pilots is flying the Cessna that's en route to San Jose. He's a very good pilot; he has IFR certification."

Allison knew what IFR was. "Instrument flight rules" meant that a pilot was certified to navigate from the instrument panel without having to rely on visibility in bad weather.

"Yes, but they were going to wait until morning. Why did they leave?"

"I don't know. They took off for San Jose in wet weather about an hour ago, and the tower called to tell me that the plane is missing from radar."

Now Allison was standing. All she could think was, *Why did they leave?*

"Ronnie—that's my pilot—said they wanted to go to San Jose and he was going to fly them. He's a good pilot," Maxine said again.

Now Allison was pacing. Her body was ready to do something, but her mind wasn't moving. It was stuck, unable to get past the question: Why did they leave?

"The last thing Ronnie told the tower was that they were caught in a strong downdraft with heavy rain and they were doing a 180 and heading back here. Do you have a phone number for someone in Paul Wyman's family? Is he married?"

The question snapped Allison back.

"Yes," she said. "Yes. Wait a minute." She put the phone down, ran to the kitchen, and pulled her address book from her purse. She picked up the kitchen phone. She couldn't allow herself to think of anything but giving Maxine the number.

"Thank you, dear."

"Yes. I appreciate you calling," she managed to say. "You'll let me know anything else, right?"

"Of course I will. And you call me if you need anything." She paused. "We'll just hope for the best."

Allison hung up. She found herself standing in the bedroom again, looking into the dark sky as rain pelted the windows. Why had they left? She couldn't get the question out of her head.

What should she do? Who could she call?

Lillian had told Allison that, as a recruiter, she was often out at night. Yes, she visited schools, but she would also talk with potential enlistees at their homes, explaining to their parents the benefits of joining the air force. If the parents weren't home until nine, then she wouldn't arrive until then, and she'd stay as long as the conversation took. But this night—it was close to midnight when Allison called—she was home. She came right over.

Lillian made Allison a cup of chamomile tea to help her sleep.

"Is there anyone you want to call?"

Allison had managed to ask herself that. "No. There's no use worrying his parents. Or mine. Until we know something."

"Then we'll wait until morning. Hopefully, we'll learn something by then." They sat huddled together on the living room couch. "They won't send out a search team until it's light. So let's try to get some sleep."

Allison was numb again as Lillian walked her to the bedroom. Lillian stretched herself out on the couch, and Allison, before drifting into a shallow sleep, was comforted by the sound of light snoring coming from the living room.

Allison woke with a start. It was 6:00 a.m. She threw a robe over her nightgown and rushed into the living room. Lillian, who had not undressed, was fully alert and watching the news on television. Allison sat and stared, but all she heard was the question still echoing ceaselessly in her head.

"Nothing yet," Lillian said, putting a hand on Allison's knee.

"I'll call," Allison said, trying to push the fog from her mind.

"Do you want coffee?"

"Yes, please." They both went to the kitchen. Allison picked up the phone and called Maxine Clement, who told her that the fire department had just sent out a search team around the area where the plane was last spotted on radar. That was near Altamont Pass, in the Diablo Range, southeast of Mount Diablo and ten miles northeast of Livermore. The team would call them both, she said, as soon as they knew something.

She walked through the apartment and feeling began to return. But what she felt was an overwhelming, heavy sadness, which she tried to will back into numbness. Part of her brain was telling her to feel nothing until she knew. She swore she could hear the air move around her.

She sat in front of the television, staring, noticing that it was now 7:00 a.m. Men were walking around steep, slick, grass-covered hills. A helicopter shot showed wind farms of large three-armed turbines churning the air. Suddenly, the world became very loud.

"Investigating the crash of a small airplane in the Altamont Pass, a few miles from the Livermore Airport."

She heard herself scream as she ran back to the bedroom. Lillian followed quickly, then hugged her from behind.

Why did they fly back in a storm when they'd decided to stay? Why did Ronnie, who was a good pilot, try to head back to Columbia when they were only a few miles from the Livermore Airport? The questions couldn't crowd out one crushing certainty.

She turned to face Lillian, who held her tightly.

"It's them," Allison said softly. "I know it's them."

PART FIVE

CHAPTER NINETEEN

Allison knew she was driving the new Porsche too fast. Route 17 was dangerous enough at the fifty-miles-per-hour speed limit; she was driving sixty on a mountain highway that was barely wide enough for passing, its blind curves obscuring any slow-moving truck or panicked deer before you were upon it. Was she the one driving, she wondered, or had Eric taken hold of the wheel? She didn't care.

She was still driving too fast when she turned off the highway onto a rural road that took her up more hills toward a small A-frame she'd rented in Soquel, northeast of Santa Cruz. She sped past the eucalyptus stands that screened a deep ravine and creek on her right. The two-lane road was the only route in or out all the way up to the winery, a couple of miles past her place, which made it a risky location in the event of flood or fire. She didn't care.

Her heart was pounding when she pulled into the drive. Speeding had been exhausting, not exhilarating. She didn't enjoy it.

Sitting in the driveway, still behind the wheel, she wondered what the hurry was. There was nothing to look forward to, no one in the house to run outside to greet her. The future stretched out before her, flat and arid.

At first, she thought she'd keep the place in Saratoga. After all, it seemed as if she and Eric had just moved in, the time they lived there barely registering as two years. It was just beginning to feel lived in when Eric died, but the first time she went out onto the terrace after his death, the evening breeze offered no comfort, the view of the mountains no peace. The space, which was just the right size for the two of them, was now cavernous, a place of shadows and echoes.

She stayed long enough to sell Eric and Paul's business; she and Paul's widow, a woman in her fifties, split the proceeds. Then she sold the twin-engine Baron that she and Eric had flown to California. If the young couple from San Jose noticed her nerves on the test flight up to San Francisco and back, they said nothing. Of course, they didn't see what she saw: the dark man standing on the side of the runway observing Allison as they took off. He was waiting for her when they landed, as well.

With money from the sales, she bought the Porsche. It was either to honor Eric's last wish or an excuse to drive something fast. She didn't care which.

She took a leave from work. Johnny, not altruistic by nature, was happy to give it to her. She suspected it was just the first step in easing her out the door. She wished that Mr. Nakamura had been in Palo Alto to provide her comfort and advice, but he'd returned to Japan in January. He'd sent a letter of condolence, and then another, reiterating his invitation to work with him in Japan.

In mid-April, shortly after sunrise on a Friday, she, Eric's family, and Lillian scattered Eric's ashes among the redwoods of Muir Park. Rina and Ben offered to stay awhile to keep her company; she hoped she'd been gracious when she turned them down. Emma begged Allison to let her and Doug come to California or to come herself to Sunflower. She gently refused but promised to visit before too long. Gerry urged her to move to San Francisco, to be closer to him. But she wasn't ready to expose her grief that way.

She went in the other direction. She crossed the Santa Cruz Mountains, as if putting them between herself and Saratoga would hide her from the despair, keep it from finding her in that little rented A-frame house on a backwoods road in the foothills.

Bundled in a peacoat, she spent the first few days sitting in a metal garden chair in the back yard, watching the woods that sheltered the house on two sides. Deer, wild turkeys, blue jays, cardinals, and birds that she couldn't identify came to observe the new tenant. Other than driving the few miles to Capitola for groceries, she kept to herself.

The stillness was soothing, but not for long. She'd hoped she could be content watching the life around her, but she soon found herself shifting in her chair, drumming her fingers on the arms, crossing and uncrossing her legs. Then she'd be up on her feet pacing the yard. She returned to Capitola and walked the beach and stalked the aisles of the large bookstore in downtown Santa Cruz and, from the cliffs overlooking the bay, watched the surfers ride the waves. She started going farther afield to the aquarium at Monterey, where she was jostled by families and school groups as she watched the sea otters play or the opalescent jellies float. She visited the nature preserve at Elkhorn Slough, where she joined a guided boat ride to see the waterfowl, harbor seals, and sea lions. The wildlife was different, and the spring air chillier, but the place reminded her of Blue Heron, and it provided a small, temporary cushion against the pain.

After twenty-one days of solitude in Soquel, she returned to Stanton.

She sat in her office, wondering what to do first. The place felt alien, the light unfamiliar, as if she'd never been there before. She'd been away for six weeks. Johnny had kept assuring her all was well, that her accounts were being looked after, and not to worry. Her desktop was clean: no memos, no mail (it had been sent on to her), nothing meant to keep her up to date on her customers' needs. She wasn't sure whether to feel relieved or suspicious. Feeling at all was something she was trying to avoid.

From her bag she took two letters: Mr. Nakamura's and the one from the Eagans' lawyers. She laid them on the desk.

There was a soft knock on the open door.

"Welcome back."

It was Johnny Schmidt.

"Word travels fast," Allison said.

"How are you doing?" He sat without being asked.

"It's good to be back. How are things here?" She wanted to get his attention off her, in case that's where it was.

"Well." Johnny folded his hands in his lap. "A little slow, to be honest. Japan slipped into a recession while you were gone, which isn't good for our growth. And it may compromise our work with Sakasama on parallel processing. They may pull back on their investment with us. And we've been feeling the pinch of slow growth here."

"The Bush recession." She may have been out of the office, but she'd been reading the newspapers.

"Exactly. By the way, Josh has been looking after your accounts."

"How's he doing?"

"He's a fast learner."

"Uh-huh. How are the Australians? Back in the fold?"

Johnny looked out the window.

"That brings up an interesting point." He shifted his gaze toward a spot above her head. "They've decided that it makes more sense to find a partner closer to home."

Where would that be, Allison wondered. *Madagascar?*

"That would have been a big account," he continued. "As you know."

It would have been ours if you hadn't blown it, she thought.

"Then there's the fact that desktop networks are eating into our business." He looked at her as briefly as possible. "Here's the short version: We're being hit by the downturn and we have to tighten our belts."

He found another spot to look at.

"So, between the economic outlook here, and the downturn in Japan . . ." His voice trailed off. She waited for him to continue, but he didn't.

"I have a letter here," she said, pointing to the envelopes on her desk. "From Mr. Nakamura." She always referred to him by his last name. "He's inviting me to come work with him in Japan. I'll work for Mr. Nakamura. That should make your laying me off easier."

"Oh, well." He pulled himself up in his chair and shifted his gaze to his shoes. "It's not just about that, it's as much about giving Josh a chance . . ."

"That's okay, Johnny. Although, if I remember my geography, Australia is much closer to Japan than it is to California."

A short time later, she carried the box of her belongings out of the office. She saw the Porsche sitting outside. Since she'd parked it there herself, she wasn't surprised, but she was caught up short as time collapsed and she thought she was looking at Eric's Porsche parked outside the Ellis Davis office in Olympia. She wiped the picture from her mind, threw the box in the trunk, and sped off, too fast, to the house in the woods on the other side of the mountain.

Two weeks later, she sat with Mr. Nakamura in his Tokyo office. She told him she was only able to make the flight with the aid of Xanax and a couple of Bloody Marys.

"That may change with time," he said. "In any case, I'm glad you have come. Perhaps here you can begin to heal."

"I hope so."

He watched her as she sat nervously in the chair across from his desk.

"Let's take a walk," he said.

They walked through central Tokyo to the Chiyoda district.

"Many Fortune 500 companies are nearby. Also, the Imperial Palace. But that's not why we've come."

They turned into a narrow street of modern shops on the ground floors of nondescript apartment buildings. She saw, at the far end, a tall vermilion-and-gold ornately carved green-roofed gate.

"This is the Kanda Shrine," Mr. Nakamura said. "It honors three Shinto gods, two of whom are among the Seven Gods of Fortune. Many businessmen come here to pray for good luck—especially men in the computer business. So, it is appropriate for us."

"All right," Allison said, unsure whether it was appropriate for her anymore. She hadn't come to Tokyo to work; she was uncertain, really, why she'd come.

"It was once an important site to the warrior class," he continued. "With your martial arts background, I thought you might appreciate that."

As they passed through the gate, he bowed slightly. Then, he moved away from the center of the open plaza and walked along the side toward the main shrine. Allison followed.

"We walk on the side of the *sandō*," he said, "so that the gods may pass down the center." As they approached the shrine he said, "Watch what I do."

From a basin standing before the shrine, he took a long-handled dipper and poured water onto his left hand and then onto his right. Next, he poured water into his left palm and rinsed his mouth. Tipping the dipper upward, he let the remaining water run down the handle. Allison saw that each motion was sharply defined; he didn't start one until he had completed the previous. When he had finished purifying himself, he put a small coin into an offertory box.

Stepping back from the box, he bowed twice from the waist, put his hands together, and said a brief prayer. Finished, he clapped his hands twice, bowed again, and was done.

Allison admired the way that Mr. Nakamura, whom she never saw ruffled, seemed especially calm and centered at the shrine. As they approached the gate after walking once more along the side of the *sandō*, he turned and bowed again.

"You may find it comforting to visit here," he said as they walked back to his office. "I find peace in the discipline. Of course, you needn't pray when you come. You can simply observe, or contemplate. But if you choose to pray, that is the way you do it."

In the days that followed, she visited other Shinto shrines. Large or small, each felt to Allison as if everyone who had ever prayed there had left a bit of serenity behind, like a patina. The same was true of the Buddhist temples, where she followed the purification rituals and lit incense. The discipline of the prescribed behavior appealed to her just as it did to Mr. Nakamura and reminded her of what she'd gained from her martial arts training: confidence, centeredness, and a lightness that came with knowing her own strength. But to think of all that was not to bring it back.

She explained to Mr. Nakamura that she looked forward to working again but was conflicted. She still had significant leave time available from her previous work and money remaining from both Eric and the life insurance policy. She explained that she didn't know what she wanted to do, but she knew that, for now, it wasn't selling mainframe computers.

"I can't put the puzzle together," she said.

"It is all right not to know which path to take," he said to her at dinner one night. "Knowing which is the wrong path is the first step. The rest will come in time."

She took the fast train to Kyoto, where she visited the moss and Zen gardens. The variegated mosses spread like frozen lakes, their waves caught mid-crest at the trunks of the maple and pine trees, covering the stones and footbridges. She walked the narrow stone pathways, watched rivulets of water move gently down channels coursing like arteries through the gardens. To wander the gardens was to be veiled in peace, the mosses laying a blanket of silence over the world's clamor and discord.

The quiet did her little good. Disturbing images rushed to fill its negative space: Allison as a teenager, sitting on Buddy's lawn on that warm summer day, realizing he'd left her; the Saturday at Sebring when she'd thought she'd lost Eric; his death in the rain and darkness of the Diablo Range; the dark man brandishing a crowbar in her living room. There were so many other images that might have flooded her mind in the contemplative space opened by the gardens, but it was these that threatened to drown her.

And then loss, in all its smothering silence, took over. She saw nothing ahead but endless desolation. No matter how lush her surroundings, she was traveling in an empty brown-and-gray plain that stretched to a far horizon.

Staring vacantly at the blue-gray blur through the window of the Shinkansen, the bullet train headed back to Tokyo, she realized that she was seeing a culture that she'd admired since she was a teenager but was now beyond her reach. As it flashed by, she felt rooted where she was. A part of her said that she *wanted* that rootedness, that stillness, that ability to just *be* that so much of this culture embraced. But this was the wrong stillness. It felt like death.

The day before she left Tokyo, she took a walk in Kitanomaru Park in Chiyoda. She tried to call up the discipline of mind that she exercised in the shrines and temples, hoping it would bring the kind of stillness she sought. She closed her eyes, concentrated on her breath, and then let it come and go on its own.

When she opened her eyes, she saw a line of about thirty grade school children, seven or eight years old, passing by on a path near the bench where she sat. They walked in pairs, holding hands, chattering softly. Their blue, pink, and green caps shone in the sun.

Allison's spirits lifted. She remembered that she was alone, and that the possibility of having children of her own seemed impossibly remote: unfinished business that would remain unfinished.

Then she felt something else rise in her, some of the old Allison. Who said that children couldn't somehow be part of her future? She could choose to have hope.

CHAPTER TWENTY

As carefully as the moss and Zen gardens of Japan were designed, the forest of Nisene Marks State Park, northeast of Santa Cruz, was rugged and seemingly untamed. Redwoods, eucalyptus, and pines quietly battled for space as they towered above Allison and Lillian, who hiked its uneven paths and steep hills along stony, twisting creeks that no Zen monk would have laid out.

As they hiked, Allison described her trip, including the sight of the school children in Kitanomaru Park.

"Do you have children?" she asked. It was a topic that had never come up between them.

"Nope."

That was all Lillian had to say on the subject. Allison sensed she'd made a misstep.

"I'm sorry. That's such a personal question."

"No harm done."

They walked for a while in silence. When they came to a lone picnic table sitting inside a wire fence, Allison called a halt.

"I'm a little out of shape." Her left hip and lower back

complained as she carefully lowered herself onto the bench. "I've been sitting a lot lately."

"You're surrounded by all this beauty," Lillian said, sitting across from her. "You should get out more."

"I know. But I need to visit my parents first. I promised them a visit."

"I'd tell you to say hello to Sunflower for me, but I wouldn't mean it. That place," she said matter-of-factly, "can go to hell."

"It's sad that we could live in the same place and have such completely different experiences."

"Sadder than you'll ever know."

Allison briefly wondered whether Lillian was being cryptic about some singular trauma—whether she'd experienced something not unlike Allison herself had with the Strangler—and if that were the case, she wouldn't pry. Lillian would tell her on her own time, if ever. But she suspected her old classmate was in fact alluding to a broader point, to an atmosphere. To a small town where children and families that looked like Lillian suddenly found themselves sharing the same space, the schools, with faces that looked like Allison's—faces that appeared much like those that had made Black people's lives hell for hundreds of years, and often still did. Lillian was right: Allison would never know that particular sadness or fear, even if at one time—younger, sheltered, naive, too often self-assured about the wrong things—she'd thought she understood it. The passage of time had changed that, and the dojo had too, in ways she hadn't expected. She'd first gone there, after all, to protect herself from Lillian. But the martial arts she learned were expressly about self-defense, not about seeking out conflict, and one day years ago it struck her: What if back at Braxton Bragg—itself named after a Confederate slaver, for God's sake—Lillian wasn't so much seeking conflict either, but rather preemptively guarding herself against the prospect of it, and especially against this girl who'd come in on the bus, into

Lillian's space, thinking she was immediately entitled to a star quarterback's jersey?

"Earth to Allison," Lillian said now, with a little laugh. "Where'd you go?"

Allison startled, then brushed it off. "I was just thinking you were right about the beauty of this place." She looked around, took it in as if for the first time. She considered sharing with Lillian her recent reverie but thought better of it. Instead she asked, "How much more time do you have in San Jose?"

"Another year," Lillian said.

"And after that?"

"It's not up to me. But I hope I can stay around here. I like it."

"I hope so too. I owe you, Lillian."

"We go back too far for that."

"It was ugly sometimes."

"Sunflower. That was one hard place to live in."

According to the guidebooks, the trail that Allison and Lillian hiked in Nisene Marks was "moderately challenging." The next day, Allison's body registered a different opinion. Her left hip and lower back still ached, and now her right knee chimed in.

Time to buy stock in drug companies, she thought as she hobbled around the bedroom, packing for her trip to Sunflower.

It had been six years since she'd last seen Sunflower, when she'd come home for her wedding. A few houses had new siding; some old trees were gone, replaced by new ones that offered little shade or welcome. She tried to remember which of the old ones she'd climbed with Bobby Sewell. What had become of him? After he told her he was moving to New York, she never heard from him again. She'd also lost touch with the Whitmore sisters from down the street. Their parents, Emma told her, had moved to Houston a decade ago. It wasn't lost on her that the only remaining friend she had from her childhood and youth was Lillian—who had hardly been her friend back then.

Emma and Doug were aging and had given up bowling and golf. They tried new ways to keep busy, since they knew that if they simply sat around the house, they'd only get older faster. For a time, Emma had taken up gardening.

"It seemed like a good idea," Emma told her, "and going to the garden center was fun. I'd never been there before in all these years."

"Warriner's? That's still there?"

"It is."

"And that creepy Russian guy?"

"I don't know that he's creepy, but there's a fellow with a Russian accent. He says he used to care for rich people's gardens in the old country."

"That's him. I remember going there with Buddy. Something about the way he looked at me creeped me out."

"I liked everything about gardening except the getting down on the ground and the getting back up again. It was something to do for a spring and summer."

After the gardening experiment petered out, Emma saw an ad in the *Enquirer* seeking volunteers for the local foodbank.

"That did it. It got us both out of the house again. Once or twice a week we'd fill up grocery bags and get to talking with new people. It was so much fun, we started volunteering other places too." Now she was shelving books at the library, and Doug spent time at an organization called Encore, where retired businesspeople shared their expertise with young entrepreneurs.

"I can't tell you, Radish, how much I've learned being a mentor," he told Allison.

"I'm sure folks have learned a lot from you."

"Yes—such as not to try selling hydroponic equipment to farmers stuck in their ways."

"What about to people who grow pot?"

"I don't think I can tell them to seek out people who grow pot."

A week into her visit, Allison woke in her old room with a sore throat. Getting dressed, she felt slightly outside of her body. By the time she'd managed to get a bowl of cereal down, she knew she had the flu.

Emma lay her hand on Allison's forehead. "May is a strange time for the flu, but then again, you have been traveling. Anyway, you're in the right place if you're going to be sick. You go back to bed and don't worry about a thing."

For the next two days, Allison lay in bed, sleeping on and off, drifting in and out of fever dreams. She was occasionally aware of Emma wiping her brow with a damp washcloth or sitting quietly in the wing chair by the window. When her fever broke, the first thing she saw was Emma in the chair, leafing through the book about the little girl who flies a red airplane.

Emma noticed her watching.

"Are you back with us?"

"I think so." Allison felt her forehead. "No temperature."

"You must be hungry."

"Just thirsty. And tired."

Emma laid the book on the bed, handed her a glass of water that was sitting on the night table, then walked to the top of the stairs and called down. "Doug, please warm up the chicken soup that's on the stove and then bring a bowl up for Allison. She's hungry."

Allison smiled.

Emma came back into the room and reclaimed her seat.

"Daddy will bring it right up. Did I ever tell you about the man I dated, oh, a long time ago, before I met your father? He was a pilot. He took me up in an open-cockpit biplane. I loved flying—but not him!"

"You never did tell me that. What else are you holding back?"

"That's the end of that story, really. He called me several times, but I just didn't want to see him again. You know how it is when you just don't click with someone? So, I didn't." She picked up the book. "I always liked this one," Emma said.

"Me too." Allison took it from her and opened it, flipping the pages until she came to the one where the girl in the red plane (also an open cockpit) is doing graceful loop-de-loops. On the facing page, only the plane's tail is in sight, the rest of the plane having disappeared off the top edge.

She stared, and felt as if she were leaving her body again. She closed the book and handed it back to Emma.

Emma saw the pained expression on her face and the tears starting to well up in her eyes. She took the book.

"Oh, I'm so stupid." She laid the book on the bottom shelf of the bookcase.

"That's okay. It's kind of hard for me to avoid airplanes these days. I couldn't exactly hitchhike to Japan. Or here." She said nothing about her need to medicate even to step foot on a plane.

"But you don't have to see them in a stupid book." Sitting on the bed, she took Allison's hand in both of hers. Allison pulled her close and hugged her. Emma stroked her damp hair and held her.

"I like being mothered by you."

"Thank you, dear. I rarely see the grandchildren, so you're the one outlet for my maternal instincts."

"I'm glad to be your outlet." She smiled at her mother. "It'll be good practice for me."

Just then, they heard Doug's footsteps on the stairs, and he appeared with a tray holding a bowl of soup, a napkin, and a spoon.

Two days later, Allison left the house, intending to walk around the neighborhood and rediscover the feelings that had made her experience growing up in Sunflower so different

from Lillian's. But walking from the house through the garage, she spotted the old green Schwinn Collegiate standing
in a corner. The one that Emma and Doug had given her on
her twelfth birthday. She wheeled it out to the driveway to see
what shape it was in and was surprised to find it still gleam-
ing after twenty-one years. There was even air in the tires. She
made a slight adjustment to the seat and then mounted it the
way she always did, placing one foot on the near pedal, pushing
off to get the bike moving, and swinging her other leg over the
seat. (This was the way the boys she once rode with mounted
their bikes, and even though hers had no bar between the seat
and steering column necessitating such a start, she liked to
do it anyway.) Miraculously, her body didn't object—not her
back, her hip, nor her knee—so she knew she was doing the
right thing. She rode the half block to Eleventh Street, where
the school bus turned and where, once she was out of Emma's
sight, she'd take off like a demon. Another surprise: The bicycle still ran as smoothly as ever.

She sped toward Montgomery Park, flying under the laurel
oaks, red maples, and loblolly pines, feeling the old freedom
surging through her gut, her legs, and her arms. The wind in
her face never felt so good. Was this it, after all? Was freedom ultimately found in speed, in movement, as she'd always
thought, and not in the stillness she'd sought in the gardens of
Japan?

As she sped up, every turn in the path, every climb that
required extra effort, every downhill through which she could
coast felt familiar and right. She returned home with a healthy
flush in her face to learn that Doug had kept the bike in good
shape, hoping all these years that one of the grandchildren, or
her sisters' children, would want it. But there had not yet been
any takers.

"We so wish we'd been there for you," Emma said to
Allison.

It was the day before Allison was to fly home, a week after her ride in the park. The two of them were sitting together on the living room sofa. Doug was out, dispensing wisdom at Encore's office.

As the warm sunlight filtered into the room, Allison felt safe and secure for the first time since Eric's death. It seemed that she always felt this way in this house.

"I'm okay," she said to Emma. Even to her mother, even safe in this house, she couldn't fully describe what the past few months had been like.

"I wanted more time with him," she said.

"I know, dear, of course." Emma looked displeased. "I hate saying things like that, dumb things, but I don't know what else to say. Or do."

"You don't have to do anything. Just sitting here feels good."

They sat quietly for a moment.

"I really wanted to have children with Eric," she said, feeling the tears coming again. "When I was in Japan, I saw a group of school children, little kids, walking in a line. Like something out of *Madeline*."

Both smiled at the memory of another book they had once read together.

"The sight made me so glad for a moment, before I realized that having children seems so . . . unlikely now."

She expected Emma to object, to say something on the order of "You never know what will happen, or who you'll meet." But Emma just patted her hand.

"Then I realized there's no reason why I can't have children. I'm thirty-two. I have time. Who knows?" Emma was still silent. "Right?"

Finally, Emma spoke. "There are so many paths to fulfillment, dear—paths that were never open to women of my generation."

"Yes, but . . ."

Emma stood up. "Why don't I get us some peppermint tea? Nice and soothing. You just sit and relax while I make it. Won't take a minute."

It took ten. Allison waited as the sun continued to spread its light into the living room and the leaves of the magnolia tree in the yard rustled lightly in the breeze. Her sense of security might have deepened if she wasn't suddenly wondering what Emma was avoiding.

Emma came back with the tea and two cups on a tray. Allison saw that she'd been crying. Emma sat and handed Allison a cup. She folded her hands in her lap.

"When I was pregnant with you, my doctor prescribed a drug that he said helped older women deliver a healthy baby. I didn't want to miscarry. I wanted you." She looked out the picture window at the magnolia, all in bloom. "Susan and Sarah, Jerry and Will didn't need me anymore, and that's all I wanted: one more healthy baby. Back then we believed our doctors; we didn't ask questions. So, I took the drug. And you were born, and you were healthy. And beautiful." Her eyes searched the yard, then the street. "We weren't told that there could be side effects." She dabbed at her eyes with a handkerchief she had clutched in her hands. "Not in the mothers so much, but in our children. They . . . might not be able to have children of their own."

She turned her face toward Allison, who had never seen her mother so stricken.

"What's the name of this drug?" she heard herself asking, as if from a distance.

"It was called DES. I don't remember the whole name. If I ever knew. You were about ten when I just happened to see an article about it. It was too late to do anything about it then." She wiped her eyes. "I always meant to tell you, but I couldn't . . . find the right time. And then . . ." Her voice trailed off.

"So . . . maybe I can't have children? Is that what you're saying?" A voice told her to take her mother's hand and offer her some comfort. But she couldn't.

Emma nodded. "I'm sorry. I'm sorry. I just wanted a healthy baby."

It was Allison's turn to look at the magnolia tree.

"We don't know for sure, do we? I was pregnant before. When I get home, I'll go to the doctor." The magnolia turned to a blur of pink, white, and brown as the tears came again.

CHAPTER TWENTY-ONE

Dr. Stein, who looked to be about Emma's age, finished reading Allison's chart. She glanced over the top of her half-moon tortoiseshell reading glasses and unconsciously smoothed her long gray ponytail. Allison, who'd been staring down at her hands, felt the doctor's gaze and sat up in her chair.

"I've looked at your ultrasound and laparoscopy exams," Dr. Stein said. "You belong to a rare breed. You have endometriosis, but no symptoms. Only about 20, 25 percent of women can say that."

Allison thought about making a joke, congratulating herself on her accomplishment, the words already forming in her head. But she didn't feel like laughing, even at her own expense. Instead, she asked, "For a long time?"

"It's hard to know, but probably. You have stage three, which is moderate disease."

"What does that mean?"

"It means that the endometrial tissue, which lines the inside wall of your uterus, has also grown outside of it, along your fallopian tubes and ovaries. It behaves the same way the endometrial tissue in your uterus does: It thickens and becomes enriched with blood, and every month, if there's no fertilized egg to nourish, it sheds itself. That's your period. But, unlike the tissue in the uterus, it has no way to exit the body. That's when most women with endometriosis will experience several symptoms—mostly pain, nausea, and bloat. Because you have stage three endometriosis, you also have what are called 'deep infiltrating endometriosis lesions' in your peritoneum, which is the lining inside your abdomen and around your organs. You also have some adhesions, as well as endometriomas in your ovaries." She paused. "I know that's a lot to take in."

Allison took a breath. "Tell me what those are. The adhesions."

"When the thickened endometrial tissue outside of your uterus tries to shed itself, it can rub against another area with it. Both areas become inflamed, and there's a chance they'll stick together, which causes scar tissue. That's an adhesion. It produces similar symptoms to endometriosis—the pain, nausea, and bloat. You don't experience unusual levels of those when you menstruate?"

"What's 'unusual'? I don't think so."

"As I said, you belong to a rarefied group."

"And the other?"

"An endometrioma is a cyst in your ovary that's filled with endometrial fluid. It can interfere with the production of healthy eggs."

Despite the weight of that statement, Allison needed to stick with the facts. "Is this because my mother took DES?"

"Probably. But I want to emphasize that it's not her fault."

"No. It's what her doctor gave her."

Dr. Stein frowned. "Unfortunately."

"Does it mean I'm infertile?"

The doctor sighed. "Possibly. We can try to remove the

adhesions, but we risk creating more in the process. The endometriosis can be removed surgically, but it might grow back. Endometriomas can also be treated surgically, but there is a risk of damage to your ovaries. They also might have reduced the quality of your eggs. In any case, we need to keep an eye on them, as it's possible they'll become cancerous."

"I see. Wow. And that's just moderate disease? What's worse?"

"Daughters of DES mothers have an elevated risk of ovarian cancer and cancer of the cervix."

"So, even if I manage to get pregnant and have a healthy child, I might not live to watch her grow?"

"Were you planning on having children soon?"

"Not right away, no."

"Then I suggest we don't go there now."

"I suppose I should have made a point of seeing a doctor more often."

Dr. Stein looked at her with sympathy. "What's past is past. Now, it's important that we think about the future."

While she didn't want to face this barrage of bad news by herself, she couldn't discuss it yet with Emma. Precisely because Dr. Stein was right—it wasn't Emma's fault—she couldn't risk burdening her mother with more unnecessary guilt. So, unlike the way she tried to hide the depths of her grief from Gerry when Eric died, Allison called him with the developments.

"Why don't you come up here for a while?" he suggested.

For the next two weeks, they walked along the Sausalito waterfront, taking in the village of houseboats that lined the docks; they browsed the art galleries, where everyone knew Gerry and greeted him as a friend, not a client or customer. When he was working in the studio, she walked by herself or sat on the balcony, and if she felt her thoughts drifting to the past, to life on Blue Heron Island, she pulled herself back to the present. She knew that the past could not provide a salve to what she was feeling now.

They paused in their walk one morning to sit on a bench and watch a group of schoolgirls play soccer in the park near the marina.

"I'd just love to kick the hell out of a ball about now," Allison said.

"Ask them. Maybe they'll let you play."

"I don't want to kick it through a goal. I just want to destroy it. Don't you have days when you just want to destroy whatever you can put your hands on? Tear it to shreds? Take every glass or breakable whatever and just smash them to atoms? Put your fist through a canvas? Just because? Because, what's the point?"

Gerry saw her lip trembling and tears forming in the corners of her eyes.

"What's the goddamn point?" she said again. "And that's not a rhetorical question."

He put his arm around her shoulders.

"I know that feeling."

"You do? What do you do about it?"

"I go into my studio and paint it out. I can be quite violent with a palette knife."

"But what about us nonartistic slobs? What do we do?"

"This is America. Everyone's an artist who says they're an artist. You have a gift. You know how to listen to people, how to talk to them on their wavelength."

"Maybe. But for what? To sell $100,000 worth of hardware and software? Unload a few hundred acres of real estate? That's how I use this great gift?"

"Come on." He stood up. "Let's find you something to kick around—rhetorically."

Late in the afternoon, as they sat together on the balcony and watched the fog envelop San Francisco in an impenetrable white cloud, she said, "I have no idea what's ahead of me. I've always been so focused. I'd know what I want to do, and then I'd do it. Or try. Now, I have no idea what's out there, what's ahead of me." She pointed to where the city lay, hidden by the white curtain. "My life feels like that."

"That's every day of my life."

"What do you mean? You have your commissions, all your work, your rock concerts; you know what you have to do, and when."

"In theory. A rock concert takes place when they tell you it'll take place, and, yes, I know I have to get it done. But having a date to deliver a commission is no guarantee it will be done on that date. Or even that year. It's more a hope than a promise. I've been known to dawdle."

"And that doesn't hurt you with clients and galleries?"

"My work's a known quantity. People are willing to wait. From one day to the next, I have no idea what's going to happen when I stand in front of a canvas. If I don't get the feeling, if nothing happens, I can't force it. I'll go on to something else. Or I'll grab a brush and a fresh canvas and improvise; maybe something will come. Or I'll take a walk or put on some music. I really have no idea what's going to happen. And that suits me."

The fog was extending its gloved hand across the water toward Sausalito, even as the sky, exchanging its daytime deep-blue outfit for a dusky-purple one, stayed clear. Allison shifted her gaze to Gerry.

"Haven't you ever thought about getting married? Having children?"

"I know that's not a proposal."

"It's not."

He gestured to the studio below them. "All that, down there? That's my commitment. I've tried, but I just don't have room in me for much else."

"Even knowing they'll all leave you in the end?"

"Knowing that from the start helps. Besides, with these relationships, leaving is the whole point. Then moving on to the next one."

The following day, Allison wandered into the studio just as Gerry, done with work, was washing his hands at the sink.

"I've come to pass judgment on your commitments," she said.

"Have at it. All positive opinions appreciated."

She made a circuit around the room. "Wait. I notice that someone's walked out on you. What happened to Lama what's-his-name?"

"Lama Thokmay? He's hanging in my gallery in San Francisco. If he sells at the price I want, I'll be able to give his school a Golden Gate–sized gift."

"Lucky him."

"If we sell it in the next few weeks, I'll give him the check in person."

"Are you headed back to India?"

"No, he'll be here in San Francisco. You can meet him if you'd like."

In his maroon robe, saffron sash, and leather sandals, Lama Thokmay cut an exotic figure among the wealthy, well-dressed ladies and gentlemen who had gathered to hear him talk about his school in Northern India.

Smiling, often laughing softly, and putting a finger to his lips as he did, moving deftly among the clutch of society folks with a wineglass of seltzer in one hand while making expert small talk like the practiced fundraiser he had, by necessity, become, he did indeed know how to work a room. He moved— almost glided, Allison thought—to a spot before the fireplace, the large mirror above it reflecting the balding spot at the back of his head, which added the right touch of humility to his polished persona. At the same time, the sun shone through the large picture windows of the opulent apartment on Union Street, lending a glow to his brown skin and wrapping him in a soft, irresistible nimbus of radiance.

The host, standing next to him, tapped her glass with a spoon, and the room hushed.

"Thank you all for coming this afternoon. Most of you know me, but for those who don't, I'm Ellen Craig, and along with my husband, Jack, I'm thrilled—honored and thrilled—to welcome Lama Thokmay back to San Francisco. Since we last saw him just over a year ago, he's enrolled six more girls from impoverished villages in Nepal in his school, the Institute for Growth and Education, in Rishikesh. We're so thrilled to support his work that I can hardly resist telling you all about it—but Lama Thokmay can do it much better than I can. And besides, he's come all this way." The gathering applauded. "So here he is to tell us why we're here today. Lama Thokmay"— she gestured toward him—"the floor is yours." More applause. Ellen moved away, leaving the spotlight to the Tibetan monk, who knew how to use it.

"Thank you, Ellen, my friend. I'm so very glad to be with you all again in your beautiful city, to bring you up to date on our programs, and to have this opportunity to share with new friends what we're endeavoring to do in our school in Northern India."

Did his eyes meet Allison's when he mentioned newcomers like herself? It seemed so to her. She also thought that Gerry's painting did not do justice to his natural charisma as he told the crowd in a fluent, lightly accented baritone about his work. He described how each summer, he and several colleagues walked from the school in Rishikesh across the mountains into the Dolpo region of Nepal, seeking children who had been made outcasts in their small, often destitute, villages. They might have a physical disability—a clubfoot, a cleft lip or palate—which was considered bad luck among superstitious villagers, the sort of luck that could be avoided only by hiding the unfortunate child away, depriving her of friends, of school, even of sunlight, for most of her life, making her a burden on the community. Some were orphans; others had fathers who had disappeared, leaving the mothers in poverty and raising only sons, who might one day earn a living, leaving the daughters to fend for themselves. Why would their fathers disappear? In the spring, they would take their wood carvings, pottery, clothing—any goods the family had made during the winter—across the mountains to sell, and some would never return. No one knew what became of them, although it was suspected that some deserted their families out of desperation. Lama Thokmay described these circumstances with only caring in his voice; he never passed judgment.

He offered the parents, often poor but loving, an opportunity to give their children a better life through an education they would otherwise not have. The school could take six children each year, train them for jobs, and seek medical treatment for their ailments. It had been difficult in the beginning, but now that the village parents knew of him and the school, and had seen the changes in the children who had come back to the villages to visit, many were willing to send their daughters (and sometimes sons) with him, in hopes of finding better lives than they could provide at home.

Leading the children to the school meant a dangerous monthlong journey over the Himalayas at altitudes of more than eighteen thousand feet. They dared decrepit footbridges over roaring, swollen rivers; crossed broken, boulder-strewn terrain; and threaded their way up and down the narrow footpaths hewed into the steep mountainsides. Some of the children, as young as three, had to be carried by members of his crew in slings, or in packs on their backs, for the entire five-hundred-mile trek.

Lama Thokmay talked simply and directly; he did not describe the villagers as victims or victimizers or dress the children up in pathetic modifiers; he didn't describe the journey across the mountains as a great adventure or himself as a hero. Everything he said struck Allison simply as work that he knew had to be done.

There followed a slideshow of the trek across the brutal, if sometimes beautiful, terrain, and then the school: the children playing games or in classrooms, smiling, happy, well nourished. The school's purpose, he explained, was to provide more than an education. It was to give the children a home, security, and most importantly, self-worth.

He talked about the costs involved to run the school and provide materials, clothing, food, and medical care for those who needed it, and how his good friends in San Francisco could aid the effort to give these young people a future. He finished by inviting anyone who was interested to come to Rishikesh, see the work being done, and meet and talk to the children.

After the presentation, when Lama Thokmay was mingling again with the group, now rather hushed by what they had seen and heard, he saw Gerry. Wrapping his arms around him in a tight embrace, he said, "Gerry! How good to see you again! Has our picture sold yet?"

"It has, indeed." Gerry handed him an envelope. "For whatever you need. Maybe some art supplies."

Lama Thokmay laughed. "When you come, they can paint *your* portrait."

Gerry introduced Allison, who had listened with intense interest to Lama Thokmay's story.

"I'm very happy to meet you," he said, shaking her hand. "Gerry is one of our very best friends."

"When," she asked, "can I come visit?"

CHAPTER TWENTY-TWO

Two weeks after she met Lama Thokmay, Allison had surgery.

"Everything went well," Dr. Stein told her in the recovery room.

"They can come back, right? The endometriosis and the adhesions?"

"If they do, we'll remove them. Meanwhile, take it easy for the next three weeks. But start walking—tomorrow, if you feel up to it. It's the best thing for healing."

Allison walked the beach in Capitola and the cliffs in Santa Cruz and spent time in the Santa Cruz library reading about India. The temperature in Rishikesh would be in the eighties if she went in autumn. A Georgia girl could handle that.

When she felt ready to tackle Route 17, she drove up to San Francisco to have coffee with Ellen and talk about visiting the Institute for Growth and Education in October. The day was typical for San Francisco in July: foggy with a chilling breeze that made the tourists, dressed in their shorts and T-shirts, scurry for warmth in shops and hotel lobbies.

"I'm thrilled you're interested in the school," Ellen said, nibbling on a chocolate chip cookie. "Lama Thokmay is a treasure."

"I don't mean to be presumptuous," Allison said, "but is he really as good as he seems?"

"He is, believe it or not. He runs the school on a very lean and mean basis; so far as I can see, nothing is wasted. And I've looked. There are three buildings—for classes, for meals and recreation, and a dormitory, all spartan—but the children are very well looked after. The staff is small; his mother and sister are the primary teachers for the youngsters. He has an arrangement with a private school for when the kids reach high school age, and we help pay for that. It's the real deal. And believe me, I can see through anybody's PR."

Ellen had worked in advertising since coming to San Francisco from the Midwest in the mid-seventies. She'd met Jack at the office; he was a client who owned a chain of men's clothing stores. "They tell you never marry the client. They're wrong."

She and Jack were major contributors to local arts and medical organizations and were well loved among the philanthropic community. "It's Jack's family's money," she told Allison. "He and I are still working stiffs. So, tell me about yourself before I have to run back to work."

When Allison described her martial arts history, Ellen seemed particularly interested. "I'm kind of a fitness buff myself," she said, "despite my sitting here eating this cookie. Please have some, by the way. Nothing fancy. A few mornings a week at the gym on weights and a treadmill, some power walking. But listen. I've got some vacation time coming, and I'm thinking about doing the climb to the Mount Everest base camp again."

"Again?"

"I've done it once, with an excellent guide. Why don't I come with you to the institute, and then you can join me on that trek to the base camp?"

"Mount Everest?"

"Not to the top, just to the camp. Don't let the E-word

intimidate you. It's a ten-day walk. Well, not a walk. A trek. It's a challenge, but you'll never forget it. You look like you're in good shape; you could do it."

Allison told her about the recent surgery, and the way her old martial arts injuries had a habit of paying her unwanted visits.

"Look," Ellen said, "it's July. If we went to the institute in late October, we could do the trek in November. That's a good time to do it. It can be cold—but it's always cold at base camp, which is about 17,500 feet up. The weather's usually good that time of year and the sky is miraculously clear. You won't believe the views." She regarded Allison for a moment. "Think about it. Something tells me this is for you."

Allison joined a gym and started running on a treadmill, which was kinder to her body than the concrete streets. When she read that squats, lunges, and jogs up and down stairs were good training for mountain treks, she slowly added those to her routine. For once, she was patient with herself, and it felt good to be working out with only minimal soreness. It felt so good that when she saw a pamphlet at the gym about the Big Sur Marathon the following spring, she thought, *Why not?* and applied.

In August, she called Ellen.

"What would you think if I asked a couple of people to join us for the E-word base camp trek? Two fit friends?"

"If they can do it, the more the merrier. Oh, I forgot to mention: Every visitor to the institute must bring something to teach the children, some bit of wisdom, some experience to pass along. It doesn't have to be deep or serious. I taught them baseball."

Allison phoned Will in Saint John.

"You always said you sail because you have to find out how far you can go. How does the top of the world sound?"

"Pretty far. What top of the world would this be?"

"Everest base camp, 17,500 feet up. Early November."

"Hmm. I'm visiting Mom and Dad in October. Let me think it over?"

She called Lillian.

"Everest base camp? Are you crazy?"

"If I can do it, you can do it."

"Who says you can do it?"

"I say."

There was a pause.

"I guess I'm going to Everest base camp."

A week later, Will signed on too.

In late October, Allison, feeling more fit than she had for years, packed her gear and met Ellen at the airport. It was only while checking her bags that she realized she had thought of no bit of wisdom to pass on to the children.

The next day, Allison and Ellen met Lama Thokmay in New Delhi.

"I'm so very glad to see you," he said, greeting them at the airport.

"Thank you, Lama Thokmay." Ellen put her palms together in front of her chest and bowed slightly.

"Hello, Lama Thokmay," Allison said, and following Ellen's example, put her palms together and bowed her head. "It's good to see you again."

"Allison, welcome to India. I'm so pleased you want to see the school. How was your flight?"

"It was fine," Ellen said, "considering that we were in the air for sixteen hours."

Allison had slept as much as she could and then walked the aisles, attempting to keep any muscle stiffness at bay. Other than jet lag, she felt fine.

"What day is it?" Ellen asked as they walked through the terminal. "It was ten thirty Monday morning when we took off."

"And it is now three o'clock on Tuesday afternoon. I promise to make the drive as easy as possible. We'll arrive in time for supper."

Lama Thokmay drove them the 150 miles to Rishikesh in a Volkswagen van that the San Franciscans had paid for. Allison sat in front, Ellen in the back, and while they tried to stay awake, they both drifted in and out of sleep.

About an hour into the ride, Allison awoke. Lama Thokmay was humming quietly as he drove. When the song ended, Allison asked him, "What's that you were humming?"

"It's a *lhu*, which means a 'mountain song.' I learned it in one of the villages we visit."

"Can I ask you, why do you do this?" she said to him. "It seems unusual for a Buddhist monk to be rescuing children and running a school, to be so involved in the world."

"I went to Dolpo with my brother to visit an uncle I'd never met. But it turned out that the most important people I found there were the children. When I returned to India, I could not erase their faces from my mind. Wherever I went, I saw them; I saw them in my dreams. The girls are married off when they are eleven or twelve. The littlest ones spend their days with the animals, watching over herds of yaks or goats, sometimes starting when they are four. There is no education for the girls. Sometimes none for the boys either. And the ones who have physical defects, they are shunned. Shunned—can you imagine? No one bathes because there is no running water and no room in their small homes for tubs. In the winter, they must bring the animals inside. That is how they live, and how they will always live, because there are few resources in Dolpo. We must help them break this cycle. I must add that it is no one's fault. Everything they do, they do to survive. I explained all this to the priests in my monastery. They gave me permission to start a school. Now when we come, mothers beg us to take their children, even if it means making their own lives harder.

They want them to have a future." He suddenly brightened. "Ellen hasn't told me what you have brought to share with the children."

"Yes," Ellen said from the front seat. "You haven't told Ellen. What have you brought?"

Allison blushed. "I don't think I've brought anything. Only my poor self."

"Well," Lama Thokmay said, "maybe that will do."

Allison dozed again. When she awoke, she saw mountains out the left side window.

"We are almost there," Lama Thokmay said. "Those are the foothills of the Himalayas." He pointed out the opposite window. "On the right is the Ganga. In English, it is called the Ganges."

Twelve miles later, Lama Thokmay said, "Welcome to Rishikesh. Many pilgrims come here, and tourists too. The pilgrims come because it's a great center of yoga practice. The tourists come because the Beatles lived here. You know the Beatles?"

"I had all their records once," Allison said. "My brother said I had too many."

"I did not know that in the West one could have too many records." He laughed. "The Beatles wrote the songs for *The White Album* here."

"Lama Thokmay is well versed on Western pop culture," Ellen said.

"I only know what is useful for living in Rishikesh alongside our Hindu neighbors."

Once past the town, they drove up a hill to a plateau, where they had a glorious view of the snowcapped Himalayas. A gravel drive led them to a small compound. Three cement block buildings formed a rough U: The building on the left was painted bright green. The center building was cerulean blue, and the one on the right was deep pink.

"Here we are," Ellen said.

Allison was surprised to see, in front of the buildings, a large, lush green lawn.

"That could be a California lawn," Allison said.

"It means much to the children. The grass in Dolpo is often brown, or patchy green. It makes them happy to see such grass."

Twelve children were sitting cross-legged on the lawn in front of the blue building. When the three got out of the van, the children clasped their palms and began to sing.

"They are greeting us," Lama Thokmay said.

Allison's eyes filled with tears. Ellen put her arms around her shoulders.

"This is why we do this."

After breakfast the next morning, Allison walked outside to get a better look at the Himalayas. Lama Thokmay was coming out of the green building, where classes were held.

"Allison, come walk with me."

"Gladly."

They walked behind the blue house, where the lama's mother and sister were putting up a volleyball net for a game that afternoon.

"What brings you here, Allison?"

For a moment, she was silent, trying to answer the question for herself.

"My husband died in an accident in March. I learned a few months ago that I probably won't be able to have children. When I heard you speak in San Francisco, something told me I should come. I guess I thought I could get away from myself for a while."

"Perhaps it will work; who knows? But usually, we take ourselves with us, no matter where we go. Often, it is loss that takes us so far from home. I realize now that I went to Dolpo to meet my uncle because I had lost my father at an early age. But the result of my journey was to find a purpose for my life."

"Wouldn't your life have had a purpose if you'd spent it in a monastery?"

"No doubt. But now it touches many more people. We never know how the good in our lives will manifest itself."

As they walked around the side of the building, Allison's attention was drawn to a row of five cylindrical metal objects, about the size of milk cans, each embossed with what looked to be letters, hung on a wooden rack suspended on vertical rods.

"Tell me about those."

"They are prayer wheels. Inside each one is a mantra, copied thousands of times: *Om Mani Padme Hum*. It's the most well-known mantra. When you spin them," he demonstrated, "it is like reciting the mantra as many times as it is written inside. This helps you accumulate merit for the next life."

"What does the mantra mean?"

"It's complicated and has many layers of meaning. But spinning the wheel creates compassion, in yourself and in the world." He touched the lettering on the first wheel. "This is the same mantra."

Allison put her hand on the nearest wheel. "May I?"

"Please."

The metal was cool to the touch. She spun it gently; it made a soft whooshing sound. She spun the other four.

"Now you have added to the good in the world."

Over the next few days, Allison and Ellen participated in the school's life. They sat in on classes, and Allison was impressed to learn that eventually all the children would speak three languages: Tibetan (because Lama Thokmay wanted them to remember their heritage), Hindi, and English.

"Most Americans will never speak three languages," Allison said to Ellen.

"Three? Most barely speak one."

They helped prepare vegetarian meals in the kitchen and served and cleaned up in the dining room; and they played volleyball and soccer with the children, all of whom played better than they did.

After dinner on the last evening, everyone congregated in a large room in the blue building. Two children accompanied on wooden flutes as the other Tibetans sang *lhus* and folk songs. Lama Thokmay introduced the final song of the evening, a folk song about the high plains of Tibet and the love of Tibetans for their land and all that lived there and grew on it. Allison couldn't understand the words, but she hummed along as best she could, and the sounds seemed to connect her to each child. The high register, and what she could only describe to herself as glottal grace notes, long strings of them, drew her into them. Joy emanated from the children, passing into her and back to them, and made her wonder even more at their resilience. They had experienced so much poverty and hardship before arriving, on foot over the mountains, at the institute. Yet, at this moment, they were singing, smiling. When they first greeted her and Ellen they were smiling; they smiled when they played soccer, at meals, even in class. She couldn't remember any of them not smiling. Their radiance was a testament to Lama Thokmay and the school, of course, but as the music passed back and forth between the children and herself, Allison was aware of the presence of something else, something in them that was indestructible.

Allison could see the stars appearing through the windows. As the song's last notes died away, the room was wrapped in a deep silence. She didn't know how long it lasted, but as she looked at all the glowing faces, she felt as if each child held her gaze, and everything seemed clear.

Then a voice broke the silence:

> *'Tis the gift to be simple, 'tis the gift to be free,*
> *'Tis the gift to come down where we ought to be,*

And when we find ourselves in the place just right,
'Twill be in the valley of love and delight.
When true simplicity is gained,
To bow and to bend we shan't be ashamed,
To turn, turn, will be our delight,
Till by turning, turning, we come 'round right.

When she finished, the hush came over the room again. Everyone looked at Allison, who was surprised at the sound of her own voice.

The following morning, Lama Thokmay was to drive them to the nearby airport at Dehradun, from where they would fly to Kathmandu to meet Will and Lillian. They had said goodbye to the children who had gathered outside to see them off, and now Lama Thokmay stood by the van as they loaded their gear into the back.

"We're so thankful, as always, for the work you do," Ellen said to Lama Thokmay. "You can continue to count on us."

"For which we are blessed." He turned to Allison. "And we were very glad to have you here. Please come back."

"Thank you," Allison said. "But I'm sorry I didn't bring any wisdom or knowledge to share."

Lama Thokmay gave her a hug. "Oh, but you did."

CHAPTER TWENTY-THREE

By late afternoon, they had arrived in the capital of Nepal. It was warmer than Allison expected, like a late autumn day in Sunflower.

"Don't worry," Ellen said. "Our coldest days are ahead of us."

The plan was to spend a few days in Kathmandu to acclimatize to the thin air. "Kathmandu's at 4,300 feet," Ellen had told her. "Then we step up to 9,400 at Lukla, and 13,000 at the Tengboche monastery, before we get to base camp at 17,500. Not exactly what we sea-level gals are used to."

Will and Lillian were waiting for them at the hotel. Allison hadn't seen Will since her wedding, more than eight years ago. Since then, his hair had turned almost entirely silver, complementing the permanent tan he'd cultivated during his years of sailing on the *Perseus*. He didn't, however, seem his usual relaxed self.

"Is something wrong?" she asked him when they had a moment alone.

"Yes, but now's not the time." He changed the subject. "I like Lillian. You've never talked much about her."

"We weren't exactly friends in Sunflower. Then I never saw her again until she called my name in a Palo Alto sushi bar last year. We were different people by then, and she was there for me when Eric died."

"We could have been there too."

She'd called Will when Eric died, but just as she'd discouraged Emma and Doug from coming to California, she'd deflected Will's request to visit too.

"I can't claim to have been in my right mind; I was wrong to shut you all out. But she was there."

By the next morning, Lillian had struck up a friendship with Ellen.

"I was an air force brat," Ellen told Allison and Will at breakfast as Lillian poured water into her glass.

"I could tell right off by the way she carries herself," Lillian said.

"By my bossy nature, you mean. My dad was an acquisitions manager at Wright-Patterson Air Force Base in Dayton, where I grew up. Once in, you're never out."

"Tell me about it, baby." They clinked glasses.

The four of them spent the next few days exploring the city: Durbar Square with its shops and temples; the narrow streets crammed with pedestrians and motorcyclists; and the two monumental Buddhist stupas, or reliquaries, which attracted pilgrims and tourists from around the world. At one, Swayambhunath, Will pointed out a small golden pagoda.

"This is the temple of Harati Devi. The legend says that she kidnapped the local children and fed them to her family. The villagers begged the Buddha to help, so he took her son, and when she came looking for him, he instructed her in the ways of compassion. Every mother, he said, loved their children as much as she did. He returned her child, and from that moment, she became the protector of all children."

"Clearly an overachiever," Ellen said.

"Can we leave an offering?" Allison asked.

Everywhere they went, long streamers of small flags stretched across rooftops; at Swayambhunath, they reached from the roofs of small buildings like the Harati Devi temple to the base of the spire on the tall stupa.

"They're Buddhist prayer flags," Will explained. "Blue for sky, white for air, red for fire. Green for water, yellow for earth. Prayers are written on them for peace, health, and prosperity, and as they flutter in the wind, the prayers are taken up and spread around the world." He pointed. "See how tattered they are? They're made to disintegrate over time, to remind us of the transience of everything."

"Our flight's on," Ellen announced on the morning of their fourth day in Kathmandu. Flights in and out of Lukla, the jumping-off point to their base camp trek, were often canceled due to the unpredictable mountain weather: Clouds could descend or winds come up without notice, causing the airport, which lacked any radar or navigational aids, to shut down. Pilots needed clear visibility to maneuver onto the frighteningly short runway; there was no relying on instrument flight rules there.

The trip took thirty-five minutes, so Allison, not wanting to risk drowsiness or lightheadedness for the rest of the day, forswore Xanax and meditated instead. There were no assigned seats, and Ellen suggested sitting on the left side for the best view. With one look at the sixteen-seater prop plane, Allison took a seat on the right. When Will sat next to her, she took his hand and closed her eyes.

"Tell me when we get there," she said.

Moments after the aircraft lifted into the sky, Allison was startled to find herself in the copilot's seat of a two-seater Cessna. Eric was sitting next to her. He smiled at her and said, "Here we go."

He nosed the plane upward; her own hands were frozen on her control column. Rain pierced the night fog and pelted the windshield; she could see nothing else.

"We'll get through this," Eric was saying. "We always do. Right?"

A long bolt of lightning illuminated the night, and through the rain, Allison could see a hill suddenly rising in front of them.

"That's not supposed—" Eric was speaking again when she felt a jolt.

A gust of wind buffeted the sixteen-seater sideways. She opened her eyes and saw the plane hurtling deeper and deeper into narrow crevices between the jagged, ice-covered folds of the Himalayas. Afraid that if she closed her eyes again she'd be back in the Cessna with Eric, she stared at the floor, trying not to register the rugged peaks or the long distance to the silvery thread of a river in the valley far below.

Finally, the airport, perched on a mountainside, came into view. The runway was half the size of a small-plane runway in Georgia or California. She could tell that the pilots had no choice but to make the landing on the first try, since in front of it was a sheer drop of thousands of feet. The plane hit the ground with a jolt, and she saw that the landing strip was nothing more than dirt and grass. But they had made it.

They stopped at a teahouse for a lunch of dal bhat (the first of many meals they would have of this lentil soup), and then met their Sherpa guide, Nawang, who had led Ellen on her previous trek. He laid out the day's hike to the village of Phakding, five miles to the northeast. They hoisted their packs onto their backs and set out.

The sky was as clear and blue as any of them had ever seen; the mountains were covered in pine; beneath them ran the icy Dudh Kosi River, which they crossed on a narrow suspension bridge. There were few other trekkers at this time of year, but they shared the trail with numerous small caravans of don-keys, horses, and yaks, which, Nawang explained, were the only means of transporting goods to all the mountain villages and towns. They saw many small stupas and, in the villages they passed through, treetops festooned with prayer flags.

After spending the night in a small, freezing lodge in Phakding, they set out for their next stop, the town of Namche Bazaar. They climbed seven miles of stony paths that cut through pine forests along the river to a height of eleven thou-sand feet. Before they began the last steep portion of the climb, Nawang led them to a clearing in the forest and called for a rest. He pointed through the opening in the trees and there it was: the peak of Everest.

"We call it Chomolungma—Goddess Mother of the World," he said.

Clouds surrounded its glinting, snowcapped peak; it wore its majesty with the ease of an immortal monarch. Oddly, the peak's greatness made Allison feel strong. Although they had six more days of climbing before reaching the base camp, she was pleased with how well she was feeling: Neither her back, her legs, nor her feet were complaining. The trekking poles that Ellen urged them to buy helped; so, she thought, did the conditioning she'd put herself through in Santa Cruz. She was Everest's match.

Namche Bazaar was a bustling little town whose many vendors and ubiquitous aroma of incense reminded her of a miniature version of Santa Cruz. After two days of acclimatiz-ing to the thinner air climbing the many steps of the terraced town, they moved on to Tengboche.

They arrived at noon. After another lunch of dal, Nawang suggested a visit to the local monastery, where the annual Mani Rimdu festival, commemorating the coming of Buddhism to Tibet, was underway. The four travelers and Nawang joined a crowd of Sherpas and tourists in the monastery courtyard to watch masked monks dance a story of demons attacking Buddhist guards, to the loud accompaniment of cymbals, drums, and horns. The demon masks were bright red, their mouths wide, tooth-filled rictuses; the guards wore broad-brimmed black hats and brightly variegated brocaded silk robes. Not for the first time, Allison marveled at the ways in which Tibetans brought such vivid colors into their lives and worship—a far cry from the brown-and-white St. George's Episcopal Church in Sunflower.

The dance ended with the banishment of the demons and the triumph of virtue over evil. "If only it was so simple," reflected Will. It was the first negative comment Allison had ever heard him make about anything concerned with Buddhism.

As they left the monastery, Will stopped outside the monastery gate. "Now I'll tell you," he said to Allison and Lillian. "The time wasn't right before."

"I'll see you at the lodge," Ellen said, and she and Nawang headed away.

"Finally," Allison said. "What's been bothering you all this time?"

He pointed to a row of prayer wheels abutting the gate. "Spin them first." They did, and he led them to a bench, where they sat.

"When I was in Sunflower last week, the news reported that someone confessed to being the Sunflower Strangler."

Lillian's mouth tightened into a grimace, and Allison flushed as she felt nausea coming on.

"Tell us," she said.

"He confessed to it in prison. He was sick in the infirmary and thought he was going to die, so he told another inmate."

"Who is it?"

"He was a landscaper, apparently. Years after the Strangler incidents, he was charged with some unrelated crimes and has been incarcerated ever since. No wonder the murders stopped not long after he showed up at your place. His name is Yuri Abakumov."

Allison felt the ground begin to shift beneath her. Her vision blurred, so she turned to look at the monastery to anchor herself, but that faded quickly, replaced with vivid memories of a visit with her high school boyfriend, Buddy, to the garden center decades ago and the salesman there who creeped her out in ways she couldn't put into words.

Her mind continued to spin until she felt Lillian and Will grip her shoulders and shout her name. She had collapsed into a pile of herself, it seemed, in the dust and snow. And once she shook off her disorientation, she found, to her own shock, that she'd begun quietly laughing, involuntarily, her friend and brother looking at her now as if she'd completely lost it.

And had she? There was certainty nothing funny to her about the deaths of Andrea Rice, Toni DiVincenzo, and others, nothing nostalgic about her and Jon's home being invaded, nothing joyful about the women of Sunflower terrified to walk the streets at night, nothing just about her classmate's wrongful conviction. But now she felt something else too, something that she'd never felt when it came to the Strangler. Something like a release, something like freedom. Something that made the already giant vistas over the Himalayas seem even more expansive.

Everest base camp was twelve and a half miles from Tengboche; it took four days of slow hiking to reach it. On the first day, Ama Dablam, the triple-peaked mountain that vied with Everest for beauty—and that Allison thought resembled a child in a Halloween ghost costume, its arms extended to frighten you—looked down on them.

"Ama Dablam means Mother's Necklace," Nawang said. "The two lower peaks are her outstretched arms embracing her children. The glacier hanging down from the high peak is the necklace. She watches over us."

Allison sensed Ama Dablam, not a ghost but a mother,

wrap her in its embrace. From the air, the mountains had seemed forbidding, but here, peace and acceptance emanated from them. She felt a strange kinship with this rugged alpine beauty, and with the necklace-draped mountain in the distance. It was almost enough to shelter her from the well of sadness that Will's news had reopened.

They reached the village of Dingboche that evening. They rested there a day, allowing themselves to acclimatize to the altitude of 14,500 feet. On the third day, they pushed forward to yet another hamlet, Lobuche, at 16,800 feet. On the fourth day, now well above the tree line, they moved slowly up the rocky and barren terrain as they ascended a path alongside the Khumbu Glacier, which would lead them to the base camp.

"This is a glacier?" Lillian said as they slowly picked their way. "Looks like nothing but rocks and sand to me."

"The ice is underneath. For thousands of years, rocks and debris from Everest have fallen onto it," Nawang said.

"Oh, so we're on Everest now?"

Nawang laughed. "If you wish."

They were amazed that anyone could live in this desolate place, but people did, in Gorak Shep, the last village before the base camp. They had climbed only 1,800 feet that day, but the temperature had plummeted to fifteen degrees when they dropped their bags at the teahouse where Nawang had reserved them rooms that were almost as cold as it was outside.

It was now four miles and seven hundred more feet in altitude to the base camp, and after another meal of dal—which had lost its luster by now—they set out. The terrain remained rocky and uneven, but the incline was gentle. Alone as they approached the base camp, they took small steps past the ropes of prayer flags tied between posts driven into the frozen ground. Before them, the glacier stretched up the mountain and, shed of its blanket of rubble, gleamed brilliant white in the sunshine.

Nawang pointed at an arch-shaped rock on which someone had painted "Everest Base Camp." "We are here," he said.

The four trekkers stood quietly in the stillness around them, looking up in wonder at the vast expanse of ice, snow, and rock.

"I've heard about this all my life," Will said, "but nothing prepared me for this."

"That's how I felt the first time," Ellen said. "And now too."

Lillian put her arm around Allison's shoulder. "We made it."

"A long way from home."

"Not far enough."

They spent the next hour walking gingerly along the glacier, looking up at Everest.

"Okay," Ellen said. "From the top of the world, the only place to go is down. Let's get going."

They rested the next day in Gorak Shep. The following morning, before starting the descent to the airport at Lukla, Allison braved the cold for a final look at the mountain. She remained pleased with how well she'd withstood the rigors of the trip.

She studied Everest and the surrounding mountains. They did not seem welcoming now, just indifferent, even hostile. She thought of Lama Thokmay's trips to Dolpo to rescue children from the harshness of the life there. The conditions here seemed no more welcoming, yet she'd seen the ways the Sherpa population brightened the world with prayer flags and festivals adorned in color. They called one mountain "Goddess Mother of the World," and another "Mother's Necklace." Were these manifestations of the world as they saw it, or the way they wished it could be? She thought about this on the trek out of Gorak Shep, as they passed small monuments of piled stones honoring the climbers who'd died on Everest.

The downward journey to Lukla put greater stress on the walkers' backs, knees, and ankles, but Allison was wearing knee and back braces for extra support. They welcomed the increasing amount of oxygen they were taking into their lungs, and Allison looked forward to a relatively easy trek; she'd worry about the flight to Kathmandu when they got to Lukla.

A few miles from Namche Bazaar, her back began to tighten. She tried shortening her stride, but that didn't help. Neither did taking deeper breaths. Finally, she had to stop. The group gathered around her.

"I'll be okay in a minute," she said in a thin voice that gave no one confidence. Then she felt herself being squeezed in a vise between her hips and ribcage. "My back is spasming," she managed to say. She took several sharp breaths, but they only made the pain worse.

"Do you want to sit?" Ellen asked.

"There's no place to sit without clogging up the trail," she said. "Let me try walking." But with every step, pain shot up her back and radiated to her hands, so that she couldn't hold on to her sticks. She stopped and, feeling helpless, said, "I don't know what to do."

"I do." Lillian handed her sticks to Ellen.

Trading her between them as if she were a large backpack, she and Will carried Allison, fireman-style, down the last three miles to the town. "Let your arms dangle," Will said. "It might help stretch your back."

Allison could only moan. She'd celebrated her rejuvenated body too soon; now she felt utter humiliation, which increased when every well-intentioned trekker who passed them on the trail asked if they could help. This wasn't how she'd envisioned the end of her triumphal trek.

In Namche Bazaar, Nawang found a Sherpa woman who did massage. Later, Allison was able to sleep, fitfully. She dreamed she was in darkness at the base of Ama Dablam, calling Eric's name.

CHAPTER TWENTY-FOUR

Once her flight from Delhi to San Francisco was beyond sight of the ground, Allison opened her eyes. Lillian, who had the window seat, was leafing through a magazine. Across the aisle from Allison, Ellen had opened a book.

Before her Xanax took effect, Allison looked at the ring she'd acquired the day before. She thought the green stone with flecks of crystal might be aventurine. Large and oval shaped, the ring was too large for her ring finger, so she slipped it on her index finger. She was still getting used to its feel.

Yesterday, her back spasms having receded, she'd wandered the alleyways of Kathmandu alone, until she found herself standing in front of a small stone building off Durbar Square, with a sign reading "Oracle" next to the door. On an impulse, she went in.

The room was small and low ceilinged; Tibetan rugs covered the floor. On a low table a handbell and a few small copper bowls sat; behind the table, two cushions lay on the floor. On a small altar standing against a whitewashed wall, three rows of butter lamps burned, lending the room a warm, golden glow. Alongside the lamps were a mirror and a bowl of rice.

"You may put a donation in the box if you wish."

Allison heard the voice before seeing the young man, no more than fifteen, to whom it belonged. He was standing next to the door.

"May I see the oracle?"

"Please wait here."

Allison dropped some rupees into a wooden donation box, and a man suddenly appeared through a door on the far side of the room. His stumpy body, square jaw, and kindly eyes didn't say *oracle* to Allison, but she reminded herself that she didn't know what an oracle was supposed to look like. He carried a carved wooden crown with five petal-shaped slats, each featuring a painted portrait of the Buddha. He placed the crown on his head and wrapped himself in a short silk cloak whose deep red-orange color reminded Allison of Sausalito sunsets. He picked up the bell and tossed incense sticks onto a charcoal brazier; the odor of cedarwood seeped into the room.

He looked Allison over from head to toe and closed his eyes. Swaying slightly, he began to moan, then hiss. He made guttural sounds like a growling dog and jerked down and up from the waist perhaps a dozen times, ringing the bell wildly. Suddenly he paused, rolled his eyes upward, and began moaning and hissing again until, after ten minutes, he stopped. He opened his eyes.

"The oracle is here," the doorman said. With a piercing gaze, the man regarded Allison. "Say a prayer for the well-being of all living things," the doorman instructed Allison. She did, silently, and then looked at the doorman as if to ask, *What's next?* He responded by wrapping a saffron-colored shawl around her shoulders.

"You may ask your question," he said.

Did she have a question? She asked the first thing that came to her.

The man closed his eyes and spoke quietly and evenly. "You know all the reasons for not bringing a child into the world. But that is not the end." He opened his eyes. He looked past Allison toward the door to the outside.

Allison turned and looked to the doorman and saw that three people had formed a line while the man was contacting, or being contacted by, another realm, if that's what had happened. The doorman nodded at her.

"Thank you," she said, and left.

At the hotel later that afternoon, Allison told Will of her visit to the oracle.

"The man wasn't the oracle," he told her. "He was the medium. The oracle is of the spirit world and speaks through him."

"Do you believe in that?"

"There are thirty-one different planes in the six realms of existence, and sentient beings exist in all of them. We exist in the realm of gross form; other beings are formless."

"Including spirits that talk through mediums?"

"That's what the *suttas*, the ancient books, teach us."

"But do you believe it?"

"Let's just say I don't have a reason not to believe it. Do you?"

"I'm open to the possibility."

On the plane, Allison looked at the ring. She could feel the Xanax begin to wash through her. What now? She could return to the A-frame in Soquel and . . . sit. But she wasn't ready to just sit. She could return to Japan and work for Mr. Nakamura, but much as she loved her time in Japan, uprooting herself so entirely didn't feel right either. "Knowing which is the wrong path is the first step," Mr. Nakamura had said. "The rest will come in time." Where was the right path?

She didn't rush into finding it. She was surprised to discover that she was content to be back home in Soquel, sitting in her garden chair in the back yard with the birds and deer. She read in the business journals that Stanton was likely to be wholly absorbed into Sakasama and wondered what would happen to Johnny Schmidt. She imagined him living in Tokyo, trying to picture him praying for his good fortune at the Kanda Shrine. Or maybe he'd send Josh to do it for him. Or perhaps he'd end up in Soquel, and she'd bump into him behind the counter at the fishmongers or an antique store on Main Street. In the event, she'd try to have compassion.

Her back healed; she learned from a local chiropractor about something called kinesiology tape that helped relieve muscle pain, reduced swelling, and improved range of motion. She bought rolls of blue, red, and yellow tape and applied them to her lower back, her right glute, and hip. *I look like a line of prayer flags,* she thought, staring at herself in the mirror. *Could be worse.* She was surprised to find herself saying a prayer for the well-being of the world.

She began training for the Big Sur Marathon she'd signed up for the previous summer. Her base camp training stood her in good stead, and she found she could tolerate running on pavement after all. She had a little over four months. She'd be ready.

It rained torrents the day before the marathon. By evening, the streets in Big Sur Village were slick and the trees dripped ceaselessly. Allison picked up her runner's bib with her identification number on it, pulled her raincoat around her, and dashed across the street from race headquarters to the hotel where the carbo-loading dinner was in full swing.

In the event room she grabbed a tray and joined the line to pile her plate with rigatoni and pomodoro sauce, mixed vegetables, cookies, and water. She was looking for a place to sit when a nearby voice boomed out, "Allison? Allison Eagan!"

She looked behind her. Coming toward her with a tray

loaded with pasta and green salad was Marty Schliemann, whom she'd not seen since he'd left Stanton three years earlier.

"Marty?"

"Hiya, kid. Let's find a place to sit. Fancy meeting you here, of all people." They found an unclaimed table at the far end of the room.

"This is my first marathon," she said, sitting.

"This is my . . . oh, I've lost count. This is my third Big Sur. I was sorry to hear about your husband. I wanted to offer my condolences, but you'd disappeared. I heard you left Stanton."

"I took some time off. Johnny Schmidt was about to make it permanent, but I saved him the trouble."

"You'll find old Johnny on the unemployment line these days. Along with most of the Stanton crew. When Sakasama took over, they cleaned house."

"That doesn't sound like Mr. Nakamura. He was very kind to me. He offered me a job."

"No kidding? Did you take it?"

"No. I had other priorities."

"You wouldn't find me working for the Japanese. Too buttoned down. And everything's got to be their way."

Allison tried not to show her irritation.

"Didn't I read something about you recently?"

He brightened at the reference to himself.

"Probably. I got out of Stanton while the going was good. Like I promised you I would."

"That was before I left, wasn't it?"

"It was a month or two after we met. That was '91. Now it's '94, and we're about to roll her out."

"A supercomputer, right?"

"A parallel supercomputer. Several thousand processors. Twenty-five hundred, more or less; 128 gigs of memory. The company's called Anima. Something or other to do with the female principle. It was my partner's idea."

"Congratulations. You must feel good."

"I'll feel even better when it's up and running in the real world. That's when the money will roll in in a big way."

He hadn't changed much, she noticed. Perhaps his hair was a little longer; the eyes, now that he was seemingly on the verge of a big success, were a little hungrier. Despite herself, Allison felt a tinge of interest. "Who are your customers?"

"We've signed up a lab doing energy research, and another one studying oceanic flow." He speared some rigatoni with his plastic fork, pointed it at her, and put it in his mouth. "You should join us. I repeat my ancient invitation to come work for me."

Allison was silent.

"Unless you're still working on those other priorities."

"Tell me more."

By six forty-five the next morning, the sun was shining, and as the marathon kicked off at Big Sur Station, the temperature was fifty degrees.

"I'll look for you tomorrow," Marty had said after dinner, "but if I see you, I probably won't talk to you. I'll be locked in on my running."

Allison was less intent than Marty on running for the sake of running. Like the Everest trek, it was one more way to convince herself that her body wouldn't slow her or bring her down. Now here she was, among a pack of strangers, leaving Big Sur Station behind, with the next 26.2 miles to do—what? Figure out her life?

She'd hoped to keep her mind a blank and just experience the run, but as she jogged with the crowd at a slow pace through the redwoods, the oracle's words came back to her. She'd asked, "Will I have children?" She expected that oracles were supposed to reply with a riddle—better an answer that could sustain multiple interpretations than only one that could prove wrong. Allison thought he'd meant "No, you won't, but have you considered other alternatives?"

Was he suggesting that Allison should adopt? The thought had occurred to her more than once since visiting Lama Thokmay's institute in Rishikesh. She could easily afford it with the money Eric had left her; she wouldn't even have to work.

But she'd always worked, at least until the catastrophe of Eric's death. She'd earned her own money ever since the days of handing out balloons at Wendy's. For years, women had been telling themselves they could "have it all," partner or no, and, unlike many women, she was fortunate enough to be able to do it on her own. But did she want to raise a child without a father?

The first nine miles had been fairly flat; now the road climbed and would continue uphill for two miles. As she headed for Hurricane Point, she imagined Doug as she'd seen him when she was a child: on the kitchen stool talking things over with Emma; in his living room armchair with his cigarette, bourbon, and a copy of that day's *Enquirer*. She remembered her parents worrying when they thought Will was lost at sea and being relieved when they learned he was safe. She saw Doug in his office at Britmar, where he exercised such easy authority, and where he told her the secret of being a good salesperson. She saw him persevering after they'd taken his job away from him.

It wasn't just the way she felt seeing him in these circumstances. It was also the feeling she'd had among the boys at the Black smoking tree and the martial arts school, the one that drew her into the world of men, the feeling that she *belonged*. She *liked* the world of men. Was that retrograde? It had given her everything, from the experiences in Sunflower to the adventures with Eric to her career in Silicon Valley. The Valley was certainly no easy place for women; it was the world of the Johnny Schmidts and the Josh Powers, but it was also the world of Mr. Nakamura. Why should she give it up now?

Yet she'd also wanted a child ever since Eric had brought her to Blue Heron Island. Now it was an urge she wasn't anxious to surrender, even if her body and the oracle were telling her it was not going to happen. *But that is not the end.*

She reached Hurricane Point, the highest elevation of the run. But it was only six hundred feet above sea level—nothing, she reminded herself, compared to the Everest trek. She'd learned the hard way that going downhill wasn't necessarily easier, but her legs, although a little heavy, were moving in the same steady rhythm she'd set once the pack had thinned out after the start. To her left, the Pacific glinted hard and green in the sunlight. The next two miles were downhill, to the halfway point at Bixby Bridge. *But that is not the end,* echoed again in her mind. What could the end be? She gulped some air and was on her way.

She crossed the finish line in Carmel at eleven o'clock, four hours and fifteen minutes after she'd started.

"Not bad!" Lillian said, giving her a big hug when they met in the runner reunion center.

"'Not bad'? I'd say 'Great!'" Allison gasped. "Don't let go either—I might fall down!"

She drained all the water from a plastic bottle, collected her finisher's medal, and as they walked toward Lillian's car, Allison spotted Marty.

"Three hours!" he said, not asking about Allison's time or how she was feeling. "Introduce me to your friend." She did. Then he took her aside. "We're not done yet. Have dinner with me."

Allison agreed to have dinner with Marty to hear more about Anima. She thought she'd recognized the word; she looked it up to be sure. Yes, the word "anima" meant "the female element in every male." If Marty had a feminine element, she thought, he was keeping it well hidden. However, the anima was also represented by the archetype of the nurturing mother. Perhaps this was a hint that working for Marty was a step on the path to fulfilling the oracle's prophecy, at least as Allison understood it.

They met at a Los Gatos steakhouse—Marty's choice.

"You need to join us," he said, tearing into his bone-in rib eye. "We make it easy for our sales force; we've got the whole thing down to a science. Your work in the briefing center will be quicker and easier because we do all the work ahead of time. Before we meet a client, we know exactly what their needs are, and we massage them to fit the software and services we'll offer them."

"Sounds a little backward to me, Marty."

"Not at all. Once they see what Anima can do, all these research institutes and universities will be lining up around the block to buy one."

"If it will sell itself, what do you need me for?"

"Can't do without the human touch, know what I mean?" He looked at her in a way that suggested business, but not necessarily the business of selling supercomputers. "Listen, you come to work for me, and I'll make it more than worth your while." He named a figure. Allison tried not to look stunned as she swallowed her scalloped potatoes. At the salary Marty was offering, she could put enough away in a couple of years to adopt a football team, if adoption should turn out to be the fulfillment of the oracle's prophecy.

The next day, she called Marty and agreed to sell Anima.

PART SIX

CHAPTER TWENTY-FIVE

1996-1999

It began with an email to every employee in the autumn of 1996. "Important all-campus meeting on October 16, 10:00 a.m. Big announcement." Allison had been on the road much more than she'd anticipated when she agreed to come work for Marty in 1994. She didn't enjoy the flying, but she preferred it over working in the briefing center, never having reconciled herself to the way Marty did business, putting Anima's needs ahead of the clients', massaging their needs, as he said, to fit the software, rather than the other way around. It grated enough that she'd talked him into letting her visit the labs with an Anima engineer to ensure that the computers and software were fulfilling the client's needs, and if they weren't, working with the on-site engineers until they did.

At 9:50 a.m., she took a seat in the auditorium. None of the Animators—as Marty insisted on calling them—around her knew anything about the big announcement.

A few minutes past ten, Marty strode onto the stage, dressed in black slacks and a black turtleneck, a wireless mic clipped to the collar. There was no podium. A rear-projection screen showed a recent iteration of Anima in a shiny white laboratory. A few in the crowd stifled chuckles at his resemblance to another Silicon Valley innovator.

Marty launched into his speech without greeting or prologue. "I want to thank everyone who's had a hand in making Anima what it is: With more than four thousand processors, it's the fastest supercomputer in the world. We've sold 137 of them, and everyone—and I mean everyone—in this room is responsible for their success. Our success. Your success." He paused, and the expected applause followed. "But the wind has changed direction, and we have to change with it. Anima Systems is about to enter a new era. I'm willing to bet that all of you Animators have noticed that the market is evolving. It's trending more and more toward computers built for consumers, with increasingly powerful chips. What does it mean when a scientist can go to a store and buy a workstation? Or when a university can buy a hundred of them and link them in a network? It means that the market for a machine like Anima, however much we love her, is shrinking. So, the first thing I want to announce is that we'll ship our last machines by the end of next year."

Now Marty had everyone's attention.

"That might sound like bad news, but I promise you it's not. Because . . ."

Allison could tell he was pausing again for effect.

". . . we have a new project and a new customer." A picture flashed onto the screen behind him of another computer, this one, strangely, in purple cabinets, and again came the expected applause, which felt mixed to Allison: Some Animators were exhaling in relief, anticipating the role they would have in whatever this brave new world turned out to be. Others, she could tell, were trying to determine the upward climb or the downward plunge of the roller-coaster ride their careers were about to take. She took a breath, exhaled, and then took another.

At first, Marty had been disturbed by Allison's traveling to labs where she'd already made a sale. "You're done with them, leave the fine-tuning to the engineers," he'd tell her. "Move on to the next sale."

"Look," she'd say. "I'm selling a package: the software, the hardware, the services to get it up and running, and the training to keep it going. I can't just hope it works out; it's too complicated."

"The rest of the sales force does."

"Being there tells them that we care about the fit between them and Anima; it tells them we're with them for the long haul. That means something to them."

It was true: Marty had heard from every lab and university that had bought Anima from Allison that her care and concern made a difference, and that reflected well on Anima Systems.

"Well," he said, fiddling with a pencil, "there's only one thing I can do. I'm making you a project manager. But I can't let go of you in sales. You're going to do both. With appropriate compensation, of course."

Marty knew when he had a good thing going. Allison also had to admit, however, that he knew the value of his people.

The travel was something else, although Allison accepted that she'd brought it on herself. She might spend up to a week at a time with the scientists, engineers, and technicians from the lab and from Anima Systems. Any thoughts about adoption were put on hold.

A slide of the White House appeared on the screen. "The new customer is the federal government," Marty said. "The new project is another supercomputer—just in case you might be thinking we're going to compete with Compaq. The power of our new baby is going to be measured in teraflops." He paused. "'What's a teraflop?' you're asking. First, 'flop' stands for 'floating-point operation'—that's any calculation that employs numbers with decimal points, which is a much more complicated calculation than numbers without them. A teraflop is one trillion flops per second—that's how fast and powerful this new supercomputer is going to be. And what else would we call something so fast and powerful"—a new slide appeared with the name emblazoned in metallic red letters—"but Hercules?"

"A Mac?" a woman sitting next to Allison whispered helpfully.

"Amazing, huh?" Marty went on. "And now you'll want to know what task the phenomenal Hercules is going to be performing for the federal government. It's only the most important task they could ask us to undertake to support our national security: Hercules will maintain and predict the performance, safety, and reliability of the nation's stockpile of nuclear weapons." Now there was a hush. Allison was startled. "This is *really* good news." There was some rustling in the auditorium. "Until now, the only way to ascertain viability was through actual nuclear testing, which has been conducted underground since 1963. But thanks to the brilliance of our engineers—and to the new Comprehensive Nuclear-Test-Ban Treaty—Hercules will replace underground testing with complex mathematical calculations. Thanks to Hercules, the United States will not do any more real-world nuclear testing. I'll take any questions now."

A man behind Allison stood up. "When do we get started?" She wondered if he was a plant.

"I'm glad you asked. That's even better news: We've started. We've been working with our partners, including four government labs, for the last two years. I couldn't announce it until now, when the government finally gave me the go-ahead." He lifted an imaginary glass. "To the future!"

Anima had brought good things to the world. Allison felt she'd done useful work, assisting labs in their work on AIDS research, developing stronger materials with which to build cars, research into the ways ocean currents flowed. There was little doubt in her mind as to how Hercules would be used: to ensure the world continued to be endangered by nuclear weapons.

"Yes," Marty said to her over lunch a week later in the shiny, luxuriously stocked cafeteria built with Anima's profits, "but now we'll know how safe or unsafe those weapons are without having to perform real-world tests."

"And the computers will also be used to help design new bombs, won't they?"

"Yes, again, but they'd be designed and built with or without Hercules. The difference is that with Hercules, the tests will all be performed mathematically, not actually. It's a win for the world, Allison."

"If I were a project manager on Hercules, I'd be complicit in the maintenance of a mechanism whose purpose is world destruction."

"You're wrong. What world's been destroyed by a nuclear weapon in the last fifty-one years? Unless I've missed something big? But who's been saved? Maybe billions. Having the bombs is a deterrent. That's a fact. And who's to say"—Marty tucked into a second helping of four-cheese macaroni and cheese—"that Hercules won't have a future doing the same kinds of research that Anima has done, but with more firepower?"

Since, as far as she'd heard, no lab engaged in such research had come forward with an interest in the phenomenally expensive Hercules, Allison had to weigh for herself the possibility of such work against the reality of performing nuclear bomb maintenance.

"Come on, Allison. To the future," he said, raising his glass.

She raised hers. "To *some* future."

Allison fulfilled her project management duties on the remaining sales of Anima through the end of 1997, then turned in her resignation. Marty asked her to reconsider; she declined. He offered her a significant raise in salary. She thanked him sincerely for the opportunity, but said she couldn't see herself as part of the Hercules team.

For the next several months she felt as if she were wandering in a desert. She couldn't feel sorry for herself, knowing that her desert was self-selected and well appointed, but the view was empty in all directions. She needed to move, but where to?

She took up bicycling again. She had to ride her ten-speed slowly around Soquel, Capitola, and Aptos, but on the roads between the towns she found the room and space for speed. She was no longer fifteen, however, as her body would remind her the next morning. On went the kinesiology tape; down went the NSAIDs. It seemed to take longer and longer each morning to stretch her limbs and torso just to be able to walk without stiffness. "I'm thirty-seven," she'd grumble. "Why do I feel like sixty-seven?"

Now was the perfect time to adopt; she had the money saved and time to devote to a child, and California wasn't averse to adoptions by well-situated single parents. But if the timing was right, the circumstances felt wrong.

Enabled by Hercules's "gift," the complicated and dangerous procedure of underground testing, and manufacturing new nuclear bombs, would only be easier. Allison conceded Marty's point that the destruction of Hiroshima and Nagasaki had prevented the further use of nuclear weapons, but that was no guarantee that a madman wouldn't come along one day and blow up the world. Moreover, less than two hours south of her A-frame stood the Diablo Canyon nuclear reactor, built between two geological faults, a world-class disaster waiting to happen. During the last few years, it seemed as if whenever she turned on the news or picked up the paper, she heard about an airplane explosion off Long Island killing eight hundred people, or terrorist bombs in Saudi Arabia and Manchester, England, or—too close to her hometown—at the Centennial

Olympic Park in Atlanta. Russians and Chechens were murdering each other daily at numbing rates; so were Israelis and Palestinians. How could she raise a child and teach them to act with optimism and joy in such a world?

In March 1999, Ellen invited Allison to come to San Francisco for a talk.

"We could really use you on the institute's board," she said as they walked one afternoon in the Marina District. "I'm thinking—and pardon my arrogant assumption—that now's the perfect time. Someday, my girl, you might even be president."

Ellen took her to Los Angeles, where Allison watched her speak to a group of women, all senior advertising executives, about Lama Thokmay and the institute. It was a sales pitch, no different from the kind Allison herself had been doing for years, imbued with Ellen's belief in Lama Thokmay's mission. She saw how easily Ellen tapped into the women's genuine desire to do some good with their money. *I could do that*, she thought.

From there they flew to New York to meet Lama Thokmay himself, who was considering opening a medical clinic to spare the children and staff round trips to Delhi. Members of his East Coast fundraising team had arranged for him to visit a children's hospital in the city so that he might see the small miracles medicine was performing, and use that knowledge to inform his own plans—while also raising money for the project. In turn, he invited whichever of his hosts were available to accompany him. Allison and Ellen went along.

A nurse guided them through clinics devoted to several specialties. The last stop was an activity room, where children gathered to watch a play put on by members of a local young persons' theater group. Some of the children had visible ailments, from missing limbs to skull deformities, and conditions that Lama Thokmay had seen for years in his trips to Dolpo, such as cleft lips and palates. Others suffered from invisible illnesses—cancers, heart diseases, lung disorders. Despite their conditions, all the children sat rapt. The young actors, performing without scenery and in just bits of costumes, invited the children to create with them an imaginary world where the reality that weighed heavily on them didn't exist.

Allison, who was also beguiled by the performance, thought the children looked lighter, at peace.

"It seems so easy," Lama Thokmay said to her after they'd left the recreation room, "for a portal to open from one world to another."

"If only they could stay there."

"We must help make such a world inside this one."

The faces of the children as they watched the play were still with her when Allison arrived back in San Francisco with Ellen. As they walked through the terminal to the luggage carousel and chatted about the week ahead, she also thought about the doctors and nurses they'd met. No less than the children's at the play, some of their faces had lit up as they'd described to Lama Thokmay the procedures they performed that could change the lives of their young patients forever.

A crowd had already gathered around carousel number eight when Allison and Ellen arrived. They joined the second ring of disgorged passengers, and Allison found herself standing behind a man a few inches taller than she, so that she had to peer around him to watch for her bag. As she and Ellen strategized about raising funds for the Rishikesh clinic, they didn't notice a third ring of patrons forming behind them. When the luggage finally arrived, they were hemmed in, front and back.

Still oblivious, they were discussing a fundraiser to be held in either San Francisco or Santa Cruz, when the man standing in front of Allison picked up his suitcase. He turned swiftly, and as they came face-to-face, the bag's momentum caused it to strike Allison hard in the right knee.

"Pardon me," he said. "Sorry." He pushed past her without another word as the pain vibrated around her knee. She turned and heard him say to the man behind her, "Excuse me, in a hurry," and he hustled toward the exit, fumbling with his bag's retractable handle.

"Nice," Allison said, rubbing the knee.

"Nice butt," Ellen said, watching him go. Allison had to admit that the soft-gray eyes behind the tortoiseshell horn-rimmed glasses, the trimmed, curly, thinning brown hair and beard, and the fit body inside the white shirt and beige slacks weren't bad either.

Ninety minutes later, Allison pulled into her driveway. She sat for a moment, staring at the empty house. Why hadn't she adopted a child during these last few years? The world was surely a terrible place into which to bring a child, but adopting a child was different from bringing one into it. First, she had told herself that all the traveling for Anima was holding her back. Then, it was Hercules and all it had come to represent in her mind, which was not only the possibility of nuclear war but the casual acceptance of the whole range of hatred, violence, cruelty, and needless death that she, and the rest of the world, acceded to every day. Perhaps she had been aware of this attitude toward, or against, life, yet hadn't fully realized it until this moment. This world was so far from the one envisioned by Lama Thokmay, and by the prayers for compassion sent into it by prayer wheels and flags, that even if she could raise one child to treat the world with kindness, what good would it do?

Yet, suddenly, these reasons that had felt so powerful, so solid, so inarguable, dissolved.

"You know all the reasons for not bringing a child into the world," the oracle had said, "but that is not the end." She had always taken him to mean that this was not the end of *her* story, that somehow, she *would* have children. Now, sitting in the car, looking at the empty house in front of her, she realized that she'd misinterpreted the oracle, and that her reasons for not adopting weren't excuses or righteous arguments. They were, she realized, simply placeholders, thoughts that prevented her from acting until she understood the oracle's words correctly.

Now she did. The oracle was talking not about the end of her story, but about *means and ends*. The ends he was referring to had nothing to do with her having her own child. They were much bigger than that.

CHAPTER TWENTY-SIX

By the summer, she was back at work. Having finally understood the oracle's words, she had found a way to put them into action.

"This year," she'd say to Lillian, swirling her tequila gimlet after a good day with a client, "the Institute of Medicine published a study showing that more people die each year from medical errors than from car accidents or breast cancer."

"So you said last time. And I know you've got the solution."

"You bet."

Her new employer was a company called Caduceus, part of an emerging industry called medical informatics, which was the business of bringing the benefits of computerization to medicine.

"We have two solutions," she explained. "First, we computerize patient records and make them available, practically instantaneously, to any doctor or nurse tied into the system. Second, we replace doctors' handwritten orders for tests, prescriptions, and procedures with electronic ones. This is where the mistakes creep in. Have you ever seen a doctor's handwriting on, say, a prescription? Completely illegible, right?"

"In the air force, handwriting is immaculate."

"My ass. A doctor writes an order in barely legible scrawl on a patient's chart. Then, it's written out again by a nurse or someone on the ward and sent to, say, the pharmacy, or radiology, or a lab. Someone there writes it out a third time for the department's records. That means there are two opportunities to misinterpret the doctor's already unreadable order."

"I follow you," Lillian said, although she knew that Allison didn't need the encouragement. In the last six years, she hadn't seen her happier than in the two months she'd been working for Caduceus.

"But when the doctor types it into a Caduceus terminal, it arrives at its destination as clearly as it was typed in."

"Assuming it was typed in correctly to begin with."

"Whenever you deal with humans, you deal with human error, but with this product, the chances for errors are much reduced. And if it's typed in wrong, it's clear who'd be held responsible. The doctors know that, so it behooves them to get it right."

"To check their work."

"To check their work. It sounds technical. But it's going to make a difference in the world."

"Here's to that."

Whether for patients' records or doctors' orders, hospitals had been slow to embrace computerization, but Allison accepted the challenge. She wasn't shy about using some of the medical research contacts she'd made through Anima to open doors, and when she talked with the administrators at children's hospitals especially, she'd tell them that she was more interested in helping to save lives than selling them hardware, software, or training services.

It was a perfect Saturday morning in September 2000 for the Walk to Support Children. The sun was shining, the humidity was low, and the visibility over the ocean was good at Seascape County Park in Aptos, down the road from Soquel. The Children's Hospital of Santa Cruz was holding its big outdoor annual fundraiser, and Allison had persuaded Ellen and Lillian to walk with her. The walk was along the beach—unusual, perhaps, but Allison had learned that's how things were done around Santa Cruz: unusually and, if possible, at the beach.

The Children's Hospital was the first institution Allison had called upon and one of the first willing to overcome their doctors' conservatism and try Caduceus's system. It wasn't the largest children's hospital in the state, but its relatively small size meant that Allison could get to know and work with more of the staff than she usually could at the larger ones (although they received their share of her attention too).

Most of the doctors, nurses, and staff at the hospital were adventurous (many lived in or around Santa Cruz, after all, and had come there attracted to its tenuous attachment to conventional wisdom) and were willing to give Caduceus a try. The doctors were the hardest to convince to give up their pen and paper, but they tended to come around once Allison showed them how simple the process was and they realized that they would never have to translate their hieroglyphs—always perfectly clear to them—to anyone again. Business had always been a personal matter for Allison, to the extent that she took her customers' needs to heart and wasn't satisfied, no matter how large the commission, if she hadn't matched them with the appropriate solutions. She never took her successes more happily to heart than she did now.

The walkers assembled beneath a purple tent to hear speeches from the hospital administrators, and then the state assemblywoman and senator. The senator first thanked the crowd for coming out, then took the opportunity to remind everyone of the important work he was doing in the legislature to advance the cause of children's health. When the hospital president finally took the mic and asked, "Is everybody ready to walk?" the crowd of about 150 cheered and set out along the beach.

As Allison turned, she found herself staring into the gray eyes of the man who had banged her knee with his bag and fled the baggage claim with barely an "Excuse me."

"Well, if it isn't Mr. Carousel," she said. "In a floppy sun hat."

"That's *Doctor* Carousel to you," the man said, tipping the hat. She couldn't help but notice the gray eyes light up at recognizing her. "Or Tom. May I walk with you?"

"I don't know. I'll have to ask my bodyguards. Lillian?"

"He seems harmless enough."

"Are you packing a suitcase?" Ellen asked.

He held up his hands. "I'm unarmed."

Lillian said, "You may proceed."

As they made their way out of the tent, Ellen whispered to Allison, "He's got a nice front too." Then she held Lillian back a bit so that Allison and Tom could walk ahead of them.

On the beach, they passed a drum circle: eight women beating out a rhythm on their drums and clapping their sticks together, a typical kind of Santa Cruz encouragement and an invigorating counterpoint to the walkers' casual pace. Once past them, Allison asked, "So, you're a doctor?"

"A GP."

"A vanishing breed."

"Well, most people go where the money is, into the specialties."

"But not you."

"I like the variety."

He told her that he had a practice in Santa Cruz but was thinking of moving it up north to Gualala, where he'd built a house some years ago. "Not right away. Gradually."

"Gualala? That's where?"

"North of San Francisco. Mendocino County."

"Must be nice."

"No place like it on earth. We have cliffs and bluffs, a river that runs into the ocean, a big sandbar that attracts whales—why? I don't know. Some days the ocean is blue; some days it's coral. The house sits in a cove; the deck overlooks the ocean. And the sunsets: purple, red; flaming orange. There's trails and golf, hawks, ospreys, plenty of quiet. One thing there isn't is a lot of people. And what brings you to this walk?"

"I'm a friend of the hospital. Through sales."

"So, this is business?"

"No, the sale's already made."

"What did the sale consist of?"

"It's a system that computerizes patient records and doctors' orders."

"Oh, *that*? I've heard about that. In fact, I supported the purchase."

"Oh, really?" Allison couldn't help but feel glad. "How's that?"

"I'm on the board of trustees. It was a big purchase, so it came before the new technology committee, of which I'm a member."

"A forward thinker. You'll be pleased. And I'm pleased to meet a doctor who believes in making doctors' writing legible." Allison paused momentarily. "So, this is business?"

Tom laughed. "In part. I like to see who our donors are who don't happen to be wealthy or run foundations. A lot of the folks here have a personal stake in the hospital. Many of them have a child whom we've treated. There are a few who've lost a child but know that we did everything that we could for them."

"That says a lot about the hospital."

He pulled a round sticker from his pocket, peeled off the back, and stuck it on her light-blue sweatshirt. It read "I Walked for Children."

"Welcome to the team."

"Thanks." They walked on for a moment in a comfortable silence. Then she said to him, "How about coffee?"

It was an impulsive offer. Afterward, she wasn't sure why she'd asked him. She was busy selling again, in the service of children and adults, and she loved it. On occasions when being childless filled her with sadness, she redoubled her efforts on behalf of the children in the hospitals she called on. It worked, except on the quiet nights when she couldn't conjure up the sounds of the Buddhist mantras of compassion, or when she dreamed, as she still did, of searching for Eric in the hills near the Altamont Pass.

She hadn't thought about dating since Eric died, although it occurred to her now that perhaps, on some level, she had. Maybe that unconscious thought accounted for a recent desire for speed—to put that possibility behind her, to outrun it. After they'd made arrangements over the phone a few days later, however, she found that she could sit still and contemplate dating, even look forward to it.

"So, why were you in such a hurry at the airport that day?" she asked him during their first coffee, at a Capitola café.

He blushed. "I was rude, wasn't I? I apologize. My flight from Dallas was two hours late, and I had three hours to get to Gualala for my daughter's rehearsal dinner before her wedding the next day. Bad planning on my part."

A daughter? And where's the wife? Allison thought to herself.

"What took you to Dallas?" she asked.

Tom frowned. "My wife is buried there."

"Oh. I'm sorry, Tom."

"She died three years ago. Ovarian cancer. Her family's from around there and asked that we bury her 'close to home.' It didn't make me happy, frankly, and we'd both thought of California as our home. But they lost their daughter, so . . . I stopped there on my way home from a conference; I thought it would be nice to see her before the wedding. But, as I say, bad planning."

"Did you make it to the dinner?"

"Yes, but I wouldn't advise driving as fast as I did."

There were further dates for coffee, which led to hikes in Nisene Marks and walks along the cliffs above the beach. In pieces she told him about training and teaching martial arts but not about the Sunflower Strangler; also about real estate, Eric, and Blue Heron. She told him about Gerry, Lillian, Mr. Nakamura and Japan, Ellen, and Lama Thokmay.

"I don't race cars or fly airplanes," he told her. "Nothing too dangerous. I ride a bike and go abalone hunting."

"That sounds impressive."

"I'll teach you, if you're interested."

"And why Gualala?"

"I built the house when Maggie and I got married; we had our kids there. It's too big for me now. But it's too beautiful to give up."

Tom was forty-six. He'd grown up on the peninsula, in Mountain View, between Palo Alto and Saratoga. "It felt like a small town then, even though thirty thousand people lived there. A lot of them worked for the aerospace industry. It's a different place now. Too crowded, for one thing.

"I'd wanted to be a lawyer, originally. My dad was a partner in a corporate firm. Growing up, I swallowed all the television propaganda about lone attorneys at law fearlessly defending the wrongfully accused, the weak and powerless, with their re-lentless investigations and cross-examinations, until the real culprit confessed on the witness stand. That's who I wanted to be: the people's champion. My dad, who refused to watch those shows because he said they made his gorge rise, told me that those guys didn't exist. In real life, he'd say, most defense attorneys are either high-powered, publicity-seeking missiles who defend rich celebrity clients, or mom-and-pop lawyers without the resources to mount an aggressive defense, or public attorneys who watch the system chew up their clients before it chews them up too."

"So, you switched to watching the medical shows, where fearless and dedicated surgeons buck the stodgy hospital administrators and save every life against all odds?"

Tom laughed. "Something like that. Come to think of it, I've never seen a television show about courageous salespeople saving the world."

"Yeah. I don't know why that is."

He told her about taking a year off between undergraduate and medical school to be a Deadhead. "I joined the caravan and followed the Grateful Dead around for almost a year. I saw them at the Paramount in Seattle, Winterland in San Francisco; I saw them in Richmond, Fort Lauderdale, Atlanta, Chicago, Detroit, Dallas, Portland. It was the best time."

Allison asked him what it was about them that made him such a fan.

"The ready availability of pot, for one thing. I probably smoked enough for a lifetime, so I was all right giving it up once I started med school. The camaraderie of the audience was another—I've never experienced that anywhere else; it was a very close and caring community. And the band most of all, of course. The way they never played anything the same way twice, ever. The feeling that they were always *right there*, improvising, listening, alive to everything the other guys were doing. Even if they were stoned or tripping half the time. Which I kind of doubt they were, at least not as often as legend would have you believe. I don't think you can be that good so consistently if you're always baked. Anyway—that sense of alertness to what was going on, the ability to experiment and improvise based on what you're hearing, that's what I've tried to do in my practice."

As the end of 2000 approached, they'd had many meals, taken many walks and hikes, but had yet to spend a night together. Allison was still practicing slowing down, and Tom was in no great hurry to commit himself to another person either. But in mid-December, on their way to a holiday party at the home of the hospital's president, he said to her, "Why don't you come up to Gualala for the holidays? I'd like you to meet my daughters."

CHAPTER TWENTY-SEVEN

More rain. Tom was at work, administering Covid tests and caring for patients in his office and at the hospital. Allison did her best not to think about it, but little helped to keep her anxiety at bay. Case numbers were rising, and restaurants, bars, and other businesses were closing every day. Tom risked exposure to the virus daily, and while he remained calm, her unease increased every hour he was away.

She tried meditating. Sitting in a wooden kitchen chair to help her remain upright, she closed her eyes, clasped her palms lightly, concentrated on her breath, and tried to free her mind. But the dread tightened its grip; she counted three or four breaths before her thoughts returned to Tom and Covid.

She gave up. The best thing to do was to go out.

That entailed its own ritual: the appeasement of her aching body with THC cream, the kinesiology tape, the stretches.

The rain had turned to a mist by the time she, creamed, strapped with tape, and stretched, made her way to the garage for her hiking sticks. She had to take it slowly on the slick, slippery grass. She wouldn't have rushed in any case: No one in Gualala—not the neighbors, nor the people in town, certainly not Tom, who took all the time required to treat his patients—felt the need to hurry.

The tranquil rhythms of the place had seeped into her bones, and she, too, had finally learned to take it slowly. One cool, sunny morning, early in her life with Tom in Gualala, had been especially instructive.

They were riding bikes on an asphalt road not far from the cliffs when the breeze through her hair returned her, unbidden, to the years when she'd sped through Montgomery Park. Seized with the old feeling of freedom, she took off, flying down the path, Tom calling out behind her.

The path was new to her, and, taking a short blind curve too quickly, at the last second she saw that the asphalt suddenly became gravel. She tried slowing the bike, but her front wheel slid out hard from under her and she went down, pulling the bike on top of her, the left pedal digging into her calf.

Tom came racing around the curve, leaped off his bike, and ran to Allison. He lifted the bike off her.

"I shouted to slow down but you didn't hear."

"Sorry about that."

"Where are you hurting?"

"My butt. My leg. My arm."

He examined her. "Nothing broken. There'll be a nice bruise there. Your elbow's bleeding." He pulled a handkerchief out of his fanny pack and pressed it to the gash.

"Hold that." He applied a bandage. "Don't worry about it. All bleeding stops eventually."

"Thanks. That fills me with confidence."

"It wouldn't hurt to slow down, you know. Watch the world go by a bit."

Now, to the east, the sun was trying to break through, a yellow smudge hanging over the town. The mist and cool air felt good on her face as she struck out for the cliff on the far side of the inlet. If she could make it there and back, the walk would not only give her some fresh air and exercise, it would also eat up a good hour she'd otherwise spend in the house fretting.

She passed the Chinese pistache, which was beginning to put out its buds. Its seasonal rhythms were a ritual too. What was life but a series of rituals meant to bring order to our activities, to connect us with some significant purpose behind the large and small things we do, to keep the chaos at bay?

She had come a long way from Emma's religion and St. George's Episcopal Church, with its blend of sober observance and the resonant voice of Reverend Hewett, which she could still hear. She remembered much of the service, although now it mingled with other sights and sounds: bells and prayer wheels, the clapping of hands at a Shinto temple, the heavy odor of incense, and the colors of prayer flags. Well, Emma had always said that the Bible was not a cookbook, that you had to think religion through for yourself.

Allison couldn't remember the last time she'd been in a church. It must have been when she married Eric. Her second wedding, in 2002, had been here, in the garden, and her entire family had gathered: Emma and Doug, in their eighties, Will, Susan, Sarah, and Jerry, all were there on a September day washed in warm sunshine. Now, thanks to Covid, Allison wondered when she would see her siblings again. Lillian, who she'd long considered a member of her family, had become a minister of the Universal Life Church and had conducted the ceremony. Tom's daughters, Jen and Paula, had made her feel welcome almost as soon as they'd met her that Christmas in 2000. Finally, after so many years of wanting them, she had children. She hadn't brought them into the world; they were grown when she met them (Jen was twenty-three, Paula, twenty), and they called her Allison, not Mom, but they were her family.

She stood proudly with Tom at Jen's medical school

graduation; cheered her postdoctoral appointment at the University of California, San Francisco; and celebrated her employment there a year later as a cancer researcher. In time, she would become a leading ovarian cancer investigator. Paula became a social worker for Santa Cruz County; by 2020, she was overseeing all its programs for seniors. When Paula was preparing for her wedding in 2008 and asking Allison for her help finding a dress, Allison thought of the one that Emma had made for her. If only, she thought, she'd kept up her sewing skills.

They returned to her when the time came for baby clothes. She made onesies and hats for both daughters' children; she even found a pattern for a baby kimono. It seemed like whenever she wasn't selling, she was sewing. When Tom asked her which gave her more joy—her work or the world of birthday and holiday parties and visits she was swept up in—she was hard pressed to answer.

She felt fine when she reached the cliff. It and the ocean were still wrapped in mist, but she didn't mind. She felt safe behind its soft white veil. The wind was blowing a little harder, but she'd been warmed by the walk. She started back.

She was two-thirds of the way back to the house when she saw him. The familiar dark figure was standing near the deck on a patch of grass browned by the salt air, watching her. She stopped.

She knew that he wasn't real, not in the corporeal sense. But he was real enough, and the sight of him still unnerved her. She had learned over the years to look away when she saw him, because when she'd turn back, he'd be gone. Now, however, she didn't look away. She had never wanted to approach him, but now something urged, *Do it. Come face-to-face with him.* And why not? What was there to fear? Yuri was rotting in prison for his crimes, and this phantom—this remnant of him, the Strangler—had no place in her life anymore. No, this would end now.

She thrust one hiking stick into the soft turf, then the other, nervously at first, as she moved toward the deck, keeping her eye on him. One stick, one foot, the other stick, the other foot.

What would he do, she wondered, when he realized that she was coming for him?

He'd turned to look over his shoulder at her, and for the first time ever, his ghostly face was unmistakable: It was Yuri's face. It would take ten minutes to reach him, less if she picked up the pace. Her nervousness now tempered with resolve, she moved faster and was rewarded with a sharp pain that shot up her right calf to her hip. She focused on her breath without shifting her gaze.

Her senses heightened. She was aware of the squelch each footstep made as her feet rose and sank in the sodden grass. Her mind flashed for a moment to a muddy football field, falling as she hurled a desperation pass to Lillian, but she pushed the image away, keeping her eyes on the figure. The osprey's cry came from somewhere above as it hunted nearby. The mist felt like ice as it fell on her face.

She was less than fifty feet away when she began running toward him, and her body reacted by shooting more pain up her right leg. Her breath came faster. As she slowed it down, her mind flashed again: She was using one of the hiking sticks as a bo staff and lunging at him, intent on killing him off, once and for all.

Hours later, she sat in the kitchen chair she used for meditation, but she wasn't meditating. Restless, she checked her phone every few minutes for an email. She flashed on another memory: "If a computer has the capacity to store that much information and can recall and calculate it super fast," she'd told Eric, "then it would be the most powerful computer in the world." She had to laugh: The phone in her hand had 128 gigs of memory, and it was hardly the most powerful model available.

To say that technology had advanced in the last two decades was like saying the Porsche Carrera was a slight improvement over her old Schwinn. In 1999, she was selling computerized patient records and doctors' orders; today, patients and their doctors across multiple practices could see their medical histories and test results on a screen. A practice could be run without a single piece of paper that might be lost or misread. Office visits were held via Zoom, a feature that was growing in popularity every day during the pandemic. Her last job before retirement a year ago was to automate Tom's office down to the tablet he now used for taking notes and consulting his records.

She tried not to watch the clock. She wandered into the bedroom and sat on the bed. Through the window, she could see that the mist had lifted; a chill breeze was shaking the boughs of the Japanese magnolia. The osprey was wheeling again over the water. What did their snug bit of acreage look like from that height?

Her mind strayed to Blue Heron and the warm evenings when she and Eric had drifted on the fishing boat through the perfumed summer air. They'd had an osprey's view of the island as they flew to Sunflower for their wedding, to races in Florida and New York, as they left Georgia for California.

Change the picture. No airplanes. No race cars. Nothing fast. Once, she would have jumped into the Porsche and sped away, anywhere. But she'd sold the Porsche years ago, replacing it with the more efficient, less speedy Prius.

Too many memories today. Stay in the present. She closed her eyes.

She was awakened by the sound of the car in the driveway. A moment later, a door opened and closed.

"I'm home," Tom called.

She woke again at 3:00 a.m. Sleeping through the night had been difficult lately. She put on a robe, went to the kitchen, turned on the light above the sink, made some chamomile tea, and sat at the table. On an impulse, she'd taken the Lucite globe from the nightstand with her.

Her last vision of the dark man returned.

She'd wanted him to show his face as she plunged the stick into him, so, gripping it tightly, she tried shouting, but no sound came out. She was ten feet away when the dark, vague shape turned. She caught a glimpse of shapeless black clothes covering a thoroughly average body, though large and several inches taller than herself. It was the face, however, that startled her: fleshy cheeks, a squashed nose, and the coldest eyes she had ever seen. With both hands she thrust the stick forward as pain tore into her right shoulder. The point of the stick was an inch from the dark man's chest when he disappeared.

She knew that he wasn't gone forever, that she would never outrun or be rid of him. He was braided into her life along with Tom, Eric, Lillian, and Mr. Nakamura. Her right hand was clenched; she realized she was squeezing the little globe. She relaxed, and revolving it in her hand, she examined its light and dark shades of blue, its flecks of brown and white that she'd once imagined were the Himalayas. She put it on the table and watched it turn. Later, she would call her siblings, check in, let them know that she and Tom were all right. Then she'd call Jen and Paula.

What was that song she'd liked to sing at church when she was a kid? The one that Will had taught her better words to, and that she sang, unprompted, to the children at Lama Thokmay's school? The words came back to her again:

> *When true simplicity is gained,*
> *To bow and to bend we shan't be ashamed,*
> *To turn, turn, will be our delight,*
> *Till by turning, turning, we come 'round right.*

ACKNOWLEDGMENTS

Writing *Chasing Air* has been one of the most humbling and rewarding experiences of my life. It would not have been possible without the encouragement, wisdom, and support of so many.

To my husband, thank you for your endless patience, grounding presence, and unwavering belief in me, even when I wasn't sure what I was chasing. Your love has been my foundation through every page.

To my children Chelsea and Justin, my family, and my close friends, thank you for cheering me on, reading early drafts, offering honest feedback, and reminding me to keep going. Your faith carried me when I doubted myself.

To the writers, editors, and early readers who shared their time and insight, thank you. A special thanks goes to Michael, whose talent and candor helped shape this story into something stronger and more honest. And thank you to Abi—your guidance and tenacity kept me focused.

To everyone who has ever faced loss, reinvention, or reintegration with quiet courage—this story is for you.

And finally, to the readers, thank you for picking up this book and giving my words a place to land. I hope *Chasing Air* finds you at the moment you need it most.

BOOK CLUB QUESTIONS

1. Allison faces a range of physical and emotional challenges in *Chasing Air*. Which moment in her journey felt most pivotal to you, and why?
2. How does the title *Chasing Air* reflect the deeper themes of the novel—freedom, loss, resilience, and reinvention?
3. Were there any scenes or relationships that reminded you of your own life experiences or choices?
4. The book explores the tension between control and surrender. How does Allison navigate that balance throughout the story?
5. Allison's relationship with risk is central to her evolution. Do you see her as fearless, reckless, courageous—or something else?
6. How did your perception of Allison shift from the beginning to the end of the novel?
7. The novel weaves together themes of grief, ambition, and personal identity. Which of these felt most resonant or surprising to you as a reader?
8. What role does nature or movement (flying, running, climbing) play in how Allison processes her inner world?
9. Was there a character besides Allison whom you found particularly compelling? What did they add to the story?
10. If *Chasing Air* continued beyond its final pages, where do you imagine Allison would go next—literally or emotionally?

ABOUT THE AUTHOR

Caroline Prince has (nearly) done it all. Raised in the South, she developed an adventurous spirit that led her to travel the world. She built a successful real estate career in Georgia before breaking barriers as a top sales executive in the historically male-dominated world of Silicon Valley.

A second-degree black belt (Nidan), Caroline has piloted airplanes, had close experiences with the adrenaline-fueled life of a race car driver, climbed mountains, and completed marathons. She approaches every challenge with humor and determination, always seeking the next great adventure.

Now, Caroline has embarked on a new journey: writing. *Chasing Air* is her debut novel.